What Are They All Waiting For?

Stories, Poems & Essays: 1944-1962

Gil Orlovitz

Compiled and edited by Rick Schober

Tough Poets Press
Arlington, Massachusetts

Acknowledgment is made to the following publications in which the works included in this volume first appeared: *American Letters Press, Art of the Sonnet, Beloit Poetry Journal, Coastlines, Colorado Review, Concerning Man, The Diary of Alexander Patience, The Diary of Dr. Eric Zeno, Discovery, Experiment, Hearse, Inferno, INTRO, Keep to Your Belly: Fourteen Poems, The Literary Review, The Minnesota Review, The Miscellaneous Man, Mutiny, The Papers of Professor Bold, Poetry, Poetry Los Angeles, Poetry New York, Quarterly Review of Literature, Rocky Mountain Review, San Francisco Review, Selected Poems, 21st Century, Whetstone, Who,* and *Wormwood Review*

Cover photos by Victor Laredo, used with permission from his estate.

Cover design by Rick Schober.

ISBN 978-0-692-11681-4
Tough Poets Press
49 Churchill Avenue, Floor 2
Arlington, Massachusetts 02476
U.S.A.

www.toughpoets.com

EDITOR'S NOTE

The works included in this collection represent only a small fraction of Gil Orlovitz's writing that was published between the years 1944 and 1962. Because they were all originally copyrighted prior to 1964 and the copyrights were never renewed, they have since fallen into the public domain.

To the best of the editor's ability, the stories and poems have been arranged in chronological order, from earliest to latest, based on their original publication dates. However, for the sake of convenience, all of the selections from *Art of the Sonnet* have placed at the end.

Great care was taken to preserve the author's original spelling, capitalization, punctuation, and formatting. Only obvious misspellings that appeared in the original publications have been corrected.

CONTENTS

STORIES

What Are They All Waiting For?   11
Ah, Kathleen   21
— Image in Static Continuum   57
The Rest of the Staff Was Out   65
Fob at Bay   70
A Deposition of Ben Berman   90
Something to Tell Mother   97
A Back Cover   124
On Such Sundays   149

ESSAYS

Some Autobiographical Words   157
The Ubiquitous Symbol: POETRY, some informal   160
    remarks on my method and intent
The Classic Offender   163
Letter to the Editor: Beat Poetry   166

POEMS

Portrait   171
Third Elegy   172
Brief Me on God   174
To St. R   175
Memo to St. R   176
Ninth Elegy   177

A Further Instruction of Hamlet to His Players   178
For George Washington   180
On a Modification   181
Lines on Lawns   182
Mug Manhattan Swinging Doors   183
Hymn   184
Solvent, a Plume Evoke, She   185
The Diary of Dr. Eric Zeno: One   186
The Diary of Dr. Eric Zeno: Five   187
On the Wonder of What Is   188
What Maxim Is a Silencer   189
Address to the Union   191
The Rooster   194
The Letters of Great Ape: 1   200
The Letters of Great Ape: 2   202
Sunburnt the Bather   204
Not   205
There Is a Man I Do Not Know   208
Wesley Thorne   209
Index (8)   212
Index (3rd Series): 2   213
Index (Last Series): 10   217
On the Nature of Suicide   219
Diary of Matthew Parson: 4   222
The Morning of a Clown   224
Flamenco: 3   226
The Diary of Alexander Patience: 29 May   227
The Diary of Alexander Patience: 7 July   230
M'sieu Mishiga: 3   234
M'sieu Mishiga: 7   236
The Impeccable Barbed Wire   239
The Papers of Professor Bold: 4   240
The Action   242
Masterindex: 35   245
Art of the Sonnet: 9   251
Art of the Sonnet: 29   252
Art of the Sonnet: 43   253
Art of the Sonnet: 57   254

Art of the Sonnet: 67   255
Art of the Sonnet: 68   256
Art of the Sonnet: 98   257
Art of the Sonnet: 129   258
Art of the Sonnet: 130   259

BACK MATTER

A Brief Biography of Gil Orlovitz   263
Gil Orlovitz Bibliography   269
Acknowledgments   274

STORIES

WHAT ARE THEY ALL WAITING FOR?

Some people repeat more and more telling certain things about their past.

Given half a chance, Teddy Poole says, "I was married to the most beautiful girl in Hollywood." He utters this in protest, with longing, and finally as a challenge, as though the listener may find it hard to believe. On other occasions the same statement will be offhand, sometimes dreamy, or pugnacious.

But none describes Teddy Poole recounting, "I'd give her plenty spending-money. After all, I was making. But soon she didn't have enough. She'd ask for fifty dollars one day. Then sixty. What do you need it for, I'd ask. This and that. A dress. A piece of jewelry. All right. But how much of that stuff can a girl use? Seventy-five dollars a day it got to be. I had to go in hock. With my salary yet. One day I come home, would you believe it? — my house is loaded with people I don't even know, only my wife — and everybody's laying around, it's full of smoke. A reefer party. I found out my wife was an addict from way back. I left my house, I never went back, I had the marriage annulled. But she was the most beautiful girl in Hollywood."

That last sentence can be described.

There is a girl in New York Teddy Poole has often been seen with, a Cissy Lee, whose real name is Hilda Dombrowski. She talks, her words accelerate, then she stutters.

Here is a story Cissy repeats. "Me and my brother fight like dogs and cats. You know every time a guy phones me my brother grabs the phone and he says to the guy Don't date my sister she's undependable. Imagine. He keeps doing that. I have so much trouble with him. He's good-looking my brother, but we fight like dogs and cats." Cissy will end on a squeal and a stutter.

Teddy Poole lives in a two-room suite, with bath and kitchenette, at the La Comtesse Hotel, east of Fifth Avenue on 31st. West of Fifth, there are wholesale fur establishments and typewriter exchanges. At Sixth, you come on two cafeterias, brightly lit, where bleak people at night sit in both sexes. Outside, pages of discarded newspapers rove the street, like stray animals.

After entering Hotel La Comtesse, you are struck in the face by the blue mirrors pasted on the lobby pillars. To the left, in an insubstantial wall cut-out, like something from a paper-box, stands a disgruntled old clerk wearing a hearing aid; behind him are pigeonholes for mail, and at irregular intervals what look to be white feathers stick out; he has a telephone switchboard too, over which the old clerk sometimes sways, addressing a mouthpiece as if it were a flute and he a transplanted fakir, wearing an American business suit, playing at the still, plugged black cobras.

If you should walk a little further, you will observe a blue neon arrow pointing to a blue cocktail bar. Ahead, near the elevator, a blank television set, where a young man may sit, biting his fingernails. Dull brass plates hardly read that a doctor and a dentist occupy the offices behind the two rear doors. The carpet is new and in need of stains. One sleeve of the young elevator-man's uniform seems empty; not quite: one arm is far shorter than the other. Two persons feel wedged aboard the slow elevator.

On the smut-green walls of Teddy Poole's sitting-room hang color shots of female nudes, which Teddy does as a hobby often enough after a stint of dialog for a television variety show. But placed between two such color photographs, a hand-tinted black-and-white picture of his distinguished-looking mother and father, who have been dead and buried for about twelve years, appears rather prominent.

Teddy Poole wants to tell Cissy Lee how many things he owns. Now, he decides, because she is loaded with Canadian Club and sitting on his lap up at the hotel suite and dead quiet, underlip surly.

"I even own a submarine," he begins. But the door buzzer suddenly nags.

"Answer it," Cissy more than suggests, "it must be the sandwiches."

"Not if you don't move."

"I don't want to."

"Then it'll buzz. again."

"Carry me and answer it, Teddy."

"Piggyback?"

"No."

"The hell with you then. Let him buzz. I'm telling you I even own — "

"You're a bastard."

"Don't call me that name, Cissy."

"Well you are. You're creepy too. Why don't you stop being stubborn and admit it?"

"You don't even appreciate all that Chanel I got you."

"I'm sorry, Teddy. I'll get up. I'm hungry. Answer the door."

Stocky, Teddy heaves himself up and ploughs ahead, putting his hand deep into his pants pocket. Cissy giggles, "Every time he goes to the door he puts his hand in his pocket."

"Well," Teddy shrugs, half turning to her apologetically, "you know. Living in a hotel. It costs.

"I was on the Coast five years. I only did dialog for pictures, my specialty, I can't plot. But give me a situation and I'll dialog. I was married to the most beautiful girl in Hollywood. When my marriage broke up, I wanted to get away. But it's hard to break a contract. Besides, you don't want to when it pays so good. You know. Lucky the studio asks if I want to go East and do TV awhile, I'd be on loan. I jumped. But when I got back to New York I didn't know a soul. Sure, showgirls, from phone numbers my friends out on the Coast gave me. For a while I took them out, but they're all so tall. And they wore high heels yet. I'd take them places, and I'd walk behind going in, like I didn't want it known I was with them — till we'd sit down. You know, I'm a shorty. I wanted a little girl, and somebody permanent. Well, a Hollywood friend had given me the name of a photography agency, very reputable. I phoned, and told them who I was, Teddy Poole. They heard, I got a pretty good rep as a dialog-man. And they sent up a little blonde. She marches right in my suite here, sees the camera setup but don't say nothing, instead cases the premises. Finally she looks satisfied and starts to strip. Okay, she says, what poses? — That's Cissy."

"Don't you like goldfish, Teddy? I love them. I have a whole tank, I could watch them all day, they're so beautiful. Swimming around. Or just looking through the glass. In the water. You'll buy me that special tropical fish, won't you, Teddy? Tomorrow's all right. I just love to watch goldfish. I take awful good care of them. But they died. And whenever one of them die, I cry."

For her loving care of the fish, their swimming and floating, and for their death, Cissy maintains a single expression on her face and in her voice: dreaminess.

To a tyro who seeks advice about breaking into show business, Teddy Poole will exhibit a comfortable fatherliness.

First he leans back in the sofa, his arm around Cissy; she squirms; he grins.

"Look at his belly," Cissy nags, "isn't he creepy?"

Teddy will hang on to the grin and pull her closer. She shrugs, as if to allow infinity shelter.

"What's creepy mean, Cissy?"

"He don't even know what it means!" The girl widely shrugs big blue eyes.

"Well I'm not in condition." Teddy sinks deeper into the sofa, patting his belly.

"I'll say you're not," Cissy whisks contempt.

"Complaining?"

"Never mind," embarrassment crossing the contempt. Teddy is reminded by the tyro that he would appreciate advice about show business.

"Oh yeh," Teddy discovers, "it took me two years to break in. Boy was my aunt wonderful. She supported me the whole time, enough to get by, seventy-five a week. So I know how tough it can be, fella. Maybe you saw my aunt's car downstairs? She was just here. A Cadillac limousine. She owns two."

He must take a narrow glance at Cissy, then turn again to the tyro and become expansive. "Boy I remember when I first got to the Coast." Once more he holds back, only to continue with, "By the way, my aunt isn't the only one who owns plenty. I — "

"You're always changing the subject," Cissy bawls, "that can get awful annoying, Teddy."

With petulance, Teddy resumes the Hollywood period, but by and by expansiveness returns. "I didn't know a soul out there at first. But through the studio I got invited to dinner by one of their top actresses. Anytime you go out her house she's got glasses on, up to her neck in scripts. She's a little girl but what a dynamo, has to do everything. Now she's got her own producing outfit. Me, I'm only a dialog-man, but damn good. Anyhow I'm there, I'm introduced and she takes one look at me through her glasses and says right off, Teddy what you need is a woman. The end of the week she phones me and says come out that night. I come in and she says, Look them over, I invited the ten most beautiful girls in Hollywood for you, take your pick. I'm telling you she's nuts. Let me fill your glass, fella," he urges the tyro, "we got plenty Canadian, I got a case in tonight. And a hamburger steak, maybe? Sirloin. You can make it yourself on the grill. I got plenty, the icebox's loaded."

The tyro declines with thanks.

Cissy presents her tiny nose. "Teddy, get a television set, huh? Gee there's nothing to do hardly when we stay here nights. And I saw the most wonderful parakeet today. I just love animals. Will you buy it for me, Teddy?"

"Sure I will, honey, if you're nice to me."

"I'll be nice to you, Teddy. Gee it's a beautiful parakeet." Dreamily.

The tyro quits the place on bended toe, Teddy yelling after him, "Come back tomorrow night, I'll have ideas, and bring your script, and don't pay for the cab, it'll be on me." Which he will always say, and habitually forget.

Playfully, after some three hours of particularly harelip television during an autumn evening, on the sofa underneath the photo of his father and mother flanked by the nudes, Cissy raises the cigarette she has just lit till it is a few inches away from Teddy's cheek. Curling in his lap, Cissy grins. Teddy pouts.

"Now what do you think you're doing?" A little sleepy, and his fat hands rest on her thighs.

"What would you do if I burnt a hole in your cheek? Would you still love me, Teddy? Huh?"

"Why would you want to burn me, honey?" Smugness drains his smile, the smile drains the broad solidity of his face.

"Oh just a teensy-weensy hole. Why don't you let me?"

"Why?"

"Didn't they use to burn witches? Their whole bodies and everything?" She lowers the cigarette, her expression full of holes of astonishment and wonder, and breathless insistence that her knowledge be confirmed.

"Sure, honey. But witches were women. Do I look female?"

"For a man you sure have wide hips," Cissy cackles.

Her disproportionately long mouth has become for the first time to Teddy the most important part of her face; and as he looks down on her upturned features, her eyes and nostrils in the cackle are echoes of her mouth. Irritation nudges him, scoffs.

"And people burned witches because they thought the witches could harm them, or did harm them. Did I do you any harm, Cissy?"

She springs from his lap to stand before him, legs spread.

"Well, maybe you did and maybe you didn't."

"How?"

"I don't know." She paces, puffing hard on the cigarette, an arm on her hip, head thrust forward, baffled and tough.

"You're nuts."

"Yeh? But you didn't answer me if I burnt you would you still love me, did you?"

"How can I such a crazy question?"

"Would you?"

Teddy rotates his skull on that short foulard of a neck. His pale green eyes avoid her bald blue ones.

Quietly, "Why should I love you if you did that?" Then, at a shout, "My father was senator from Vermont! A banker, he — "

"So what! Maybe you don't think I'm as good as you are."

"I didn't say that."

Cissy leaps into the sofa beside him, grinning, holding the cigarette close to his cheek again.

"Just a teensy-weensy hole, Teddy?" her grin melting into the holiest petition, she the sacrificial offering. "Please?"

With a clumsy twist of his torso, he seizes and kisses her, his fat child-like hands pushing and pulling, digging and clamping her body, and then yanking her loins back and forth across the sofa. Her arms lay loose; her cigarette was nearly a butt.

Teddy had almost forgotten how tall some of the illuminated tops of the buildings were, and took an impulsive glimpse through the small square window of the hansom he and Cissy were jogging along in through Central Park. She had insisted on the ride, suddenly, after they had left a bar, and started to stroll aimlessly down Park South about two-thirty that morning; to Teddy's protest that it was too late and getting too damn cold, Cissy had countered, with all the summonable extravagance of one who becomes all at once aware of the possibility that anything, anything in the world might have more value than anything else if one has missed experiencing it in all one's twenty-one years on the earth — that she had never, never ridden in a hansom through the park, and that she absolutely had to, now. So they had gone, and here Teddy was with his squat nose juggling out the window, thinking how strange the skyscrapers were, almost like some mythical creatures he remembered once reading about: they had been illustrated as naked men from the waist up, but beneath goat-like and woolly; and here, above the woolly masses of the trees they rode by, emerged the buildings, clean concrete torsos, some shining at the apex, which thrust a light that seemed to dig out and burn the cloudy night. Teddy shrank back.

"You a greenhorn or something? My God the way you look at the sky-scrapers," Cissy said, her small face a dim vague heart — it could have been a locket — shifting inside the, hansom.

He had never been able to get her to listen, but now Teddy felt he really had to insist on telling her how many things he owned. Besides, it was his birthday; not that he had informed her, because she might make fun, but certainly he should at least celebrate it for himself by listing his properties to someone who hadn't known him too long a time, like Cissy, which would also increase his significance to her. Still, he would prefer doing that in the warmth of his hotel suite, rather than creaking coldly along here in the dark, the heat of Cissy's body, though close, quite ineffective; and he wanted to do it before it got light, when his birthday would end.

"Honey let's go home, we been on the town since nine." Teddy tried to cuddle her.

She shouldered into her corner. "You'll mess up my coiffure."

"Cabby — "

"No. I want to keep riding."

"All right," he sighed, shivering a little, and mentally reviewed what he would catalogue for her. His two houses in Vermont, the one with the fourteen rooms, which a caretaker and his wife kept in constant readiness, and the other a six-room cottage on a lakefront. His Cadillac convertible and Jaguar, neither of which he used in town because it was so much simpler to take a cab, even though, as he put it, "it cost." The full-length mink he intended giving Cissy as a surprise. His thirty-five-thousand-dollar-a-year income. And, most important of all, the submarine — but then Cissy stalled him above the steady clopclop of the horse's hooves on the macadam and the creaking carriage wheels.

"The television set's starting to get creepy. I don't know why you had to go get that cabinet in dark wood," she said.

"You could've told me that a couple of weeks ago when I bought it."

"Well you just went right out and got it, you didn't ask me what color, that's how you hurt me and don't even know it and I can't let you know it hurt me." She started to stutter.

"What color."

"Gee in that creepy joint what they call blonde wood. Yeh it should be a blonde cabinet, Teddy."

"Christ you didn't even have any decent clothes when I first met you and I give you a whole wardrobe and now all you can think of is you want a blonde wood television cabinet. Christ you got more feeling for goldfish and parakeets than people."

"Ah you don't know nothing about people. All over the world there are just two kinds, rich and poor, Teddy, that's all."

"Is that so?"

"Yeh that's so." She thrust out her underlip.

He smelled the strong living odor of the horse, and the old leather reduction in the carriage. "Well let me tell you something, Cissy. When I was in the army I saw the crematoriums where the Germans burnt the Jews.

People aren't just rich and poor. Some are good and some pretty lousy. I'll tell you what I wanted to do when I saw those crematoriums."

"So go ahead."

"That's not what I wanted to tell you, Cissy." He tried now to remember the list of things he owned, but couldn't.

"You tell me what you wanted to do in Germany."

"I wanted to burn all the Germans!" he blurted, knowing this wrong to say, and unable to help himself.

"Well some of those Jews deserved the crematorium," she snapped. He, the Jew, was absolutely impassive. She went on, furious. "You know my mother's German."

"Yeh," he said, dully. "You know I didn't mean your mother, Cissy." Once more, she crouched away, staring straight ahead. He huddled in his jacket, and then leaned forward again to look through the little square window, frowning to recover the list of his possessions, his shoulders jouncing to the hansom's creaking and giving: everything in its structure gave, a hundred little grumbling adjustments, but somehow done comfortably, a grudging youth in its age, its emotion quite clearly expressed by the occasional snort of the horse. The cabby had grunted, and they were traveling along at a fair clip. Teddy lifted his eyes: there the peaks of the Manhattan range, swathed at irregular intervals by high-powered spotlights which themselves bored into the cloud-rolling night sky: they made empty and isolated holes, outlined by the dark. Did empty holes always have to be outlined? the question took Teddy, and he felt his thinking had got awfully strange. And another: Was that outlining a sort of punishment for emptiness? A round throbbing pain sinking through his eyes and the cold wind blowing on his face shuddered his shoulders, and he slumped back in his seat. He concluded he was temporarily nuts: how could there be punishment up in the sky? Besides, he should be grappling to recover the list of things he owned. But Cissy's rasping had resumed, and that cut his memory to rusty ribbons. All he could think was, how could he shut her up?

"Oh boy that wonderful aunt of yours," she was babbling, "you know she was pretty mean to me last night, asking me what I did all day seven days a week. You know I don't think she likes people. I'm sorry for her, Teddy. Oh boy how she loves you, her dear darling Teddy. Maybe I should've told her how when I woke up yesterday afternoon I caught you in the front room sitting right under that photograph of your mother and father looking through your album of naked models one after the other, real slow, and boy were you grinning, like you were eating those pictures. What's the matter, Teddy, aren't I good enough for you? Well I don't think you're so smart sometimes, like keeping on living at that creepy hotel for instance. Why do we have to keep on living there, Teddy? Gee every time I walk through that lobby it gives me the creeps. Those creepy blue mirrors. That old nightclerk with that hearing aid, he squints his eyes each time he tries to hear better. And that elevator guy with one arm shorter than the other, like he don't want anybody to see that arm, it's like he shrugs it all the way up into his armpit. And that kid sitting in front of that television set near the elevator — it's never on and he keeps looking at it and biting his nails. What's he waiting for, anyhow?" She was stuttering badly now. "Everybody in that lobby looks like they're always waiting. What are they all waiting for? It gives me the creeps. Why don't we move out of there, Teddy, huh? Why don't — "

"When' s that husband of yours getting out of the pen, honey? How long they send him up for on that narcotics charge?" Teddy broke in, quietly. She clammed up.

Now he could tell her. In celebration of his birthday. With the rhythm of the horse's hooves, a steady trot. Regular. The horse was solid. Teddy should have been able to think of everything he owned, because the horse's hooves weren't disturbing; they gave a good and continuing foundation. But the only item he could remember was the submarine. The rest blank. He couldn't understand why. He was getting afraid. He'd better tell her about the submarine, at least. Before the morning light would fall on him and end his birthday. If he didn't, he might even forget the submarine. And he just couldn't take such a chance now: what kind of man would he be to forget absolutely everything that he owned on his birthday?

"I guess you didn't know I own a submarine, Cissy. Well, I do. My father, the senator, left me controlling interest in his marine salvage company. The Navy sold us a sunken submarine for salvage — we thought at least it would make good scrap. Then we sent down divers — it was at the bottom of the bay — to estimate it. They — " and he halted, feeling that it would be difficult to express the rest, but then went on, swiftly. " — they said it wouldn't pay to raise it. So it's still down there. But I own it, Cissy." And he added, in a voice that trailed off to hushed indifference, "We got a marker on the water right above it, though." The musty leather inside the carriage was quite strong to Teddy, yet somehow, though he heard the horse distinctly, he couldn't smell it at all. His fat hands were very cold, and he shoved them in his pants pockets. It costs, was what he thought, it costs.

"I want a drink before the bars close," Cissy said, in a reasonable monotone. Teddy told the cabby to take them back to Park South.

When the hansom paused at an intersection, to turn slowly onto another drive, the light of a park lamp fell through the window on Teddy's face as Cissy turned to him wanting to say that she'd be real nice after she'd had a drink, and her glance fell on his cheek. Her eyes went down, and her head went down on his chest; she linked an arm with his, and with the other she lightly lingered a finger at the spot where a neat round mark from a cigarette burn could be seen on his cheek.

"It's nearly all healed, isn't it, Teddy?" She spoke softly the moment it was dark again inside, the hansom jogging along.

"Yeh." He freed a hand from a pants pocket and put an arm around her, and something struck him funny: America is the land of brands, Cain could've got along here swell. I sure am a good dialog-man, anyhow. I can think of all the switches.

AH, KATHLEEN

Outside, the nights had begun to white and cool. People accelerated; tongues pointed out thoughts with greater elan, and concealed feelings, in response to some protective urgency, by more effective sham.

Inside the Giotto Bar, in Greenwich Village, the ending of summer and another matter coincided with a solemn round of beers. The girl and her three male companions, who sat at a booth, drank them as he would have: pauseless swallows till the glasses were emptied. Then, like four dies synchronized, they punched the glasses down on the name-gouged mahogany table. They exchanged meaningful looks; not one smiled.

That Saturday night the bar's patrons derived from McDougall Street, the University a few blocks away, and the fey brownstones of the West Seventies. Mistresses and paramours were being illiberally traded; and the decline of civil liberties deplored. Somebody laughed about the Bobbsey Twins of Fire Island. A sensual blonde, short but pithy, known far and near by the soubriquet "Moonbeam McSwine," was drunk and vowed herself the most adept bed-partner within hog-calling distance. Provincetown had bereted admirers and prancing cold shoulders. Even so, the girl and her companions paid the scene no heed. They continued a ceremony. Had she stood up, she could have been seen just short of a long girl, whose willowy richness winked breasts through her dress when she walked or swung for a kiss; her legs quipped at the ankles and relaxed, fully, at the calves; a sword or velvet puff could have suited the hips. She was a young lass of nineteen who, sitting up schoolgirl-stiff now in the booth, proclaimed that "he'd've wanted it this way," and reprimanded chestnut curls, that had rushed pups over her forehead, by a burst of brushing palm, though she let them crowd back upon her neck. Unmarred except for the bruise on the lips, still a little painful, the faultless oval of the girl's face, and the complexion that found the most shy topaz, were displaced, at least, by the wide, stinging, deep blue quartz of the eyes which, while her voice might carol or be mist-lidded, would never less than accuse. Her name was Kathleen Malone, and she had, abruptly, fallen silent in the midst of an impersonation. The companion whose premature balding, high cheekbones and tight polished skin seemed to have stripped his skull down to an arclight glare of youth, blinked slow concern. Like assistant angels, the other two males hovered their heads to fill out the Florentine effort; save that in the background two barrel-chested bartenders Flemishly bawled.

"And I won't see Stan again, either," Kathleen broke her hush, and shot back both hands to stifle the curls, for a moment, behind her ears.

The balding boy pitted himself against the absent and brawny Stan. "Him? Well..." his tones high-pitched: they would tighten, by several notches, so that he might deprecate. On either flank, the angels stirred soft chuckles beneath the quick-lofted tapers of their fingers.

"Well nothing!" the girl clubbed. But they need not have quailed: the next instant, remembering, she relented, and exhibited mellowed martyrdom to dedicate an epilogue. "Stan would take me walking along Madison Avenue. There were the shops. The frocks..." The stroll paused. Then: "In the windows, my reflection within the frock. I could have been a model. Oh, easy. Or the wife of — of a diplomat." Only Kathleen could have summoned to her cheek that dimple defined by faint pain. "And worn expensive gowns. Stan said I belonged in them. And I did want to be an actress." The three males hung, transiently insatiable sympathizers, on each frill and flounce. "He'll never visit me," the girl concluded, as if she had chosen shaded corridors. While her hot fingers enjoyed the cool of the beer glass, she glanced off through the flesh-hung bric-a-brac aslant and awallow at the bar, and through the animals that paced back and forth in tweeds, dirndls and bearded leers. Kathleen could register no tick-tack-toe talk, nor contemptuous riposte, nor raised eyebrow in avant-bored colloquy; she was staring beyond the particolored liquor bottles that tilted back upon themselves in the mirror behind, far beyond the reflections upon reflections.

The tight and shiny-skinned one conceived himself muscled, and would contend vain, proud sacrifice. "But you can still change your mind," was his epic challenge. His acolytes murmured a brimful "Yes, Kathleen, yes," in unison.

Perhaps by way of reply, she resumed the ceremony. Her frame quivered, her mouth steeled itself to a quake; yet from somewhere she borrowed slyness to present the show. The companions watched, consciously supreme familiars. Kathleen lowered her head to the table. There, after a taut interval, she flung her head back up, and the same instant reared her entire body to stand and crow "I am Wesley Swift!" She was quick to sit down, though, and flushed through the light topaz, the blue eyes angry. The girl's mouth, however, sent up little balloons of titter.

About the only reaction from the Giotto turmoil came from a passing stolid post-climacteric female who baritoned to the big seaman at her side, "What will these children do next for a thrill? Obviously the girl's been needling herself with hormones. She probably will never know how suddenly one can become butch. My sweet, I know one woman who in the midst of acquiring a new lover..." the rest lost in the marcelled screams of five linked young men scooping into the place.

"Wesley would rear up like that at parties," the tight-skinned skull said, "while he'd sit on the floor."

"Or just before the curtain raised on a new ballet," the second one recalled, embarrassed, "while he had his black cloak around him in the mezzanine."

"Or out on a raft, in Provincetown Harbor," the third mewed.

"He'd tell each new boy he'd meet that he had the best air-foam mattress in Manhattan," the balding boy said, "but he'd always be drunk, drunk, drunk. God!" he addressed the Fates. "He had thick glasses, black crewcut hair, a short powerful physique, physique —"

Kathleen cut him short, severely. "He isn't here, but we can stand the corpse up in the corners of our minds instead, can't we? and get drunk? Wesley would've sneered at grief, wouldn't he? But he'd've howled at us remembering him by imitating how he moved and acted."

"Yes, Kathleen," they thrilled at her command.

"Well, we aren't through yet." Kathleen prepared to renew the wake, not before, however, she shut her eyes a moment, as if to prevent something or somebody else from a look in, perhaps her own projected image. So that might not at all have indicated tiredness. Certainly Kathleen's immaculate oval face, eyelids down, slim hazel brows casual arches, and lashes like the trailed fringe of a coverlet, betrayed no single line nor shadowed fluff that might have resulted from her having gone nearly two days without sleep. Then again, it might have been an unconscious echo of one of her old habits, common, really, to many people who, after they dial a phone number, close their eyes a few seconds while they listen to the buzzing sound, just as Kathleen had done in a booth about six-thirty the other night, waiting for Stan to answer, at a large restaurant-bar near Central Park South, where she worked the hat-check concession.

He was taking long enough to come to the phone. She calculated the distance between the front room of their four-room apartment, where Stan studied amidst a record collection, mostly his, which boasted, aside from the standard items, the now fashionable ethnic music, in the main drumbeats fast, slow and medium from the surfaces of lightest Africa, to which guests would listen, startled and ecstatic, quite sure that they could observe, their amazement later always controlled, how the functional modulated to the symbolic — and the rear bedroom, which housed their sex and telephone.

By the insistent ringing, he should at last have been aware that it was Kathleen. After all, ten years were due by plane; three seconds could have marked Stan's long-legged stride to the receiver. A 2nd lieutenant had stridden from the Malones' parlor. A major now. Kathleen stood up, the small whirring fan at the top of the phone booth chilled her forehead; she stamped a foot and switched it off. Ten years. Then, hearing Stan boom over the wire, she could have lectured him about natives, drum skins stretched taut, and functional ethnic music; and glozed, with highlights, how Wesley would have left little anthropological grass grow under his feet had he to answer a phone. Nevertheless, there was no doubt that she loved the major; he had had a right to quit her mother. Wesley had left him — but that was another case, and perhaps he shouldn't have; perhaps Wesley belonged with a mother. Oh yes, she loved her father, Major Dennis Malone, Public Relations, U.S. Army — Kathleen trailed the nomenclature behind, swinging, like schoolbooks when she was nine, so that, as she asked Stan what he'd been doing, it was with impatience and annoyance cradled in daughterly pride.

"Working on that old thesis, I guess. Well you just drop your snow-gods and summer-gods for a minute and listen. My daddy called — he's flying in from Washington. He's meeting me right here around eight-thirty."

"Aren't we due at Connie's party about then?" Stan sounded as if brain and tongue were still distantly cross-indexed.

"I haven't seen him for nearly ten years!" Kathleen wondered whether Stan needed her at all, even to discharge his most elemental gratifications; she remembered, not long after they had met, that he hadn't in the least missed suspension of sexual relations a good six months before his wife had separated from him; however, she recalled too that that had been apparently belied once he had flipped Kathleen between the sheets. His buckteeth thereupon grinned to mind: they persisted in plumbing her cavities; unlike Wesley's, white, small and even, that sometimes she would have liked to brush, a wish impossible to voice. Besides, Stan was almost thirty, so much older than she; this quickened her each instance it recurred. She really had to get back to work: the manager walked by a second time. "Stan, we'll make the party the latest — oh, ten-thirty. Daddy flies back after an hour or so. I know it's awfully short notice, but don't you want to meet him?" Then, in a rush, declining to press him: "Look, if you'd rather, I can see you later at Connie's."

"You'd like me to be with you when your father comes in, wouldn't you."

"Not if you're going to indulge me." Her ear hurt, the phone tight. Wesley would have acceded right off, simply, and all charm. Kathleen shook her head no: one must halt such adolescent comparisons, now. She caught a whiff about impulse.

"I said, Kathleen, your father had a sudden enough impulse to see you. After so long. It sounds odd."

"Afraid of him?" She might as well sit down again, she scorned, and did, flicking on that toylike fan. The manager could go to hell; let him shake his finger. Men. What had Stan said to her, smug, once when he'd been drunk? Oh, that he walked softly, and carried a big stick in his pants. She giggled: she could have it out with him — on any difference of opinion, or course of action; with daddy, after all, she'd never been able to. The girl slashed at her hair; it had stuck to her brow, coldly. Stan hadn't answered the question; he had moved elsewhere. Or had he?

"Didn't he leave you and your mother when the war began in '41?" his voice weighted, and a shade insecure, which Kathleen had never before detected. As on prey, she leaped:

"I don't know what you're driving at, Stan, but you don't have to be here." Delighted at her toughness, a new toy, perhaps an adult teething ring, Kathleen anticipated thorough indifference to how he might react. That new fleshtoned fingernail polish had started cracking. Why was she compelled, always, to buy cheap merchandise? Her dress. And the cheapness of the underclothing repelled her belly. Her lousy cheap job. Her — . Damn him! Stan was being just as tough. Still, she smiled, and found herself relaxed in his definitude.

"I'll be there at eight-fifteen," he said, and hung up. Chuckling, Kathleen tickled the mouthpiece with a little finger, returned to her job and mollified the manager by a twitch of a breast, convinced that he would consume a steak at dinner while Wesley would forget to eat altogether, though his parents did remit him a lavish allowance. How incongruous that the stocky Wesley owned a button-nose. Tenderly, into a fragile handkerchief, she blew her own. Her father's, now, should still be wide and humped, like a bicep.

"My father used to tell me," she volunteered later, quite animated, to her friend Grace, in the restaurant section roped off after eight o'clock, "he was the only one who could make a muscle in the middle of his face — his nose!"

Grace felt spared that she could abbreviate response by so token a measure as a toss of her mouth, because she was obviously applying lipstick, and covertly reflecting upon her own complexities.

"Oh there's Stan," Kathleen stood up, thankful in spite of herself, and waved to the blond, broken-nosed tall man who seemed to have center-plunged through the revolving door. When he sat at the table, Kathleen having brought him coffee, Grace's problems got overt, which befitted, creaseless, a snug waist, a chirruped chest and long russet hair, here being combed, that could ripple a certain ingenuous malice over her flat cheeks in a bedroom. Kathleen fixed her gaze on the door.

"Maybe you can help me," Grace pitched sideways from her mirror at Stan, who nodded absently and counseled Kathleen that she shake off anxiety about her father's advent. Grace didn't mind the defaulted attention: her puzzles could wait, bowered by fragrant question marks.

"It's not what he'll think of me I'm worried about," Kathleen murmured toward the door, "or what I'll think of him either."

"No?" Stan hunched a wide flat chest over the coffee; a forefinger rubbed buckteeth. He sat opposite that part of the restaurant which trapped coupon-clipping, buzzing widows, scooting collegiates working next semester's tuition, and chattering career women careening food down their throats in a decor that was by far more corseted to film-thin sandwiches and evasively-signed cocktails than the consumption of meat and potatoes.

"But I can't tell you what it is," Kathleen sounded helpless, "because I don't know myself," and rested those never less than accusing blue eyes on him. Her forehead, Stan trailed beyond, displayed not a line: had it been worn smooth from things that forever slipped off? Really, he grasped a light counterweight, she was much too young for that. His brawn went afloat, then; he shifted, to recapture anchored weight. He remained silent; search would have negligible point: he hadn't yet mapped the site of what transpired in her, if anything. Perhaps, perhaps her father's appearance might cause, so to speak, Kathleen to geologically reshuffle. Since she was of course too young to be settled. Such youth, Stan self-chastised, shouldn't be deeply loved. On the other hand, she had been visiting Wesley rather often these past few months. But Wesley. My god! His simper and lisp to each new boy that he had Manhattan's best air-foam mattress; at parties, drunk before women's feet, his incessant smug barrage that all they desired was to fornicate. Why, there couldn't even be a mother-son relationship between Kathleen and Wesley. More like a mother-doll. And the girl hadn't reached the period where she'd invest a doll with flesh and blood. Why would she want children, at that? If you can sensualize a girl from top to bottom, fill her with demanding and getting you-ness, which he absolutely knew he had done to Kathleen — then children were quite superfluous. On general principles, though, damn the materialization, soon, of her father. Still, that wouldn't be so bad, Stan struggled to appraise, had not Kathleen seemed to judge it essential that he, Stan, attend her during the visit, because it wasn't for moral support. Possibly — something dormant in the girl, that she sensed existent yet indescribable, and therefore felt urged to awaken and bring out, if only to recognize it; such debut could require both father and Stan; and should that debut not now occur, it might later, anyway. That did not mean, however, that Kathleen would in consequence accept what became known to her. She might reject. The girl's worry might be stemming from a prescience that she would have to accept or reject; perhaps she'd never made choices before, and tonight would see initiation. Stan ruefully pictured himself an elder, of a primitive tribe, watching the rites of the end of adolescence — without an ounce of pride. Wait a minute, he reined back; for Godlessness' sake, you're carrying anthropology too far! Let up. He had a habit which led him to face matters before their features clarified. Had he carried in a draught from outside? It lay now between his clothes and skin. The nights were cooling more than he had suspected. He could have worn a topcoat.

"Got more coffee?" His manner was casual.

"Oh I'm so glad that didn't upset you." And, as if to throw a line out for an indispensable solidity, Kathleen gripped his shoulder.

When the girl returned with the cup, Grace had begun to consult him about which of three eligible men she should choose to be exclusive. Amused, brown eyes quarried deep behind his cheekbones, which added a kind of bitten-off expression, Stan listened, puffed at a cigarette like someone bent on hacking away at its end, and here and there glanced seriocomically at Kathleen, the possible implication that he might make the decisive fourth for Grace.

Were that the case, it could only here have been minor to Kathleen: she was concentrating on the revolving door, thinking what a long, detailed letter she would write the next night to her mother in Maine, about how her father might look, what he might say and leave unsaid, and the little intimate things, for instance, whether he still kept his clothes fresh and pressed, or let them go flabby. Critical or admiring, her mother would seize at what Kathleen wrote. That would consume some of Nancy Malone's time which alone tenanted her brain as a little girl who hopped, terrified, from one foot to another, and hid bits of string, empty medicine bottles and old sheet music in drawers, and forgot where, in that Portland house, clean and modest, where Kathleen had been born and raised, and her father a newspaper editor. Had she been Dennis Malone, she would also have got bored with Nancy and fallen out of love. What had taken her father so long to discover mother's shallowness? There must be a certain handsome stupidity about him as well. Kathleen felt a trifle unnerved: she resembled her mother closely. Physical loveliness wasn't enough, for a man or woman. But how would you find out if you were stupid or intelligent? Perhaps too great a physical attractiveness limited your intelligence. How would you find out? And could you really be an actress? Why hadn't you been taking night courses at a dramatic school? Part of your leisure you preferred spending with Wesley's mother, conferences on what perhaps could be done for Wesley — didn't you? Or giving a party. Or rambles to girlfriends over the phone. Or having Stan take you along Madison Avenue to examine the shops. Perhaps if her father had stuck it out with mother, then she, Kathleen, wouldn't have become such a gadabout. He had waited ten years before locating her. Had she mattered to him at all? Was Major Dennis Malone flying in to see his daughter from sheer curiosity? Clinical interest? Kathleen remembered him dashing and debonair: that type could be quite clinical. Yes, she'd write her mother that too, how clinical the major might be, and how less than dashing and debonair at an amble through the revolving door. Kathleen caught herself. Because — if dashing and debonair no more, then he might be coming not out of curiosity, but because this could mark the first of many future periodic visits. He hadn't said no, had he? It was possible, wasn't it? Since he might want to be with her often. To be her father. The anonymous anxiety she had mentioned to Stan had receded.

"I don't think we ought ever to invite Wesley to our apartment again," Kathleen said between Grace and Stan.

Grace gave her russet hair a last savage curry. "George and Bob are both taking me out tonight, that's how much they want to be with me," and stood up, her makeup weapons packed into a navy-blue kit. "I can't make up my mind as easy as you, Kathleen. You can phone me if you feel like talking to me," she zipped the kit up, the zipper almost wrenched off. "Goodnight, Stan," she flipped a speculative speck from his shoulder, smiled, and made for the Ladies' Room, in five feet one inch time. To summon authority, Stan leaned back from the table, and shook a forefinger at Kathleen. "Now look here —" he began, and stopped. Kathleen was rushing to the revolving door. He rose, coldness in his loins, and rubbed his teeth.

Kathleen had broken her race, and now was tentative toward a somewhat stooped figure, who displayed the gold oak leaves of a major on his rumpled uniform; he had just entered. Another person, however, hung to him with more than rococo design, and flourished a grin as floppy as her undulant, wide-brimmed hat, a most voluptuous creature, Stan could note from his distance: medium height and in her medium forties. Why, still, did the coldness grip his loins? Kathleen's excommunication of Wesley should have fortified him; instead, her sudden tentative approach to the major increased his fear, brought closer a winter season, somehow, to his bowel. Try and put a topcoat on your innards! he mocked himself. On the outside, anyhow, he was more impressive than the army officer, whose sandy hair receded from forehead, chest from stomach, and lustre, Stan supplied the final detraction, from the eyes; why, the major should be taken care of, looked after — and the emergence of Stan's solicitude tended to thin out his fear. Perhaps the accompanying woman would thus minister to Kathleen's father — for so the officer must be — and fear shook him; he hoped then that she had had a protracted relationship with the man, that she had failed in respect to mothering him, and that their intimacies soon would dissolve. For the moment, that presumption interdicted his fear; until what strongly recurred was that perhaps their rapport had quite recently developed: coldness recaptured him. But how was all this connected to Kathleen? His brawn, and the memory of playing quarterback in college football, which he often conjured up for tense situations, did not an iota aid him here; now, theirs were sardonic thrusts.

Kathleen beckoned him to her before she greeted the major, who stood near the door, a bit doubtful, as he twiddled words with the woman on his arm, and darted glances in every direction, that the girl making for him was his daughter, since she had so abruptly slowed her pace.

When she had first caught sight of her father, Kathleen had wanted to overwhelm him with embraces and, at the same time, place Stan by her side so that she could squeeze his arm and swiftly whisper to him how joyous she was, having both her father and him to love. At this point, it wasn't that she no longer wished these actions and words, but that she would have liked Wesley Swift's presence too, which would also have allowed her to maintain the spurt toward her father, had she not experienced, immediately following, a light distaste on her mental evocation of Wesley: that baffled her; because, when he so occurred, she pictured him vaguely superimposed upon the demode lush figure, she had decided, of the nearby woman whom Wesley, she knew, would have detested and burlesqued. And how could she write her mother about Wesley or her father's woman? The girl had been constrained, then; and discontented herself by stepping close enough to Major Malone to award a bright kiss on his cheek.

"Still making a muscle in the middle of your face, Daddy?"

"Kathy!" his leather-beaten face saddled snapshots — his daughter: age one to nine — and galloped into a grin at Kathleen nineteen. Nevertheless, his pride, that this was his daughter, and beautiful at that, warped; he felt that the girl had been cut out from under him by her beauty, which must have acquired numerous, adequate substitutes for him in the decade of his absence, including the rather oafish young man with her here. The possibility that such a thought could have indicated his unwillingness to assume responsibility for Kathleen, and that the very motivation of his decision to visit her after ten years could have been his urge to prompt any sensation of vestigial responsibility in order, should it yet own a breath or two in him, to cast it out — did occur to the major, but he flipped them aside, unwelcome cards in the kind of professional deck he was accustomed to deal: a gambler rapidly evacuates unmarked possibilities. Yes, she was far too beautiful; and she projected, at least to him, the feature of specious untouchedness, which only attains its gloss by having been touched and smoothed in numerable instances. That presented a localized danger to the major: in the process of losing her as a daughter, he might risk wanting to gain her as a woman. So that, with the swiftness he had taken hold of Kathleen, he let her go, not before, though, she registered his brandy-bound breath, which she found repugnant, a reactive ethic she had never elsewhere suffered. They both scrambled to introduce each other's witness, Agnes Tyler in the major's case, and, in Kathleen's, Stanley Davis, who had been waiting a little bent over, gingerly, like tall, large-framed men sometimes will.

Kathleen, at once incapable of small talk, composed a secretive, blank expression, and then wrinkled her lips to a soiled smile, biding. She need not have strained: her father had begun to insist they repair to some other spot. This place couldn't do. The major said it looked like a culinary terminal for the middle class; his nervous vivacity a breeze now touching Stan, now Agnes, now his daughter and, from moment to moment, himself — that it might convince him of his unadulterated animation. He asked if either Kathleen or Stan were acquainted with an old bar where well-heeled newspapermen headquartered their polite abandonment. Neither did. He stressed: somewhere between Madison and Lex, central midtown. Were they quite positive they had never passed it by? Stan said it would have been outside his anthropological line. "Oh I wouldn't be too decisive about that," the commodiously curving Agnes Tyler spoke her sumptuous Southern brogue, and slid a ramp of hat along Stan's shoulder: what with its stretch, she estimated his buckteeth more endurable, however long, she qualified, she and the major remained here. At Agnes' socially acceptable cuddle, Wesley faded from Kathleen's consciousness; while Stan sensed the coldness in his belly to some degree supervened by the desire to yank out Agnes' breasts, which, by the neckline cut, were sacrificial, and slap them down on a counter, like his father had done to raw meat in his butcher shop. Major Dennis Malone still scratched his memory for his old hangout. After all, it had been a little over eight years since New York had last involved him, he apologized for his absented sophistication. Kathleen almost blurted that he was directing greater concern toward a saloon astray than the potential address of fatherhood; nonetheless, on the grounds that this could constitute his groping communication that he was adjusting to her, wanting to find her as his daughter, and that after so long a period, it was terribly, terribly hard, she managed to suppress her temper. The girl laid claim to Stan's arm, and dug the muscle, from which Stan boasted a glance at Agnes, who swiveled onto the major, "Well, honey, we do have to make up our minds, don't we?" The major then suggested that they hop a taxi and cruise fifteen minutes or so: the place was either on East 49th or 50th, and he'd recognize it the instant they passed by.

When they stepped into the street's deep blue shadows, which seemed to buttress the tall structures by which they were cast, while a full moon hollowed their interstices, and buff streetlamp and scarlet, yellow and aquamarine neon signs monogrammed the night, Stan registered fuller impact, beyond the actual mild coolness, from what he determined the nearly wintry air. For him, summer had all but withdrawn. His sudden sexual surge toward the major's woman had subsided; hollowed out, he might have described it. In spite of having lost no tangible link to anyone, Stan was affected by loneliness, even though Kathleen broke her silence to murmur, to him alone, about the evening's clarity and the stars' sting, but spoiled it through intermittent glances at her wristwatch while the major loped down the street to hail a cab. "Just making sure we won't be getting to Connie's party too late," was her innocent reply to Stan's frown. She was lying, he guessed, and let it go: he refused to become twisted up, and insisted on being amused at Agnes Tyler trotting, her body magnificently unconfined, by the major's side.

In the taxi, the conversation desultory, superficial and tense, Agnes, Stan and Kathleen forced themselves to sparse clatters of laughter at Major Malone leaning over the cabbie's shoulder to direct him first down one street, then another, after 49th and 50th had been explored in vain, stopping and starting, the major incessantly tapping the irritated cabbie's back. Soon Kathleen dropped out from the motions of making talk and chuckles; and, grateful that Agnes was stuffed between her and Stan, surrendered to worry about the fact that they wouldn't have more than twenty minutes at the most once they located the bar, and still her father hadn't mentioned when he'd see her again. Washington was so close to New York. It should be easy for him to visit her regularly. But he'd been stationed in Washington a long time. Why hadn't he ventured the trip before? Of course: that Agnes must have been devouring him. Kathleen framed a quick picture: Wesley suspended by his fingers onto the windowsill outside his apartment; which vanished at the point she reflected that her father might be detaching himself from Agnes: they appeared rather casual with each other, as though it little mattered whether they severed their relationship the next hour or shrugged on another week or two. Good. And Kathleen, in a remote way comforted and quite warmed by the sensation of Agnes' pouring flesh by her side, thought how snug it would be to go to bed with Stan now, to have his shoulders shut out the ceiling. Still, the time, the time. Her father was squandering it in this insane, stupid, childish search for his bar, his, his, his. Any bar could've done, dammit. Oh no, it had to be his. She could have beaten his shoulders with her fists, and he would have felt it all right. She had power in her arms. She could have struck at his neck and really hurt him, crippled him, paralyzed him. I'm Kathleen, she wanted to yell at him, sitting right behind you, your daughter, Kathleen Malone, daddy. Please, let it be any bar at all, or please, let's find the place soon; you'll have to be flying back. Daddy, I don't want to go with Wesley, honestly I don't. He wants me to go with him, but I don't. I want to keep on living with Stan. I love him. I love you, daddy.

Kathleen clenched her thin, bony hands: the anxiety had returned, no longer anonymous. The girl leaned forward, arched, rigid, thinking nothing now, the neon signs and streetlamps spasmodic phosphorescent teletype.

Nor was she, when the elusive bar loomed up a few minutes later, in the least relieved. But during her attempt to shake off rigidity, as they sat at one of the white-clothed tables in a section called the "Editorial Room," the other compartments "Straight News," "Sports and Human Interest," Kathleen felt encouraged for the present that nobody singled her out, since, after her father had ordered a round of Scotches, and Welsh rarebit, everyone mechanically acquiescent to his choices, Agnes was having an exchange with Stan, which the major, the girl noticed, seemed rather artificially bent on.

Kathleen had to loosen herself up. And get through to her father. Her bony fingers closed around the whiskey glass, and enjoyed its cool sweat; still, while her eyes glinted and accused, her lips refused to move. How could the deferential waiters be so relaxed? How could the pink-shirted, ruddy-faced men, with their handsomely-ravaged cocktail-women at the bar, lounge so much at their cigarette-holder ease? But in spite of herself, Kathleen recorded the catechism at her elbow, which Agnes fetched in a rubbery drawl while blinking at Stan great gray eyes, whose leaden lids inverted the trough-and-billow motif of her hat. The Scotches had begun to burn low.

"Now anthropology, as I understand it," the Tyler woman was saying, "concerns itself a good deal with primitive cultures, does it not?"

Stan saw himself pushed into a shaky area, not in terms of his formal knowledge; no: associatively. He took a long breath. "A fair amount does, Miss Tyler," he said. Major Malone ordered a second round of Scotch.

"Agnes, Stan."

Apologetic, Stan rubbed his teeth. The Tyler woman rested her bosom on the table and went on. "Well now this here is no reflection on you, but do you think you might say a person who finds himself inclined to study primitive cultures may be expressing a sort of unconscious contempt for modern man in his so-called civilized society?"

"I'm afraid this whole subject can get pretty ramified, and I think perhaps the major might want to — well," Stan trailed off, shrugged, and smiled from Malone to Kathleen.

"Oh no no," the major hoisted his lower lip, "it's perfectly all right for you two to go on. We're all very much taken, aren't we, Kathy?" he turned to her, bobbing his head, and winked with merry goodfellowship. "How is mother?" he added, all brisk beneficence, positive that she would not elaborate.

Kathleen looked down at the charmingly tarnished silverware, which seemed about to melt on the snow-white tablecloth. Her eyes were full of snow. She giggled, and then gazed full at her father. "You remember, you were just like a boy, it just came to my mind, daddy. One of the first memories I have is of you dropping a snowball down the back of my dress, and how awfully cold it was. How awfully cold. You remember," she stated, flat.

"Of course, of course, Kathy!" his hand came around to finger the nape of her neck. "How is mother?" he warned.

Let me remind myself to get rid of this bastard, Agnes noted, her breasts becoming heavily unimportant. And Stan wanted to whittle him down by words, to parallel his father hacking a side of beef. Mastering the impulse, he wondered how long he could, since it would at least have warmed his own gut. But such an action, Stan considered, might harm his own relationship with Kathleen, though why he could not ascertain, because it looked obvious on the contrary that Kathleen would be grateful for a retributive shriveling of her father since the major was so grossly minimizing her. But you may, possibly, be blinding yourself in thinking Kathleen would desire that, Stan admonished himself. This, however, vanished with the actual diminution of his fear at what sharply occurred to him: that it proceeded almost beyond doubt that Agnes did not here act as if she had just entered a liaison with the major; rather, terminal signs cropped up. Not that Stan could discern how a termination, and its consequence that Agnes would no longer, if she had at any point, shelter and coddle the major, was germane to Kathleen, for certainly numerous women could assume Agnes' place, Stan multiplied at once, rendering Kathleen's enactment of the role unnecessary, he ticked it off. Nevertheless, while unable to divine its connection to Kathleen, if any, perhaps refusing to do so, he adjudged the severance of Agnes and Major Malone positive, and therefore good for him, Stan. He smiled. All his warning signals were down. No fear or tautness assailed his stomach. Maybe he would tear into Kathleen's father. He would see. The major deserved that, by Stan, especially.

"Mother's all right," the girl mumbled, and took swift swallows at her Scotch. All I have to do is listen to my father, she sniggered to herself, and I don't need reducing pills. Again she remembered Wesley hanging outside his window, counting to nine. Never beyond. And always a roomful of people around. Though there was always the chance he might count to ten. Only she, Kathleen, might stop him from deciding on the last number. Wait; she was ahead of herself. She must be. She clasped her hands in her lap, as she would have years ago on a school desk, before a class began. You must have discipline, she thought. Daddy would come to see her often. But, what if not? Oh, then — then Stan might beg to remain with her. She lifted her chin. If no force from her father, then she'd have to possess force, she'd become powerful. That would be something new, wouldn't it? Still, she'd rather the major always be with her. He could even wangle a transfer to

New York. And on Easter, for instance, she could saunter down Fifth Avenue, arm in arm with Daddy on one side, Stan on the other, and everybody would admire her — look, the people would whisper among themselves, what a lovely lovely young young girl, and two handsome men paying her court, one middle-aged and one almost a mature thirty. What a lucky girl! A tremble fluttered her throat; she merely nibbled at the rarebit. Daddy's saving his wonderful news for the very last, she determined; he'd like to surprise me. Oh, Stan, she wanted to rub up against his shoulders and murmur to him, Daddy's going to surprise me. She had forgotten the passing of time. Now she sipped the Scotch, a warm blur round her ears.

"Naturally, before going into the personal psychological implications," Agnes was rushing her words to Stan, trying to smooth over her own anger with, and embarrassment at, the major, "I should have asked you first what you're dealing with specifically in the field." The major, calm, masticated the rarebit.

"Well," Stan bent over the table, even so continuing to dwarf the others, "it's on something I'll be getting my doctorate for."

Agnes suddenly believed that an immense inhibited warmth lay in the boy — that, as she peered at his deepset brown eyes and observed, from the way the overhead illumination fell, hard sparkles there, as if, she gave inward chuckles, lights sprang up from inside him, and tried to break ground.

"My thesis happens to deal with traces of ancient Near Eastern ritual and myth — Babylonia, Canaan — in Greek Drama. The Bacchae of Euripides is one of the places, for instance, where they're evident, very strikingly in the first choral ode, of old ritual patterns of periodic renewals of life, that were done in many primitive cultures throughout the world, as you probably know, to assure the earth's fertility, good crops and the like." Stan threw up his hands and laughed and pushed his chair back. "Really, I've no license to lecture at such a time!"

"Go on, son," Major Malone urged. "Smart lad you've got, Kathy," he patted her thigh, "haven't you?"

"Mmm," Kathleen nodded. That pat on the thigh was very nice. There'd been a newspaper account of a man's heart ceasing to beat during an operation; the surgeon had lifted up the heart, and held the heart in hand and massaged and stroked it till the heart had begun again to beat. How daring, how wonderful. "Mmm."

"Yes," the major said, "you're very stimulating to listen to. Helps the digestion too." He stretched a broad grin.

"Does it?" Stan said, quiet.

"So doctors say." The major forked a hefty chunk of the rarebit.

Agnes cut in. "I'd be most charmed to learn, Stan, if in the course of your studies you come on any contemporary parallels?"

"Would you?"

"Well, you see, I'm studying law nights at the university in Washington — I work during the day as secretary to a senator," she declared her energies, no parasitic lady of leisure she, "and of course it's so important to discern how old Anglo-Saxon laws are embedded in our present-day jurisprudence. Therefore — "

"Only a side issue or so," Stan interrupted. He lit a cigarette and smoked as though he would tear it. "Like mock combats between an individual impersonating Winter, and another Summer — the former, for instance, in furs, and the latter in fresh leaves and flowers. These still take place in certain sections of Europe. Summer, naturally, always wins." Unaccountably to himself, he glanced at Kathleen, and, just as unaccountably, he added to Agnes while he ground out the quarter-smoked cigarette in the ashtray, "But from the weather outside, you'd think Winter would be winning, wouldn't you? But it's all a mock combat, Agnes. Death never really wins at any time. Only temporarily. Only temporary castration."

Mystified, Agnes started to ask, "What are you — " But Stan guffawed, his monstrous buckteeth exaggerated.

"You understand, Agnes. Life is essentially heterosexual."

He lit another cigarette and avoided Kathleen's stiff gaze at him. Her whiskey-blur had dissipated; she sat straight up. Agnes, puzzled, but painfully sensing a carnival of disguised conflicts, fell silent. Kathleen bit her tongue hard, a childhood habit developed when she couldn't have her way. Now she felt ugly: when was her goddamned father going to tell her about his next visit? And she had a notion to urge Stan to take Agnes the hell away from here, take her to their apartment, and take her. She felt like blurting their address to Agnes. She felt like phoning Wesley, and screaming at him to race over and walk her, Kathleen, out of here, and then she'd rip the telephone off the wall, and let the receiver dangle. She could see it dangling all right. What was her goddamned father babbling now? He was yapping everything except promising he'd move to New York. Her goddamned father was trying to belittle Stan, shocked by what he couldn't possibly understand. That must be his code, Kathleen snorted to herself: disparagement of the person he concluded was expressing obscenity in women's presence.

"Is someone financing you to research this sort of thing?" Major Malone managed a snide pleasantness.

"Yes," Stan replied, his tones low and even. "A cultural Foundation. Grants are made."

"They support you?"

"Yes. Like the Army does for a number of our citizens."

"Well, otherwise we should not have been able to intervene, as we have in Korea, by means of a police action. You approve, of course, our action there."

Both Agnes and Kathleen wanted to shut them up. But all that could occur to Agnes might be the suggestion that she and the major had to make a plane schedule; and, reluctant to separate the girl from her father until the last possible moment, she held her tongue. Kathleen could have said something to Stan, to change the subject, and stopped it there and then. She did want to, yet the antipodal desire, that her father and Stan hurt each other, closed her mouth. She was getting not to care very much if the major would ever see her again. There were limits to such a tenterhook. And limits to staying in one position, no matter how much Stan financially supported you, which wasn't by the way altogether, because only by her job could she buy essential clothes, the cheapest possible at that. Limits to your refusal to assert your own supreme, incontestable individuality, which had nothing to do with being either a man or a woman, but everything with you as a person called Kathleen. Individuality went beyond sex. Nor did it involve Wesley, a peg to hang your individuality on, a method of arriving at it; that's all he was; she drummed it in her mind to convince herself. And Stan — what an idiot to deprecate her father in turn. Did Stan believe that that could minimize the major's importance to her? and Stan gain by expanding to a more important figure for her? Oh no, she laughed to herself then, not in this tangle he wouldn't. She wouldn't need Stan at all once the major was severed from her. Let them wound each other. Or let them have enough sense to shut up of their own accord. If the latter, they'd then be considerate of her, Kathleen, they'd be thinking of her first and foremost, they would prove they both loved her. Daddy, daddy, she yearned, why don't you prove that you love me? and you, Stan, why don't you?

"I approve our action in Korea," Stan said just above a whisper. "And my younger brother Don does too. But I think this would entertain you, major. I had a letter from him today. Contrary to regulations, three months after induction into the army, he had been sent to Korea and the front lines, carrying ammo to machine gun positions. But he was lucky. The outfit he'd been stuck with had been up front for a long time and, after he spent a week there, it was pulled back for a rest. So he went to the commanding officer of the area and told him his story. Of course, his records were immediately examined, and he was reassigned to a personnel outfit, put in charge of casualty lists, where he read beguiling human-interest stories, like the one of the kid not too seriously wounded put in an intermediate hospital, where while he lay on his cot a sniper shot him through the head. Killed him."

"In a complicated undertaking," the major shrugged, "errors are bound to be made, son."

"I wouldn't argue that, Major Malone. Besides, we all know it's been a mock combat over there."

"I don't think I follow."

"Well aren't we all certain that the summer and fertility of Western Democracy will vanquish the winter and sterility of Oriental Communism? Don't we all know the outcome? Doesn't that make the Korean affair a mock combat? Surely it's entirely unimportant, therefore, whether my brother lives or dies, major. I think you wanted a contemporary anthropological parallel," Stan quite graciously turned to Agnes, who decided at that moment she would contact Stan another time to pursue all sorts of parallels. Then Stan tacked on, for the major's benefit, smiling: "Now there's something for your Public Relations Department."

The major stared at him, a deep sickly flush, as from a stagnant pool, backing up along the lines of his years on his forehead.

Their waiter approached, white-coated, bent at the middle, like a fatuous open mouth swimming toward the table without body. "Will there be anything else, sir?" he asked, a stalled hoarseness.

"What's the check?" Major Malone barked, and the waiter departed. An eager Stan tried to catch Kathleen's eye, but her brows hunched, and she leaned toward her father. Well, Stan contented himself, I can show her later how much she can appreciate what I've done. He faced Agnes, and she was searching her handbag. Smug and sardonic, he lifted an eyebrow, and downed the last of his Scotch.

"Do you really have to go so soon?" Kathleen said to the major.

"There's a lot of work to be cleaned up on my desk, Kathy, and at least two early-morning conferences."

For an instant, the girl's blue eyes, for the first time, were less than accusing; that instant, no quartz stung there, and the lids lowered, so that they did not seem so wide. Shaking her chestnut curls, resting elbow on table to cup that oval topaz face, reconnoitering the white tablecloth, she was far less than nineteen that instant she spoke to her father, chastely chiding, sitting on his knee by way of her elbow, "But it won't be very long before you visit New York again, will it, Daddy?"

Stan ran his knuckles over his teeth. He tasted salt on his eagerness. And he could hear faint drumbeats from one of his ethnic records. Eagerness equalled hollowness, and a nameless dark pygmy, from an unseen blowgun, blew a dart into him.

The waiter brought the check on a little silver plate, and then stepped back a few paces, bent at the middle. While the major took out his wallet, studied the check and removed some bills, he remarked, gesturing at the waiter that he was ready, "Oh. You've got to understand, and I'm sure you do, Kathy, that the Korean affair, and Europe, are somewhat more important than personal desires, no matter how strong they may be. Especially at this time, the army can move me at a moment's notice, and I expect to be." He made a mock fist and pushed it gently against his daughter's cheek. "So it's really pretty hard to say when I'll be able to see you again. You'll remember me to your mother, won't you, Kathy?"

"Yes." Her voice floated from the end of a long cool corridor.

"Can we drop you two off anywhere?" Major Malone briskly volunteered when they stood outside. Their shadows on the sidewalk bestowed the illusion of support.

"No," Kathleen said. "Thanks no. We're walking." Stan, behind her, loomed, yet somehow less substantial than she.

With a hidden sigh of relief, the major kissed his daughter quite hard on the mouth, bruising it, and thereby discharged, as far as he was concerned, his feeling that he ought to sense in himself the deeply paternal toward her, that necessity itself convincing him that he actually did possess a profound fatherly emotion for her, but that he was compelled to inhibit it by virtue of the war situation, which made it impossible to predict where he would be tomorrow or next year. He simply, he concluded, did not own the right to hold himself a father. His sigh of relief he forgot. The hard kiss, he described to himself in postscript, signified the wide dimensions of his affections, and his stoic decision to deny them to, and obliterate them in, himself. He hoped Kathleen discerned that. Being his daughter, she would. He dismissed the trace of her blood on his tongue: it was only, after all, a trace. He had not in the least perceived that Kathleen's mouth had not a whit responded.

During this short interlude, Agnes had contrived to slip her personal card into Stan's jacket pocket; he, much too intent on Kathleen, felt the act and no more. The next thing he knew, Agnes and the major were waving goodbye from a taxi.

"Good luck with your anthropology, Stan!" Agnes shouted. Her hat flopped along the window, and her smile on the side of her mouth. And they were gone, identity lost amongst the dense traffic honking and trailing whiffs of incoming fog down the street.

When they could not possibly have seen her, Kathleen waved in return. The girl knew she had nothing at all to write to her mother.

"Do you have a piece of Kleenex?" she said. Stan handed it to her, and she patted the few drops of blood from her bruised lips, which, got from her father's hard kiss, only stung a little now. He asked if they hurt much.

"No." She wadded the Kleenex into a tight ball and flipped it into the gutter, where the dampness relaxed it. "Let's go to Connie's party," she said, and they started to walk toward the West Side.

They were silent. Stan had no desire to remind Kathleen how he had deflated her father. Minute gusts of damp shifted from one part of his body to another. The weather had turned altogether bad, for him, anyway. The mist which had thickened, and the wind, were running and whirling and waving arms with tattered papers. Apparently Kathleen was unaffected, even with that thin cotton summer dress. He had never known women to be bothered by climate, anyhow. The men would in Korea, though. His brother Don would be totaling casualty lists. He wished Kathleen would say something, but he wasn't going to force her. Her last remark about Wesley had been that they ought never invite him to their apartment again. Beyond that, in regard to his, Stan's, status with Kathleen, his mind refused now to go. Besides, it was more important to ruminate on larger issues, like Korea, and war in general. Casualty lists. Would the earth take a census of the summer leaf casualties? They would fall soon from the trees he and Kathleen were ambling by. Or would the planet drowse, like the coachmen on their hansom tops, lined up on the park side, the horses four-footed patiences, and their masters querying, unemphatic, if they would like a jog around Central Park.

"When we're middle-aged," Stan said, in that deep-rumbled kind voice, to Kathleen, taking her skinny hand, no other part bony about her, he pictured, the rest such a tactical construction, so cunning, that, by her side, or merely thinking away from her, he was ambushed, hemmed around by the sweetness of her form, the urgent perfection of her face, zeroed in and shot by the blue quartzing of her eyes: he could not lose the girl. I must not, he swore to himself between the clenched teeth of his heartbeats; and crushed her hand, as one, uncertain of response, might do, realizing unconsciously that one could cancel the risk of the other not squeezing back by rendering it impossible through the force of one's grip, keeping it thus, to claim, if the other loosened, well, she pressed back, but I couldn't feel it because I clutched so tight. Nor could he tell whether she replied or no, since in further defense, which would in a few moments be adulterated without his awareness, his ideas and emotions had already rushed on to camp at the larger issues. Five years ago one war had ended, and then the country had got partly embroiled by one more; first he, now his brother. A chain of blood relationships to international conflict. There would be no end, ever, to conflict; which was probably, he negotiated transient contentment, how both the individual and the race managed to evolve. But that observation must have been recorded as long back as the Golden Age of Greece, Stan thumbed on. You get goddamned tired evolving; weary, in obedience to an allegedly unchangeable biologic law. Why must you necessarily evolve? progress? become more complex? develop a larger brain pan? For the sake of the sequence? the follow concept? A new god, or an old one: God the Follow! Be glad you're a link to the Higher Forms expected later! For this, you could presume that the Higher Forms would decorate you — with death. Sorry, he fumbled the mordant forward pass, I haven't been introduced to them. Who were they, these Higher Forms? Was he himself one? grown five years after the Second World War more capable, talented and perceptive? Odd, it charged in, that if he had grown at all, he would identify the link, to that advanced state, with Kathleen, and his loving her, whose deft profile he caught softened by the fog from tuft, huddle and hide-go-seek among and around bush and tree along Central Park West. But how did she look upon herself as a link between the inception of the Second World War and the Korean affair? With her father walking out on Kathleen during the former, visiting in the latter and parting from her the second and probably final time, what had she, at this point, evolved into? And his brain could no longer refuse to proceed beyond her spoken decision to exclude Wesley from their apartment. What, really, did the girl now feel about Stan? You're funny, he told himself: how else that comic draught around your groin? If only he could hack a thing into clearness by physical, tangible means — again like father had done to bloody meat on the butcher shop wooden block, or he himself in his college days by a plunge through the middle of the line. And if only he could by sheer force erect a vast barrier against the endless cycles of war and peace, of fertility and sterility, against the farcical march of the seasons themselves, halt once and for all the giant circle of spring and autumn and summer and winter. The silence to Stan had become overwhelmingly oppressive. But before he could utter a sound, Kathleen had taken his arm with both hands and pressed up against him, and was saying, in compassion, "Hello Stan. My goodness, we really haven't seen each other all evening, have we?"

"I guess in the circumstances it sort of couldn't be helped." He struggled to prevent a stutter. He wanted to sit down a moment with her, but the benches were too wet, he decided, and unimprinted: nobody would tarry here in this weather. Not too many people were out altogether; even the gay boys weren't cruising, they and their jelly eyes, that you would like to tear out sometimes, and substitute stone. No, he slammed his teeth together, he wouldn't dwell on homosexuality. Concentrate on the traffic, rather; automobiles and taxis, the slick stuck sounds of their tires on the misted street, like rubber rollers on saturated paper. The traffic, back and forth, the maneuvers of the drivers, the green and red lights, the sudden speed pickup, the quick brakes. Impersonal. Ignoring Kathleen and him, ignoring the empty benches; they were passing so many emptinesses.

"Wasn't that Agnes a bitch?" Kathleen merrily demanded.

"I didn't think so. Why?"

"Oh, if you didn't think so ..."

"Well tell me why you felt she was."

"No reasons, Stan. A woman just feels those things, that's all."

"You ought to have reasons."

"I just can't think of reasons now. Because I've got the funniest story to tell you."

"About what?"

"You'll just love it."

"Well what is it?"

"It's about Wesley."

"I don't want to hear it."

"You've got to, Stan."

"No. I'm not interested."

"Why not?"

"I'm not in the mood to hear stories about Wesley."

"Oh one can always be in a mood to hear stories about him."

"I'm not an always, Kathleen."

"Well I'm going to tell it anyhow. Even if I have to talk to myself."

"I'd rather you wouldn't."

"I don't care what you'd rather. It's very funny. Very." She had released his arm, and walked, a stiff, erect carriage, beside him.

If he could have encircled her slim waist, brushed a breast, stopped her mouth — but he was impotent. As though the impersonal traffic along the street had been detoured between them. Still, perhaps it was for the better that he could not now bring himself to such intimacy. Her story might be an emergence, with which he could grapple, that which she had evolved into.

"All right. I'm listening. But by the way, before you start, I want to tell you I'm sorry about how your father treated you."

"I'm not sorry, Stan. Not in the least." Kathleen ran a doubtful tongue over her lips bruised from her father's last kiss; they hurt less than she had expected.

"That's curious."

"Everything's curious to you, Stan, and complicated. Nothing is simple."

"That's right."

"You know it doesn't really matter one way or the other, complicated or simple."

"Maybe. But I want some things to matter, at least to me. I'll try to make them matter."

The slightest of weights pulled down a corner of the girl's mouth, and then snapped off. "As you choose, Stan. Now, will you enjoy this anecdote about Wesley?"

"Go ahead." He said that calmly, and had the quaking impression that his girl, his Kathleen, had marked her birthdays beyond his own with a swoop the moment the rites of the end of adolescence had been completed. He was somehow, he told himself, no more a tribal elder. Her flawless face blurred a little from the thickening mist as she began to recount how Wesley, some years ago, still using his parents' residence as a base camp but maintaining his own room in an East Side fifth-floor walk-up, had inveigled a drunken sailor there.

Stan trudged big and hunched by her side, hands plunged in pants pockets, a sodden cigarette sunk between the tight droop of his lips, his broken nose stuffed by phlegm, which he sniffed in savagely every now and then. His deep eyes niched against the fog, by which, across the street, the granite patches of the Ethical Culture building shifted mass. His mouth seemed a bit sore, steadfast over his buck teeth. What the hell was Ethical Culture anyhow? the irrelevancy heehawed through him while he listened.

"Anyhow, after Wesley and the sailor were through," Kathleen skipped on, jaunty, zooming an occasional hand to skate thin fingers along a park bench and fling the collected wet, as if to preface the presentation of her aristocratic crested card, into the features of the mist for a duel, "the sailor naturally asked to be paid. Well! That was too much for Wesley. He thought he'd done the sailor a service. So. He picked up the Beethoven bust he kept on the mantelpiece — you know he loves music as though it should be grateful — and brought it right down on the sailor's head — who was lucky he wasn't killed! It was awfully strange, though, the sailor didn't lose consciousness, but bled like a stuck pig, didn't say a word, just opened the door, staggered down the stairs leaving a trail of blood all the way, got out to the street and disappeared. The next morning the landlady naturally saw the trail of dried blood down five flights of carpet, and just then Wesley was coming downstairs. She opened up. She raged at him, you know? What sort of house did he think she was keeping, and all that, and positively screeched her demands to know what had happened. Well. Up to then Wesley hadn't said a thing, just stood there quietly. But then, to her howl as to who was responsible for the bloody trail, he drew himself up to his full five feet four inches, struck a light to the Russian cigarette that drooped from his long holder, blew one puff of smoke into the landlady's puffed-out face, and said, 'My dear. If I've told you once I've told you a hundred times. The altitude. Nosebleed.' And with that he marched right past her and out the door. She was left, Wesley told me, with her sails stooped! Isn't that a perfectly marvelous story, Stan?"

Kathleen's skittish laughter dappled her whole body as she flung out her arms, confronting him at their pause before an intersection that curved in from the park, almost hidden now by the fog's rumpled tarpaulin which seemed to have been hurled from the grandiose vertebrae of the apartment buildings on the opposite side of the street, where several window lights wriggled.

"You're getting a helluva lot of sadistic pleasure out of it," Stan spoke more roughly and loudly than he intended; guilty at the overemphasis, he was nonetheless glad of it. Something nagged him to ferret out negative qualities in her, to invent them, if necessary; and, should they really be there, per se, to magnify them. Yes, paralleling, his flesh shivered, his limbs weighed him down, and a cry sounded through him: if only it were possible that he wouldn't be pushed to utter independence of the girl; well, perhaps he wouldn't be, but he'd view her as she actually was, too; he'd keep her defects conscious, constantly. And though another part of his mind fought to remember some of his prior analyses, feelings and supposed intuitions about Kathleen, her father, and Agnes, the contest was in vain: those had become irrelevant, and superseded by the cardinality of what he judged the larger issues, which, beginning to flare up, could alone validate his cry that it might be possible to prevent being compelled toward thorough independence of the girl, by his explaining to her how they worked on her, so that he would not have to dwell on Kathleen's negative aspects. But why was he so ahead of himself? She had merely spun a story about Wesley. Just a story. Nothing more, surely. What was this awful nonsense of being independent of her? He loved the girl.

In spite of the fact that the red light at the intersection restrained the traffic, Stan and Kathleen lingered at the curb, their eyes meeting.

"There's nothing about Wesley, nothing at all, that makes me feel sadistic, Stan," Kathleen said, her chin lifted, her willowy richness arched. "He's a very weak person. I know he could use someone's strength. He needs strength, Stan. Gee, I know I shouldn't spring this on you, but I've been thinking about it for a pretty long time, and I might as well break it to you clean now and not hedge. I've been talking to Wesley's mother about him pretty often, and she even said many times how it would be so wonderful if her son had a strong woman to take care of him. You know he had five years of psychoanalysis and it didn't do him a bit of good. You remember I've told you how often he threatens to commit suicide, how he gets outside his apartment window and says he'll count to ten and then drop. Well so far he's only counted to nine. Well I don't intend he go further. I can prevent it. I think I can, anyhow. A person should try, Stan. A person should leave no stone unturned. I think I might be able to give Wesley the strength he needs by going to live with him. And I've decided I will live with him, Stan."

Mechanically, he cupped her elbow and guided her across the street. He had perceived, of course, and was to his satisfaction now completely convinced by, the key to the fundament which underlay Kathleen's announcement, and her true motivations. No, she had no faults. No. That Ethical Culture building awhile back possessed as much irrelevance as those prior analyses and sensings he had harbored about Kathleen, her father, and Agnes. Those were nothing. He had forgotten them. The paramount larger issues solely mattered: war, death, sterility. Despite his terror at the prospect of losing the girl, he would demonstrate to her how these cardinal factors had worked on her: that might bring her back to him, though those forces would probably prove too much for him. He nevertheless could not surrender her without a battle. Although he visualised himself seizing her whole body to crash it down on his father's butcher counter, there to bludgeon her into submission, he knew he could not physically compel her into anything. For him there obtain no more the straight-arm plunges through the center of the line; no more the immense luxury of abandoned protoplasmic expression which once had supplied him such tremendous gratification. You could not be that physical with someone you loved. You cannot make people love you by beating it into them. His mouth was dry. He dared not look at her. He was almost inarticulate, as if the fog were stopping his mouth. Ethical Culture! the mock careened through his mind. Irrelevant, irrelevant! But he couldn't explain outright to her the decision to leave him. There had to be preliminaries. Yes. His big body huddled around its shrunken, cold spine. There were faults in her! he shouted to himself.

"Your loving me," his voice a difficult stretch above a whisper, "that's been a lie, then. Kathleen the liar. The faultless-faced liar, cleancut blue-eyed hypocrisy, shining sham —" he began to enjoy himself, his tones unkinking, deriving pleasure from their motion, becoming louder when she broke in to insist that she would refuse to discuss the subject.

"If it's a fact you love me, there's an explanatory debt," Stan said.

"I do love you, Stan. But beyond stating the reasons I already have for wanting to live with Wesley — I won't go. You can just supply what's behind them yourself. I won't be under any debt." As though she stamped her tongue rather than a foot.

"What makes you think he'll accept you?"

"He's asked me."

"Well, I — I'm asking you to stay with me."

"You'd better shut up, Stan. I don't want to laugh at you."

Now he wanted to fall down on the sidewalk. Now he wanted to claw at one of the apartment house doorways they were passing, and sink to the sidewalk, and cry. His throat was wet, and his nose full, and he had to blow it hard.

"You will make me laugh if you keep blowing your nose so hard," Kathleen remarked.

"Kathy. Please stay with me." He went blind a moment. Could the mist have composed a cataract over his eyeballs? But he must keep walking; one leg, then another: so.

"Do you want me to get you a doctor?" She sounded rather irritated.

"What are you talking about?"

"You seem hysterical, Stan. I never thought you could be. You're so big. It doesn't look right coming from you, doesn't fit. You should be so much older than hysteria too."

"You sound like a sarcastic fishwife."

"That's better. Keep it up."

"I really don't want to."

"Go on."

"No."

"Please. Explode, Stan. Why don't you? For once in our relationship — explode. Nothing underground, nothing concealed. Yell."

"I don't think I have to."

"Too bad," she flipped it, shrugging.

No further preliminaries, he thought. He would have to tell her now why she had decided to leave him. Laboriously, a gross effort in the mist and cold, Kathleen was faultless. If the girl couldn't understand, that constituted no defect. Did he hallucinate? Impossible; the mist, of course, clothed the approaching people with illusory furs. It couldn't be that cold. He wore no furs. Had it not been for the fog, the park trees across the street could have been witnessed all green. He wished he could rip off that gray fur from both the trees and people, and announce the world still green, that he strode without a topcoat, see, he himself yet sunburnt from the days Kathleen and he had spent at the beaches this summer when he had sported varicolored swimming trunks, the Hawaiian type, floral, fronded, warm. It wasn't quite the end of summer. Not quite. Yes, he must explain to Kathleen the great, cardinal forces that had worked on her. He must try to regain her.

They had turned down 84th Street, having some blocks to go before they reached their friend Connie Harvey's place near West End Avenue. The brownstones thicklipped and voodooed from the mist; and that last subway rumble a remote roll on the drums. From a third-floor apartment a brilliant oblong of light, coinciding with a fog-strip slipping away from the brickwork above, revealed the horseshoe form of shallow stone inserts which curved over the windows beneath. Stan and Kathleen noticed the charm, and abased their gazes to the sidewalk.

"Look, Kathy," his voice, a dogged patience, bore down, yet carried an enormous attempt to project considerate comprehension. Kathleen skipped a hand the while over fenders of parked cars, and her eyes darted about: she never knew when she might miraculously discover a lost coin, or a scatter pin, or perhaps a ring with a semi-precious stone, or a bracelet minutely glittering. She could always use a ring; Stan had never given her one; it didn't matter that they couldn't be married: he could at least have made more pretense, because a girl's certain finger feels awfully naked sometimes. "You see," he said, "what's motivating you to leave me is rather tremendous. Perhaps if it's really clarified, you may not want to go."

He rubbed his teeth with a forefinger. He had the sensation that an ice-muscled wrestler had penetrated him, a sub-zero antagonist who grappled his heart and intestine, unfairly because inside, glacier-weighted. He heard his own laborious huskiness. "You may not. No. You see, Kathy, it's been twice. You loved him, deeply. Your father. You were bound to. Daughters must, you know? Well, he's male. A procreator, heterosexual, unconsciously embedded in your mind as the continuator of the race, of fertility. Don't you see, Kathy? It's so very simple. Then, when you need to express your love toward him, and need him to have him express love toward you, the war made him leave you when you were very young. You were only nine, then. He left you, the male did, the potent one, the heterosexual; the war made him leave, ripped out the whole potential of love between the two of you, left it vacant, Kathy; he was drawn over to war, which held not love but death, held destruction and the possibility of the end of the race, impotency, war the homosexual, war the fairy, Kathy!"

His blood pounded, clusters of anger wound up his throat, ice and flame oscillated over his body. "All right, listen, now," but he could not look at her, as though in a sense he contended as well with a de-ovarized woman within himself. "Listen. That must have been a great shock to you then. But somehow you must've carried in your mind that it could only be temporary. That that father, the male, the continuation of life — would return to you, and that you would still receive love from him. For ten years you hoped he would come back. Tonight he did. And once again he leaves, probably for good. It is the second overwhelming shock upon you, Kathy! Don't you understand? So now you react, violently, obviously, in the opposite direction. Once again war made your father leave you, for death and destruction, for impotency. Once again, your unconscious says, he prefers the winter of unprocreation rather than you. Once again he gives his love to that which cannot be fertilized by love."

His skull had a wizened ache, which the mist could not cool. "Once again fertility rejects you. And I, Stan, must also represent the male to you, the begetter, the affirmation of the going-on of the race. You are overwhelmingly shocked the second time. Who, now, can you reject in turn? What must you reject? Certainly you must turn away from all that is truly male — and yet, yet, Kathy, you must love that very thing that your father was compelled to love — you too must come to be what your father was compelled to desire: non-fertility, non-procreation. So that you oppose me, heterosexuality, and reject me; and decide to be with an individual who will corrode the love you still have for me; and finally love him, that individual conveniently present in your constellation, Wesley, homosexual, incapable of race continuation, a death, a destruction. In short, you decide you will love your father's war, link up with sterility in the person of Wesley, and sever your connection with fertility in my person. But what, Kathy, has been the overriding, gigantic force which has twice visited this shock upon you? The force that, larger than your father, took him from you and now is taking you in turn from me? The force greater than any of us. The force which, however, if you recognize its working through the medium of living things, you can fight and possibly be equal to. That is the force of death, destruction and sterility in war — that force it is which in essence alone is responsible for your reaction now, your severance from me, your acceptance of Wesley. And if you will ask me who or what is the mover of such a force, I cannot tell you, I do not know, I do not know — but see it, Kathy, I beg you, see it and do not go away from me."

His broad-shouldered hulk half-turned to her. He thrust out a long arm and grasped her shoulder, halting the girl near the curb. His buckteeth displayed a cross between a grin and a devour, like a type of African mask. The mist obscured their feet; and they were a little unsteady, their bodies wavering.

Kathleen's answer was thin and cold. "That sounds very stupid. Your throat must have an awful lot of phlegm in it. You better blow your nose again, Stan. I'll keep a straight face."

Stan let her go.

They crossed Columbus Avenue, then Amsterdam, then Broadway, where the concentrated scintillance from cafeterias, delicatessens, bars and drugstores poured through the mist over Kathleen's proud carriage. Who was the tall hunchback ambling by her side? Stan self-queried. But that was irrelevant, he evaluated, like the sudden conviction that tomorrow he would receive another letter from his brother Don, in Korea, who would have written that he lay in the hospital because an unforeseen bullet had deprived him of his masculinity. Such an event could only matter to Don, not Stan. Trivial too. As only in his mind now trivia chattered replies to Kathleen, which he refrained from voicing: "My nose feels sore." And, "I'm tired of shaving; women are lucky they don't have beards; I won't shave tomorrow. I won't." And, "I hate to step on cockroaches." And a trivial essay at a joke, "American alcoholics are bromosexual." He could summon up nothing important. A vacancy in him. Like that doorway, on which hung a frost-lettered sign, "Vacancy — Room For Rent." Trivia. He glanced at Kathleen. She was very beautiful, Stan nodded assent. Still, if he had her in bed this moment, he would fall asleep. A few more trivial irrelevancies occurred to him, which he could not resist uttering, inventory-style.

"Before you met me, Kathleen, you had eleven affairs, each lasting no more than a couple months."

"Twelve affairs."

"Excuse me. All right. You see how durable ours was?"

"Of course you still haven't divorced your wife. Now you can just fulfill your intention of eventually going back to her."

"That's irrelevant."

"Yes, Stan. Anything more?"

"You told me once, not long after you met Wesley, how one night you were walking with him in Washington Square and he had a sudden impulse to hit you, and he did, in the mouth, and the blow was strong enough to make you lose balance and fall, but that you did nothing but giggle. And he has lots of money too, hasn't he?"

Kathleen stopped and read a number over an entrance. "Isn't this Connie's, Stan?"

While they ascended the stairway, Stan thought how the fog outside had apparently begun to thin, portending a starry sky, so that much later on it would be sharply stimulating to march back to his own place, superbly drunk from party whiskey, through such a crystal-clear night. After all, the Cardinal Forces operated outside him. He wasn't responsible for their acting on others, Kathleen for example. Nevertheless, he must get quite drunk. To fill his vacancy. Dully, he rubbed his buck teeth. Already, he felt a bit drunk, devoid of tension, and somewhat warm: as though he were clothed by furs. A huge dwarf in furs.

They paused just inside the apartment door to try and discern who was who among the torqued bodies on the studio couch, the chairs and the floor, the scene blanketed by cigarette smoke and the radio tuned full blast to the last movement of Beethoven's Ninth Symphony. Then somebody squealed "Kathleen!" at the top of her nose and charged up at them from the studio couch tangle, where she had been inflicting desperate love on a young blond man, of the cowlick-face genus. The charger was Connie Harvey, wide-hipped, narrow-shouldered, with thick muscular legs and cliffhanging breasts, stubby-statured and possessed of girlish grandmother features, exquisitely old-fashioned, around large warm brown eyes, over which sparse black hair straggled.

"I didn't think you two were coming!" she complained in a maternal singsong, and smiled, her perfect white teeth adazzle, which at once gave way to worried compassion. She grasped Kathleen's bony hands. "Gee you don't know how awfully sorry I am about Wesley, Kathy. Wasn't it horrible?" Her tones, a rich grief, spiraled from the most sumptuous chocolate engagement.

Kathleen, silent, parted her lips; they were stinging from the bruise of her father's last kiss; her complexion went snowy; gradually the girl pulled her hands away, and one reprimanded her chestnut hair, wild and contorted from the mist, by a burst of brushing palm, which she let then stay at her temple. Connie concentrated on her helplessly. Kathleen vised her tongue between her teeth, and slowly sank them into it, and released — jaw slack. The stinging blue quartz of her eyes ranged wide with rage over the interlocked bodies before her, at last to rest again on Connie. Stan thrust trembling hands in his jacket pockets; curious, that Kathleen appeared blue cold, the blue of her eyes a kind of glacier moving down, and ice surfacing from under her flesh to meet it, the girl taking possession of all that was rigid and frozen; he touched the hard card Agnes Tyler had left him, pulled it out, scanned the name and address and returned it to his pocket; he might write her in the morning. But Kathleen: he must certainly still try to help her. He reached out for her shoulder, and she dipped it from under, turning.

"Let me alone!" she cried, and then to Connie, "Wasn't what horrible?" the sound thin amongst the laughters and dissensions of the party, the dense cigarette smoke and the immense-throated choruses of "All Men Are Becoming Brothers" in the thunderous Beethoven Ninth.

Connie shook her head vacantly. For all she knew, Young Cowlick might have shifted his attentions to another woman. She checked, and was reassured by his smug, drugged expression. Her doctor would countenance her right to make aggressive love to Cowlick; it had been most fortifying to discover that they were both patients of the same psychoanalyst.

"Wasn't what horrible, Connie?" Kathleen insisted.

"Oh, why the way Wesley died. You know," Connie said, distracted, wondering if enough whiskey remained for Kathleen and Stan. "Let me get you two drinks."

With the utmost looseness, Stan declined one for himself. "Thanks all the same, Connie. But how about you?" he asked Kathleen, his frame magnanimous against the wall, a hand, pocketed, edging Agnes' card, and a sort of sky-written obituary high on his mind. A homosexual sterile misfit has been extirpated. How a stiff wall could feel like an easy chair sometimes. Go or stay, Kathleen my love, he sang. The winter, though not far off, could never be permanent. And his brother Don, in Korea, would never have any really vital place of his anatomy stricken.

"I hadn't heard he died," Kathleen ignored him, with a hint of threat at Connie. "And I don't want any of your damn commiseration. I just want to know how he died."

"All right," Connie said.

Stan eased himself to the floor, and quizzically peered up at Kathleen. Under his breath, in time with the radio, he hummed the Beethoven chorus.

"He and three of his boyfriends," Connie recounted rapidly, "oh, about nine-thirty, tonight, were on the subway going downtown. They'd just had dinner and drinks at the Pierre. They were going back to Wesley's place, and one of them happened to be talking about what a wonderful place the Giotto Bar was — you know, in the Village. Well, it seems Wesley hadn't been there for years and he said he had a sudden desire to visit it, right then and there. They were all a little tight, Kathy. That's how these things happen. God it's awful, just — "

"Nine-thirty?" Kathleen interrupted, smiling. "My father and I — "

"I didn't know your father — my god — after all these years — "

"Stop mentioning my father!" Kathleen said, her voice high-pitched. She still smiled, though, and rubbed her bruised lips, as Stan would his teeth, with a forefinger. "You hear? I wish to know about Wesley. Wesley. Come on."

"I simply won't stand for this kind of pressure, Kathy."

"You're my friend," Kathleen said, a plaintive, abysmal girlishness, and pouted. "Besides, Wesley ... " she trailed off.

"Yes," Connie said. A migraine had begun to pound at her again; she worried about Young Cowlick, and was nearly tearful, for a moment, about Kathleen; she wanted to switch off the Beethoven, but there were simply too many bodies between her and the radio, and she must finish with Kathleen. Stan could at least have dropped humming the music — he'd been inaudible before. How could he just sit there, at their feet, and peek up, that big buck-toothed doggy man — why, he should have embraced Kathy and dragged her away from this noise, smoke and confusion. If she, Connie, had ever had the urge to go to bed with that guy, she must have been crazy. She could step on him now, big as he was, little as she was. And poor, pitiful Wesley. But was Kathy so weak to be really concerned about his death, deeply? She, Connie, wasn't. Must she have such weak girlfriends? Poor pitiful Kathleen. What was Wesley that Kathy couldn't take his death in her stride? A shame, of course, that Kathy had to get the news here. She had thought surely that Kathy had been advised; and would never have believed that the girl cherished profound feelings toward that fairy, which was why she hadn't been surprised when Kathy had sauntered in so calmly. So the girl had been with her father, eh? She must sound that bottom later, Connie resolved. The damn cigarette smoke and the Beethoven. And where had her man gone?

"Connie, please," she heard Kathleen. The girl's shoulders were drawn up high, arms stiff at her sides, like a uniformed marcher in a suddenly-halted parade.

"Oh. Anyhow, they'd just got to University Place Station on the subway. The train was at a standstill. Wesley bawled to his companions he had to go to the Giotto Bar, but right away. They said fine and they all started for the subway doors, which right then started to close. Wesley had tried to be first out. Anyway, he kept the doors open with his shoulders. Well, it rarely happens, but it did this time: somehow, no trainman saw him, and the train started to move, and his friends and everybody yelled for Wesley to let go and come back in. In the confusion nobody thought to pull the emergency lever to stop the train; besides, I guess everybody thought for god's sake he'd certainly have sense enough to come back in out of the doors. But he didn't, and the train kept moving and picking up speed. Then they got hold of him and tried to pull him back in, and nobody knows how he was struggling — whether for them to let him get further out or to help them pull him back in. They did get his shoulders loose and back in but his head got stuck or he kept his head stuck between the doors which closed in right on his neck. Oh god it was just horrible, Kathy. Gee I'm awfully sorry, darling. Do you really want me to — "

"Yes."

"There wasn't much more, Kathy. The train kept going. And by the time somebody did think to pull the emergency lever, Wesley's head had been banged and mashed and nearly torn off his neck, except his thick glasses," she said in momentary wonder, "that were found later along the track, undamaged. It must've been awfully messy and — " She fell silent. Stan had sprung up, and extended his hands toward Kathy tentatively, his face sorrowful, but the bared buck teeth giving the illusion of a grin. Kathleen had backed away, her eyes fixed wide on Connie, consumed with an ice-blue blazing fascination. While the Beethoven crescendoes, the laughter, drinking, political discussions and lovemaking on the floor, studio couch and chairs became utterly ensnarled by the fog of cigarette smoke.

Kathleen then wanted the names of Wesley's three companions. Connie complied.

"I've got to find them." Kathleen was matter-of-fact, head high. Her tongue, rather contemplative, licked the bruise from her father's last kiss.

"I think I ought to go with you," Stan said, making as if to encircle her waist.

"I don't want to be touched," she said, body clenched. "And you're not going with me."

Connie approached with similar intent.

"I said: I don't want to be touched. By anybody. Ever again. I don't want to be touched."

And Kathleen marched through the apartment's open door in jaunty step, much like a small girl would swing schoolbooks at the end of a strap, just as someone switched off the Beethoven "All Men Are Becoming Brothers."

Stan started to follow, then stopped, shook his head dubiously, ran a hand through his blond hair and then rubbed his teeth with a forefinger, his lips drawn back, his broken nose and forehead rutted and crinkled.

Connie absolutely had to stand there and observe what, if anything, he would do, her Cowlick for a few seconds shelved.

Stan removed the Agnes Tyler card, and tore it into smaller and smaller strips.

"What are you tearing, Stan?" Connie said, amused. "Kathy'll get over this you know."

"Uh-huh. This is just an old card that's been lying around in my pocket for months, Connie."

"What'd you shake your head for then, a moment ago? Oh Jesus, somebody just turned on that damn music again," she added, and wondered again where her man was. "Wait a minute before you answer," and she went off through the maelstrom of torsos to search out Cowlick, but Stan, deaf to her request, had already begun to reply, staring at the carpet where he scattered the pieces of the ripped-up card.

"I don't know," he was saying, while the final Beethoven strains played, "it's just that — well, a — a man died, and now, right now, I don't like that," he said, his wide shoulders a bit hunched, his brown eyes, still downcast, quarried deep behind the cheekbones, which gave his expression that bitten-off quality, "I don't like that, somehow, because, finally, you're left right in the middle, the way you began, because you've won, and you've lost, and you've won again and somehow lost again, but it's never been winning or losing either, not quite either — you don't know what I'm talking about, really, and neither do I, quite, except that I know the winning and the losing close in one upon the other, blurring each other, so that you're at the middle again, finally, as you were at the beginning. Whatever that means," he said; his feet did little shoves at the pieces of card. "And I guess I'm not sure how that can be fitted into graduate anthropology and the cycle of the seasons," he let out a short laugh, and then looked up, and saw that Connie wasn't there at all, and probably hadn't heard him. That was just as well. The Larger Issues, the Cardinal Forces, he thought. Who was he deceiving? Or was he? He glanced around, trying to sight Connie in the mass of people. He guessed he wanted a drink of bourbon. Maybe even two. No more than that, though. He knew he had to drink a little, anyhow. But not too much: you had to strike a mean. Perhaps, in a day or so, he might consult a lawyer, to ask him how soon he might initiate divorce proceedings against his wife.

"I wonder if Stan has already gone back to his wife," Kathleen mused aloud to her three companions at the Giotto Bar.

Her eyelids blinked slowly. She could hardly keep awake, now, what with all the liquor she had drunk, and not having slept at all for two days.

She and her companions had finished the ceremonial mimicries on Wesley Swift some hours ago, but they had stayed on in the booth, none of them saying very much anymore and becoming increasingly uncommunicative with each beer and rye highball chaser.

It was near closing time; at the bar, two customers perched on the stools, hunched over their drinks like two ancient clerks scratching away with quill pens in remotely nagging dialog. Two sluggish bartenders rested their elbows on the mahogany counter; a third cleaned and polished glasses and lined them in neat rows on a shelf. The mirror behind reflected the particolored bottles too, and the indecisive emptiness of the place.

"Kathy," pleaded the tight and shiny-skinned boy, he of the stripped skull and the high cheekbones, on which arclit youth glared, "if you feel that way about Stan, why don't you contact him?" The other two males opened their mouths soundlessly in supplementary supplication.

It was probably the faintly misty sharp early morning air marking the ending of summer and venturing in through the now undisturbed swinging doors that caused Kathleen to shiver a little. At any rate, the lass of nineteen, stifling thick chestnut curls severely back from her forehead and temples with her thin bony hands, breasts winking through her dress by that swift motion of her arms, the girl Kathleen looked away from them, her eyes now quite unblinking and wide, as if they stared from behind very thick glasses, or their lids had been shored up and stiffened, the stinging deep blue quartz of her eyes for the second time far less than accusing, their blue now muted and dark as though they had moved into the shadow of a long cool corridor, and she smiled with painstaking piety, exhibiting that dimple of hers defined by faint pain, her bruised lips from her father's last kiss no longer hurting, and said, confronting them with her profile:

"Do you think — do you think I'll look lovely — as a nun?"

Her three companions, as one, breathed, "Ah, Kathleen," sweetly sad, inclining their heads to one side, for all the world three angels, each of whom had the fingertips of both hands, extended upward, touching, as if in prayer, as though they were straight out of an early Renaissance painting, at least in the foreground, where neither Giotto Bar nor celestial cloud could be descried, the three hovering in gravest concern over a Mary, Mother of God, the faultless oval of her face touched with the sheerest of topaz, where now, for the very first time, at the outside flesh-corners of her eyes, could be seen the tiniest of lines, like the lightest of iron filings demonstrating magnetism, or the stigmata of force, possibly because a child was missing from the canvas.

— IMAGE IN STATIC CONTINUUM

There are other stories that ought to be told about Alec Cornwall, plus the one I'm going to tell here, the way he passed it on to me.

How, for instance, that soft-featured, cat-loving artist died. Just a few months ago — he was thirty-eight at the time — at the afternoon preview of his first one-man show in the Lubin Galleries, while a bearded confrere, Ariosto Nikolaides, a fat and fussy fraud with the bad eye caught eternally at the outward corner, tried to spray Alec's ex-wife, Jean, with passion via wheezing diminuendos. Cornwall was standing about seven paintings away. In one pudgy hand he held a cocktail too tightly, and puffed at long intervals on the ancient corncob pipe he negligently fingered in the other. From the rear, his spreading rump wadded into unpressed pants. Reversed, he showed a face from which the dregs of a vague bliss petered out as he occasionally replied a loose-jawed drawl to a handsome blackhaired lass, who hadn't quite made up her bipsyche to ride to glory on whoredom or art, and managed to quiver on the spot reminiscent of both. The late gray decor of the place successfully dimmed the drafts of voluble ladies shaped by Modigliani, and the mordant sallies of men bent from El Greco. The blackhaired wench was shaking her pre-Christian rosary at Alec when his cocktail shivered and he collapsed, the drink spattering the girl's frantically-colored frock and Alec's non-objective painting on the wall to her left, listed in the catalogue, "No. 8, Image In Static Continuum," because as he fell to the floor he flung up the glass. He kept clutching his pipe, though, but its fire and ashes scattered. In a moment or two, the point at which Jean squatted close to his bluebrushed lips, he was dead. The hospital ascribed the immediate cause to heart-failure, brought on by various complications, malnutrition included. The latter could have been avoided, really, had he eaten decently in the last couple years, and the five-thousand-dollar bank account he left for the care of his cats could have enabled him. That two-year period had seen a painting society, made up of Grammercy Place dowagers who anchored themselves to easels Tuesday evenings only, become so fluttered over Cornwall's work that they proteged him by purchasing canvas after canvas.

So he had had the money, but somehow he couldn't or didn't want to relieve himself of eating hotdogs or pies or pickles for meals, a habit begun fifteen years before when he realized the populace wouldn't accept his paintings on his say-so. Still, he'd be pleasantly damned if he'd petition the world to stopgap him by letting him squirm women's feet into shoes, or salivate ten-dollar bills in a bank-cage, or preen a compromise at any tidy tide-over to gain admission into art on triple-amputee hours. Not that he had bitched: he merely grinned, pliably, three front teeth evacuate, and proceeded to live off Jean, who had married him out of maternal pity and kicked him out a few years later on its inexorable change to independent contempt.

From there on, Alec Cornwall sponged on friends who detested him. Financially stable intellectuals, for a while, enjoy an indigent artist they regard as a quiet, childlike fool, on whom they can heap roast beef, sarcasm and commiserative dessert, finally, while they bare their teeth at the artist's jungle position in the capitalist status quo. "Yes," Alec would agree, sweetly, "you're right," incapable of further comment swallowed in the shortcake bounty. When he couldn't persuade meals from them, he'd chuckle in rather a paternal way. "All right, but how about half a buck, huh? Two bits maybe? For a water-color?" a blond cowlick hovering to tickle his humped, then spatulate nose, which one felt any moment would spoon his chin. With the coin he would buy the pie or hotdogs, but halt satisfying half his appetite to delegate most to his brood of cats, By and by, his enmitous friends thinning out, he wouldn't eat at all for two or three days at a stretch.

I don't know. Perhaps by the time the Grammercy Place ladies started to fill his pockets, he had said everything he possibly could on canvas, and knew it, but couldn't stop his brush, so that he starved himself to taper off life. Then again, the explanation might have been that the years of painting without critical or financial recompense had ruthlessly roughed up his resistance, drive, flexibility, which had got him quite tired. He did look that, enormously, at the last party I caught him at, oh, about three months before his one-man show, down in one of those scented, whitewashed ratholes off Washington Square. At least seventy-seven people had assembled to stuff themselves with chive cheese, crackers and beer to sink the a-b-c of relativity with the X-Y-Z of Mondrian. Though it was a squirmy night in tight heat, Alec wouldn't remove his weary, heavy, wool sports-jacket because, he embarrassedly put it, the white shirt underneath had sprung too many holes ringed by dirt. His puffy round shoulders had sagged as he sweated through the party, and his face tolerated again the bedraggled smile on wilted leash, a cuffed, floppy-eared dog of a smile, while he knelt with increasing frequency into large mugs of beer.

But that's another story too. And there were more. How he left a banal notebook, "The Artist in Society," which a few self-conscious brother painters posthumously published. How he never cleaned his Greene Street studio, above a warehouse, for fear he might overly disturb his lounging cats, with whom he slept. Sometimes an indulgent acquaintance would let Alec sleep over elsewhere, in a fresh bed, but Cornwall, when he arose after his donor had departed, and himself decided to go, would wander off leaving a trail of unlocked doors, wide open in the bargain. How Alec never would show anger; at least, nobody ever observed him angry, or annoyed. And how he kept painting, slowly, stealthily, year in, year out.

And the story of how, finally, after his body had been removed to Philadelphia, where he had been born, Alec Cornwall was buried in the rain. Ariosto Nikolaides came, one of his odd skinny arms from his grossly ballooned torso spinning around Jean's shoulders, and his bubble-lips close to her ear, as if he had elected himself to suck out her sadness, although Jean, the rain straggling her red hair, was gaunt enough already. Alec's mother and father were there, of course: they hadn't been in contact with him about ten years. Theirs was that parental grief founded and permanently fixed on the day sons or daughters exit to pursue opposing ends and homes. Mr and Mrs Cornwall had anticipated this afternoon, and were prepared to watch their son lowered into the grave; consequently, at the Methodist minister's intonations, they stood together, two small black sticks, topped by white frowns, the mother who had baked the most succulent pies, and the father who had built up a modest security in automotive parts. Saul Ritter had trudged to the cemetery, too, the middle-aged lawyer who during his spare time labored on an apparently interminable volume on rhythm, which he purported constituted the paramount element in each art, whose manuscript he steadfastly refused to allow anyone a glimpse; celibate, he lived with his mother, and was an old intermittent condescender to Alec; under an arm bulged four books, constant companions, while an umbrella sprouted from the other, his rubicund, square-rigged countenance studiously dolorous. And I was there, perhaps worst of all, come to see what it would be like. I felt that the people Alec had known had been strangers to him, and he to them; that, somehow, he had rebounded off us all, not quickly, nor smartly, but in medium motion, and an ever so faint a cling, the slightest stickiness. Soon the coffin hit the deep, and the grave-diggers began to shove the sticky earth over Alec, to cover up the hole.

Well, as I said, it had been raining at the funeral, mistily, and then it petered out, and the sun appeared, like that day in Provincetown when Alec told me the story I wanted to pass on to you before I became sidetracked on the others, which should be really completed, if Alec Cornwall could ever be filled out. I'm coming to think that a little doubtful: people, trying to remember him, for instance, would shake their heads after an indistinct sentence or two, baffled, and trail off. But let's get to his tale.

The way I recall, Alec had managed to hitch up to Provincetown where I'd been staying the summer about five years ago, after I'd been discharged from the army. He dropped in on me with no warning whatever, his old practice, but since I had a few extra bucks I asked him to stay awhile. One drizzling day we decided to visit that lonely beach-strip fronting the bay, where the lighthouse was the single vertical. Alec thought that if it would clear up he might do a watercolor or two, so he brought his box of paints. Leisurely we ambled over the slippery breakwater rocks, to which an occasional wave whitely bowed. In the rock crevices great gray spiders refrained from spinning; instead they crouched in balls, perhaps inactive till the drizzle would end; tiny opalescent lanterns of wet plied the webs; and, here and there, a caged fly lay dead, at which Alec shrugged.

He seemed a little springier then, but got winded much too quickly: it took us half an hour to make the beach. There we sat on top of a high dune, which gave an enviable sweep of the harbor and bay. Alec puffed, slow-paced, on his corncob. The misty drizzle dragged fragile gray webbing in the sea. The gulls' approaches, merging as they did even at intimate distances with the grayness, could hardly be seen till they were hard on the beach. One gull alighted, and tried taking to the air again, but couldn't, its wings flapping vociferously. I started to rise, vaguely wanting to help. Somehow it must have sensed my intent, for it suddenly footraced away down the sands as Alec put up his hand to stay me, remarking, "It's too fast for you. You couldn't catch it. Besides, it's obviously hurt, and must be by itself. You couldn't tame it by offering help." I thought he might be laughing at me. But his expression bore the gentlest of open explanations, the kindest of instruction. I sprawled on the dune again; and we stared out on the wide waters.

Breaking, the combers showed their teeth, and then cast white-speckled green feelers onto the sand: they flatnosed around fish-skeletons, little burrow-scurrying sand crabs and half-buried driftwood torsos, only to back down into and under the next lap behind, slipped into the ever-widening, ever-narrowing noose of endlessness.

I turned to Alec, who turned to me. The sun had burned a hole through the drizzle. The sky stung blue glint, and the harbor savagely shimmered in green, orange and gold. I saw that Alec was grinning, the three front teeth nowhere to be found. The blond cowlick tickled his humped, spatulate nose; and the light ruddied his day's growth of beard. For once his watery eyes concentrated all their available blue in a merry sparkle.

"What's so funny?" I demanded.

"The sun coming out of the rain. Reminds me what happened the first day of spring this year, in Washington Square," he drawled, easy on the corncob, a buttery shoulder curved into the tawny dune. And he talked at greater length than I had ever heard him before.

"Late afternoon it was, right after the sun poked low out of the drizzle, so the bunch of us — we'd been drinking coffee at my place — walked over to the Square," Alec went on, the gulls ruthless now through the drumming dazzle of air on water, the great hot fish-stench flapping innumerable fins over our nostrils. "I don't think any of us'd eaten for at least three days. Brother, were we hungry."

"Who was the bunch?"

"Oh, Ariosto Nikolaides, in his dumpy black suit with the canned-salmon stains. You know his beard? To me, full as it is, it always looked like a black puffy flesh-beard hanging down. Let's see, sure, there was that coked-up Garry Turner, dressed in a French sailor-outfit, a red pompon on the cap. His twin brother, who was holding a residence in psychiatry out-of-town, hadn't sent him his regular remittance that week, I remember, so Garry, with his healthy Christ-face, was nuttier than usual: he'd kicked out his wife and two kids from his apartment and was trying to interest every broad he talked to to come up and meet that stupendous St Bernard he owned. And Kewpie Whiting — you remember him? Had six sisters, no brothers. He was studying harmony and counterpoint, after six previous years mastering electrical installation, transfinite math, plumbing, archi-tecture, stage-lighting and automotive engineering. He'd get bored after learning as much as there was to know about each and never contribute anything original and go on to something else. Twenty-three and bald as a crystal. And me, plus Trotsky, my newest cat. All starved. Sitting on a bench in the Square.

"There must've been a thousand people around, all out after the hard cold winter and the war. But even if we were ravenous, the sun felt good. Peaceful. You never minded the army rejecting me, did you?"

"No." I scooped up some sand and tossed it at some scraggly weeds nearby.

"They didn't think my ticker could take it."

"So?"

"So even the checker-players were in their corner, moving their pieces. Imagine kinging light and shadow. And the late afternoon sun trailed along green leaves, grass, and the bleeding quartz in the sidewalks, like some invisible ants were dragging bright tiny loads.

"Brother, we were ready to eat. We wanted to jubilate. But not a dull coin between us. And the people around: they looked contented enough, but like they were composed figures in an ensemble. Even the kids on scooters and playing catch. Sure they were moving, but almost as if it was their duty, even the mothers with baby-carriages. It was spring, but where were their big laughs? The spread-out joy? They seemed to wait for some kind of wand, trick, a magic gimmick — to make them appreciate the big special wonderful joke of spring after war and winter, so that they'd roar with belly-laughs.

"And we were hungry. I was getting disgusted. Me, disgusted. It never happens. I knew there had to be laughter and food. I thought and thought — how?"

Alec sprang up. "Let's get closer to the sea," he urged. So we slid down the dune, took off our shoes and socks, rolled up our pants and waded a little way into the waves, so shiftily shocking they were underneath that I felt they were winking intimately next to our shy calves. And there, our eyes chasing out over the horizon, where a sailboat looked as if it were being pulled ever so slowly along by a cable attached to somebody on the unseen shore beyond, Alec Cornwall puffed staccato at his corncob now, and slapped the waves in glee.

"How to get food was the problem, wasn't it? Any food!" he waved his pipe like a baton. "And suddenly I think of a chain of bakery-shops. I looked at how I was dressed. Nondescript. Old army tans I'd picked up somewhere. Sure, I could pass for a bakery truck driver. My face was, is — just as, well, ordinary — fades into a crowd with no trouble. I didn't need a cap. Hell, it was spring. Nobody'd ask questions. It's almost the hour, too. When at this particular store in the chain a truck'd come around to pick up all the pies that hadn't been sold that day.

"Could I pull it off? If I could just beat that truck there, make it about five minutes before the regular schedule nobody in the store'd notice. What's five minutes one way or another? The employees at the shop gave at the end of every day — out of habit!

"So I hand Trotsky over to Ariosto Nikolaides, tell him to watch her so she won't get her head bashed in — and promise my hungry friends I'd be back with food. They look at me as if I'm nuts — and I'm off.

"The bakery-shop's three blocks away, right next door to that cafeteria that's like a badly-lit cave, you know it, where the esthetic troglodytes gather. Before I get there, I muss up my hair a little more than usual, I half-shut my eyes — and there I am, right in front of the blue plate-glass window where the smell of the Orient's coming from, the storybook part — spices, jasmine, cedarwood, jade, wine, magic-carpets, opium, myrrh, frankincense, drunken poets dipping ladles into the moon drowning in the water — all that rolled up in the scent from the bakery-shop.

"I almost couldn't go on. I almost wanted to stand there on the spot, smelling, smelling — feeling, what the hell, the smell's so good it'll probably be a meal in itself floating down to my belly. But no. What of my hungry friends? Could I bring back the smell to them? Impossible. They'd murder me — in cold smell.

"So I really didn't even hesitate. With half-shut eyes I open the door, I walk in, I clump-clump-clump to the counter where there's a girl in a spring-green uniform, the perfect color, she couldn't possibly refuse me, six people are milling around looking over cakes bread chocolates buns.

"And real deadpan, my voice strictly through the nose, I hold out my arms in front of me like my elbows are half-stewed, and I say, 'I come fuh da pies.'

"The girl in the spring-green uniform turns around to a guy stacking cakes down the other end of the counter and she takes up the chorus: 'Hey Joe they come fuh da pies,' and he doesn't even look at me but right off he turns round to a whole big stack of pies, picks them up and without a word brings them down to where I'm standing and loads them in my outstretched arms and very carefully but not too carefully I turn around and a little old lady with bright red hair and a hat with purple flowers swings open her eyes like a big gate and opens the door for me and clump-clump-dump I go out of the store, past the cafeteria like a badly-lit cave, turn the block and in two minutes I'm back in the Square where I dump the load into the laps of my astonished friends.

"'Here, eat,' I command them, and then I stand up on a bench and yell but my friends are piling their mouths into the pies so fast they couldn't be surprised anymore by anything I'd say or do but lo and behold all the people in the Square who'd heard me and seeing us dive into apple and blueberry and quince and lemon meringue like a bunch of animals who hadn't been fed since Noah — all the people around, including the kids on bikes and scooters and playing catch, and mamas wheeling baby-carriages, start to point and laugh like crazy, the big laugh, see, the spread-out joy — because I'd stood up on the bench, spread my arms in front of me like my elbows were half-stewed — and yelled loud as I could through my nose with a real stupid look 'I COME FUH DA PIES!'

"And christ, man, nearly the whole Square takes up the chorus till 'I come fuh da pies' rings through the laughing like some damn new Gloria — and that was the Gloria, that was the song this year, brother — brother to this year's spring that was the greeting-song!"

Alec stopped, tossed his corncob on the beach and grinned so many miles wide that damn gap in his teeth looked like the entrance to Coney Island's Tunnel of Love, and I'd swear that all the children of the earth up to ten years of age suddenly had the wildest convention since the human race began right there on his face, and his blue eyes were shouting to them from the stage "I come fuh da pies!"

Then, with his clothes on he started to race into the deeper water. "Last one in's a snowman!" he bawled out, and I, feeling as absolutely loony as he did, raced right the hell after him with my clothes on, and only the lighthouse could see the two of us racing and plunging into the wheezing, green and white crashing waves, the sweetest cold sea that was ever smacked and dove into by a couple of howling maniacs.

And I'm thinking now, now I'm thinking that maybe all the other stories about Alec Cornwall, the painter, should never be written or told at all.

THE REST OF THE STAFF WAS OUT

Of course, what do you expect? Certainly they're laughing. I can hear them, clearly, through the window, the voices dropping into the courtyard, hanging out their laughter in the night as they would the morning wash. What could they know of him? or want to know?

I can place him, if necessary. It really doesn't matter. But you demand the concrete surroundings, eh? The frame is necessary. A bedroom, a forest. Otherwise, incredible. A person has got to be somewhere, hasn't he? And in relation to something — a post, a victim, a bankbook. Otherwise you lose sight of him, do you? Or what? Would you, then, in desperation connect him to yourself? And you'd rather not. We don't want another's invention, or record, to become our personal concern. Naturally, to concern ourselves with a new weapon is perfectly admirable, or the latest car, or fashion. But we must fob off an invented individual to another relationship. What's wrong? Is it that there's nothing really invented? or recorded?

If it makes you feel any better, I think I might note that his name was Sokoloff. It must have been: it was printed in gold letters on the leather case he carried his glasses in, which stuck out of the pocket of his short-sleeved summer shirt. And he sort of blindly, with his head down, shoved through the open door of my office, looking neither left nor right but straight down at the large manila envelope he bore with both hands.

He bore the manila envelope, it was a load for him, believe me. It had large letters scrawled on it, crossed out. He kept staring at the words in utter disbelief, and utterly baffled. You could see Sokoloff was a baffled man.

You might ask: Why does a man have to become baffled? Is there any reason on earth why anybody should let himself feel baffled even if he actually was? We all say, no. We say, even if nonplussed, even if cul-de-sacd refuse to feel that way. Tell yourself that you see all possible outs, that you know precisely where you're going, that if anybody would suggest any clarification you'd be highly insulted. And, as a matter of fact, you'd entertain a sneaking compassion for the person who tried to help you. Poor, poor idiot, you'd mutter, he must be baffled; and out of the completely topsy-turvy goodness of your heart, you might retort, Is there perhaps something wrong with you, my good man? I myself need no clarification, but you sound as if you do.

Sokoloff might have been just the man to ask you if you need help. As it turned out, he asked it for himself.

He came straight for my desk. Naturally, it was a special desk, with folders on top of papers, and papers on top of folders and within them. Does it make you feel better, now, that you can picture the kind of unique desk Sokoloff headed for? A connection? Impersonal? And yet familiar? You can relax? His manila envelope is removed from your tired back? from your calloused fingers? How easily you do it. What is the magic by which you shift men away from you? Is it a special human gift, do you think? That luxury of letting a weight carom off you? Like going to the bathroom, possibly. Our emotions constantly heading for the men's room and the women's room, where we meet all our friends. Nothing quite like the luxury of developing friends in the very process of feeling you can be rid of them, are rid of them, really. Part of evolution, probably, eh? The developing art of isolation in the midst of relationship. There may be something positive to that, though. Think of it, at birth you may never have to greet your mother, nor she you. It lets everybody off with a clean caul, and clean hands. Can't you see us, right at the beginning? — with the cauls? a huge horde of little monks.

As I recall, and this will help you fix the man in mind too, give him a certain concrete characteristic, you know — as I recall, Sokoloff looked like a little monk, too. But not at birth, quite. He was a man nearly sixty. White-haired. Stocky. A little bull-monk. Nor was he tired so you're not permitted to pity him. He was freshly-shaven, his black shoes shone, his shirt was clean, the hair on his chest abundant, the belt around his dignified belly a new one, his trousers neatly pressed. His black eyes were a little startling under the nylon-stiff white hair. No, he wasn't tired, but the manila envelope was a load.

Without taking his eyes from the envelope, Sokoloff muttered, assuming a settled, definitive, concluded, no-mistake tone. "Bernanos." But staring at the envelope incredulously.

"Who?" I was a little confused.

"It's Bernanos," he looked at me. "It's here." His brow was furrowed. His whole soul concentrated on placement, location, whereabouts, that a matter should be fixed, as opposed to fluidity, that a thing should stop, as opposed to the chimerical. At least one thing, anyhow. In the whole world of a day, let at least one piece stay in one place without moving. You could see he had been moving, up and down elevators, against red lights, through America's

most shining automobiles, clutching at America's most illustrated recep-
tionists, this Sokoloff, this nearly sixty years of age, this stock energy, this
man whose muscles could be seen in his throat, moving, muscles gulping,
Sokoloff in gold letters on his leather spectacle-case.

"We have no Bernanos," I said, as respectfully, as gently as possible.

"Photographs inside, I think," he offered. He unloaded the manila
envelope onto my hands. Not to my desk. Hands to hands. God forbid the
envelope should rest on something inanimate. That would be a violation,
because the coming to rest should be after a transfer to another's hands,
something living. If you gave to the inanimate, you might never be able
to retrieve your missive, not that you didn't want to let it go, but that it
shouldn't drop into a hole. I wasn't a hole, somehow. That was being paid a
certain honor, believe me.

I opened the envelope. Photographs of a factory-machine. Utterly inap-
plicable here, no relationship. I handed it back to Sokoloff.

"It's not for us," I said. "I'm sorry. This isn't the place you want."

"Not Bernanos?" Something was lying, his face said. Not I, not a human
being, but a thing was not telling him the truth, his ruddy face said, his
black eyes crinkling, his lips scoffing. "I came right in," he said, as though it
was absolutely the most natural action, that it was impossible that he could
do else. You see, as much as you might think a matter inevitable, it isn't: the
inevitable, we all find out sooner or later, must be trapped.

Sokoloff has stubby powerful fingers; they held the missive now as
though to rip it, but forever unable to do so.

"It says on it Bernanos," he was surly. "You could change your name,"
his voice cunning, low, detestable.

I didn't want him to be this way. I was offended. You shouldn't do this
to my extending, compassionate heart. I was entirely willing that day to suf-
fer the weight of puzzled humanity: each of us has such a day, we look forward to it, it's part of our schedule. Really. Not to be able to go home and tell
one's wife that you wept for an inferior that afternoon — why, it destroyed
one's faith in one's superior humility. When somebody won't let you extend
condescension, it's an unforgivable insult. You'd like to kill. Why, the whole
social system was, at least in America, geared to have an individual one day
a week say to another: There, there, little man, I know you're little, I know
how difficult it must be for you. I understand: live for one more day because
I understand you.

And Sokoloff was denying me.

"Why should I change my name?" I said, quietly.

"We're all immigrants," he replied.

It was very quiet in the office. It was lunch-time, the rest of the staff was out.

Sokoloff held the envelope under his arm now. He rested on his feet stockily, planted, a little massivity, a piece of whitehaired statuary. "Change your name," he insisted, a little dully. Proudly, somehow, the gold letters of his name were stamped on the spectacle-case; proudly, somehow, it stuck out of his shirt-pocket. "For my sake. I wouldn't have to go anywhere else."

"You're wrong."

"Yes." Sokoloff smiled. "But you'd like I shouldn't be."

"I don't know. Maybe I like that you're turned away, turned away many times."

"You're imagining," he said. "You think you have to have proof you feel bad anybody is turned away. That's a damnation, young man."

I sweated. Sokoloff was cool.

"If you find the place for your envelope," I nearly yelled, "you think that's the end?"

"You wouldn't like I should think that?"

"It's important to understand you've got to break down."

"Me?"

"Anybody," I practically snarled.

"In little pieces, I suppose," Sokoloff said sadly, "in millions of tiny little pieces, so they can lay down on the pieces, they should be comfortable, yes?"

I was silent. He took hold, then, of his envelope with both his hands again. Sokoloff. A man with nylon-stiff white hair. A wonderful bulging nose, you could see the pores in it, like knotholes.

"Let's go back," he said.

"We have to?"

"Well?"

"Not altogether," I said, feeling hurt, hurt, like a cool spring coming out inside me.

"That you don't like, the not altogether."

"That I don't like."

"Force yourself."

"It doesn't take much power," I said, nearly in a whisper, utterly punished.

"No, I don't" Sokoloff was staring at the envelope. "It says here Bernanos."

Now it was time. I think you will agree, to be classic, restrained; time for the formal ending; time, too, for the feeling that a faintly grave ceremony be performed; something like a half-droned ritual between Sokoloff and myself. We should all recognize, I believe, a terminus. I understand that this is called mature: awareness of endings. And I would hesitate — indeed, I refuse — to impugn our concepts of the finish.

"I suggest," I said, my hands beginning to turn over the papers on my desk, and my eyes turning over Sokoloff, so that the gold stamped letters of his name on the spectacle-case blurred, "I suggest you look over the list of firms on the board near the elevator at the end of the hallway outside. There are other business-firms on this floor, Mr. Sokoloff."

"Other firms?" he said, his lips dryly running over the name on his envelope.

"Yes. Maybe Bernanos is one of them."

"Maybe."

"I myself have never heard of that firm."

"Never."

"No."

"Outside?" Not a glance did he give me.

"Yes."

"Ah."

Sokoloff turned, the little bull-monk with the stiff white hair and the startling black eyes, and strode toward the door, a little bent at the waist, shoulders hunched, something like a football-player, and he held the envelope before him with both hands. At the door he paused and presented his profile, with that wonderful bulging nose, whose knothole-pores I could no longer see, and, without peering at me, said rather absently, "Thank you."

"It was nothing, Mr. Sokoloff," I said, in the voice of a wavelet lapping at a small shore.

But he had already left for the interior.

FOB AT BAY

I

Julian Kipperworth, called Kip by all and sundry, a tall blond lean lech of a man, except for his unkempt belly, no matter how he tried to conceal it by fur-collared overcoat and over-ample sports-jacket, which only expanded the impression that he had suspended a wicker basket from his midriff — straight-armed the restaurant door that late winter night, "hardening of the arteries weather" Kip would have dealt it, "good only for the likes of me, a bon survivant," to permit his two-stop subway mistress precedence, one Heather Sankey, a desultory actress, equally the kind of blonde at whom one would stare with the sensation of proceeding rapidly through the medium of her blue eyes from the comparatively opaque to the full flush of transparency.

The parallel may be dismissed, however, at the point where Heather was his stature's square-root. His Chippendale nose frowning, a red mitten at its tip, while her narrow-gauge forehead took considerable freight, Heather let Kip retrieve the mink-dyed muskrat from her scuffed shoulders, "Hang it by the sleeve, dear," to drape it on the coat-hook commanding a surly view of the large booth into which they lowered themselves, Heather then bouncing on the seat several times, before settling, to ascertain the degree of its despondency, if not hers.

"You've still got your parka on, dear," her voice, clipped cactus and steel wool, remained unforgettably on the surface, roughly speaking.

"Man has been ever the non-objective artist," Kip countered. He would have preferred to hang his sentences in a gallery over his paintings, but had never surmounted the obstacle of assaying that the latter were inadequate titles for the former, and had contended himself with displaying his pictures nakedly, mediocrity unaccompanied, far more persuasive than talent elucidated. Nevertheless, he dredged himself from the fur-collared silt and piled it in a corner. Their heads on elbows, Kip and Heather became aware of each other as tripods.

"It's all for the birdies," she chirped, as much as one could possibly swallow that, "but I'm having another drink anyway." Kip shrugged, for his shoulders a feat, and Heather ordered two bourbon and waters from a handsomely-ravaged waitress referred to as Pearl, at her menopause with the thickest possible lipstick, who, after lugging the drinks back from the bar, protested to the proprietor over her shoulder that Gale, who had occupied an apartment adjacent to Pearl's, "couldn't've been more than twenty-two, Mike. And pretty as they come. Why she was just on television last week. I saw her, Mike. I tell you I'm all broken up. I was her best friend." But gray-haired, terror-eyed Mike was analyzing cash-receipts, his tennis-shoe fingers deep in the register, so that Heather placed her own over Pearl's hand when it lingered, square-toed, beringed (amethyst and opal, infinitely semiprecious), after the bourbons.

"What did she do, Pearl?" Heather weathered her own wail.

"Took gas," the waitress indicated, though as red-lidded as if she had applied a ruthless rouge, "and died;" she brushed aside the grim formalities of her graying hair, withdrew her hand and the blithely crimson circular Coca-Cola tray, and pulled out for the kitchen, her great breasts waddling, and flameless gray jets hissing mournfully and incessantly from her eyes.

"Isn't that awful?" Heather hopped on Kip, who sagged, nimbly, and edged on the burro of his knuckles in the opposite direction along his hacked-out mustache, and, after he hung a modest crepe pause, pleaded, "You were going to tell me, Heather, if you loved me exclusively."

She skimped her mouth, already no more than a fizzling scarlet sketch, and trailblazed, "You'll have little meaning for death!" At college she had majored in metempsychosis.

Kip straightened up like an electrified doodle. "I insist on casting my rot with the living, Heather." The overhead light scoured and split his blond hair, Heather vowing to herself that she had caught it in the very act of balding and drooping for shame about his ears, those large phony weights drifting from his antelope-like skull.

She laughed.

Kip read his fingernails oracularly; pleased, he slurred, "I'm glad you've returned to my senses, Heather, Now — I think you should make a decision as to who you — "

"Isn't this a homey restaurant, Kip?" she bounced in, her powerful calves bulging at her throat, her buttocks bitten by springs, and she threw her eyes around the place, in a kind of visual ventriloquy of which Heather Sankey was the sole extant practitioner.

The term "homey" could have been remotely subjective. It might have been partially evoked by the name of this particular eatery and bar, which had been hit on when Mike Pasture, the proprietor, had bought it some twenty years ago and was casting about for a suitable synecdoche; he had happened then to have been exchanging soliloquies with one of the interior's more enfeebled habitues, a man who seemed bottled in tweed, and found that his customer occasionally was attached to the Museum of Natural History, a hideous hut in slab and baffled battlement two blocks away; Mike, terror-eyed even at that time, but considerably more curious about man's specialties than now, inquired the tweed's vocation, to learn that it was archaeology, which struck Mike that, if shortened in the naturally necessary way it should be, so that we might endure the ancestral length, it would compose the perfectly respectable designation for his restaurant. "The Ark" it became; whose insides at night, under the fluorescent illumination, were strata of powdered intensities in blue and white, which circled too a deaf old man and a middle-aged spinster in the booth opposite Heather and Kip, and a brooding very drunk magnificent redheaded girl sitting at the counter across the way, at which one oilyhaired blackhaired young man was throwing scraps of enticement, as a spectator would taunt an animal at the zoo.

II

To his circle of admirers, one equally frigid evening inside his warm six-room apartment of West End Avenue near 96th Street, the decor in gray rug (reminding one of Persian lamb), gray drapes, and canvas and wire chairs, Kip was eloquently recounting the banal circumstances.

He stood near the draped window in the casual mantle of indirect lighting, his balding blond hair considerably muted, his shoulders extended by the pads in his blue lounging robe, beneath which, when it parted by his motions now and again, could be observed the pearl buttons of his waistcoat, gleaming touchingly. On a wall within buttoning distance hung one of Kip's paintings, whose titular subject was that of a dismembered clown, on whom pompon buttons made eyes, mouth, navel and anus.

A woman with a flatchested face had interrupted him to ask if his wife Victoria and his baby would return.

Kip gulped the rest of his scotch and laughed in what was intended to be an immeasurable dimension, after which his mouth proceeded, as it does on certain long-lipped men, to blink rapidly. His large quaking belly was barely discernible through his ample and loosely-tied robe. The prevailing dimness masked the pointilliste effect of his freckled flesh.

"I trust not. I can't abide either Victoria or the child, although both have certainly proved invaluable. You may possibly know that my parents could present cannibalistic credentials on the grandchild score. I must tell you that one of my many experiences has been office work. I became weary of it; I quit; my parents were horrified; how will you live, they inquired; I shrugged in reply; how will you eat, they inquired; I shrugged; you have responsibilities to your wife, they shouted; I shrugged; your baby has got to eat, they shrieked; I said I would not work; our baby, they wailed; I said I must paint. I received a check from them to pay the rent, and weekly stipends to provide nutriment for myself, for Victoria and, finally, for the child. Victoria …" he mused, the circle of his admirers in taut radii.

"I shall always remember the voluptuously thin Victoria with her booming black eyes, her nose like an elbow, and her teeth like large tumblers of graying milk; she had the kind of body that, no matter how exquisitely gowned, seemed gragged. She inclined toward gold evening slippers. Once, when she thought I was not within earshot, I heard her blush: a friend had asked her if he might not kiss her foot, since he felt his fetish utterly untied that night … And it might be added that Victoria wrote the kind of poetry one might accompany — oh, on a zither. But have I finished with Heather?"

His sleek chorus, the woman with the flatchested face, the eighteen-year old boy with creeping-vine features and the basso voice, the grayhaired gentleman with the remotest lisp, the buxom-eyed female efficiency in heavy wool, begged Kip to continue.

"I don't believe I'd quite done with the decor," he momentarily fetched his upper register, his index finger lightly reproving the frame of his dismembered clown painting by a swift lap around. "And is one ever? It is, after all, the surfaces of things that contribute so much to their depth. One really cannot go deeply without the initial imposition of a limitation."

The admiring circle abased its head in the humility of thought.

"Part of the decor of The Ark," Kip went on, "was the presence in a booth opposite Heather and I of a middle-aged spinster and a deaf old man. I should like all of you to know that I abominate disabilities of any sort." His voice had taken a singsong savagery, inevitable when he delightedly kissed the wriggling, dirt-caked toes of his emotions. Kip was smiling, the smile of a priest in a dedicated plush gray room, a priest filthy with the accreted greases of his victims. "The cripples, the disabled, are the elect of the world; when they are not exposed to die, they are lushly succored;

they are deferred to, toadied to, borne on the palanquins of the masochistic; as if, perhaps, the crippled were certain manifestations of death, that they must be therefore mollified and paid homage in order that one gain another day's grade. The essential aspect of Western Christian Civilization is indeed the excessive consciousness of and payment to death, which we have the effrontery to call humanitarianism. Can you then imagine that spinster in the opposite booth shouting at the top of her voice to that deaf dismalness, 'Well how do you like New York well how do you like New York,' her eyes with their bright punctual love a blinding callous to the deaf man himself, underneath her pulpy corneas the sensitive retinal bone too utterly tight in the skull-shoe, the squeaks of pain from her inner sight mincing along to her final end — can't you hear her saying to herself, If my skullshoe but got loose again, but for another day, another hour of youth, when the retinal bone was so wonderfully loose, when everything seemed so much to fit.

"I assure you," Kip's songsong savagery heights of mocking moan, "that that was the sole element of conversational exchange between the two, each five minutes or so, complete with his pompously bellowing back, 'I like New York, a fine city, a fine city,' his skull nodding, a fat fumbling skull, whose roof seemed caved in. And Heather's eyes would bounce to and fro the deaf old bastard each time he bellowed, her eyes bounce, become as sudden targets, widen, you see, as though he were finding her mark, or that she herself were leveling unerringly at her own sight, in terror that she was so accurate.

"Oh," he poured himself another scotch, and then sat crosslegged on the persianlamb floor, musing now, brow an affecting furrow, "I think I wanted to love her very much at such points; I felt a definite need to consent to such a feeling."

Since his blue lounging robe was now quite ajar, his belly promoted the picture of a comparatively young man training for the traditional form of a Buddha in a pearl-buttoned waistcoat. Amidst the circle of his admirers: flatchested face, creeping-vine features, basso voice, grayhaired lisp, buxom-eyed wool.

It was altogether gray in the room, though this evoked no discomfort, much as if ashes from a fire, that their faint warmth be indefinitely preserved, had been rubberized and carefully laminated over chair, table and floor.

"It was ferociously brilliant in The Ark," Kip played with his scotch, itself gray, slipping his circled palm from the bottom of the glass to the top, then letting the glass slide down, as though he were once again a child on some beach on a rainy day, letting the sand run through his hands. "Intense blue and white powdered light, around all those salvaged from the cold night outside, two by two. That magnificently handsome redheaded woman, for instance, sitting bowed and crosslegged at the counter, wearing the blinding white parting of her hair straight down the center, the rift through the Red Sea one might say, and thoroughly and dumbly drunk, a sea drowned in a sea, an ocean dropped to the bottom of another ocean; while a blackhaired oilyhaired young man, undoubtedly the pursuing Egyptian — I could have sworn on the Old Testament, I am so subtly jejune," he jeered at himself Jack of all Jeers, the fabulously percipient, " — the oilyhaired young man kept twirling his automobile keys before her, his tones the friendly nasal indifference, the nasal quality in his eyes, his nose in his fingers twirling the keys, 'Come on I'll take you home you want to go home huh come on I'll take you,' his nose sinking down between the rift of her breasts, into her sea within the sea, fishnose poking around, driving his convertible nose around her dumb depths, the propeller his keys, twirling."

Kip had the aspect of freckled gray vomit, his antelope skull, with his large phony drifting-away weights of ears, balanced on top of its mound. "And there was Mike the proprietor at the cash-register, and Pearl the waitress. I hope I'm boring you," he lightly interjected to his circle. "Admirers are meant to be bored. Admiration is the central feature of boredom. To admire is to be bored, to admit vacancy, to be parasitical. Boredom allows one to feed on the host, whatever it is. And the host, in this case myself, must admit it enjoys being fed upon my own lounging robe," he leaned more caricaturedly forward, its lapels bulging, so that one might almost have the illusion that breasts were enclosed, "in the mammillate attitude, Buddha the big-breasted," Kip cackled, "from whose starry nipples hang and suck all the forces of the universe. Sweet Kip, adorned with the hanging boredom of Babylon. I demand the pulling weight of boredoms, you must know. I dare to hope they will make a curious kind of inverted stigmata, you must know. As though the wounds on such men as I must be made, in order to counter Christ (we are known, not as the anti, but as the Counter-Christs), by pulling rather than by puncturing. Christ was female, you understand: She would be punctured. Whilst I am male, you see," he giggled, and threw back his enormous thin skull, antelope-like, to laugh shrilly, his Adam's apple scooting up and down, so that one nearly expected a bell to ring each time it went up, like that game of strength at fairs where one brings a sledge-hammer down on a nub, and a weight bobs up a graduated column, at whose top is a bell, to show the highest point of one's power, Kip laughing louder and louder, one feeling, watching his Adam's apple, that surely, surely now a bell must clang in his skull, and the prize of an enormous cigar erupt the pearl-gray room in which he and his circle of admirers sat.. Buxom-eyed heavy wool, grayhaired lisp, basso voice, creepingvine features, flatchested face — all sat around seeming faintly ill, as though, indeed, the milk from their admired host had turned faintly sour, but their martyrdoms reassured them, sufficiently compensatory for any indigestion.

Kip stood up, pulling their eyes up like guy-ropes to support his big top. He had suddenly sighed. "If you will recall, I had requested that Heather decide if she loved me exclusively." He paused to turn and waddle to the window. "I had repeated the request perhaps twice: she retorted with ter-giversations." He paused, again, to grasp the drapery-cords, one of which he pulled with an astonishing show of strength, though that may have been all his remaining power saved for demonstration in just such a missionary moment — and the gray draperies parted widely at the top, the lower folds trailing their billow, much like a woman in an evening-gown descending a grand stairway. Revealed through the skimmed milk sheen of the window was the chopped dark stretch of the Hudson River among the tall slats of the apartment building.

"I like the river by night," his voice gazing out, and trickling to his circle from the back of his scraggly neck, "I like the way the lights on it seem to trickle through the dark fingers of the waters."

From behind, his tall body had a specious solidity in the spacious blue lounging robe; if he could have managed it to his own satisfaction, he would always have preferred to address his audience thus; but insofar as he could bear any independence, he could not permit himself to be dependent on his own imagination; Kip found himself compelled to face his admirers after not too long a time, which is, after all, a kind of strength: it requires a certain positive ability not to evade a mirror, the more so if one witnesses in it the illusion of perfection (of course, the sceptical might adduce that the motivation in this case could just as well have been Kip's omnipresent weariness, which would have rendered most improbably, had he broken the mirror, that he stoop to pick up the pieces). Therefore, pouting knuckles along his scraggly mustache, Kip gently reversed himself, one arm grace-fully gesturing at the scene beyond the window, a sort of blackboard with chalk points in depth, as though he chose to regress his circle of listeners to a kindergarten, grown to be Manhattan at the provocation of his wand.

"A moment or so before Heather became somewhat pertinent," Kip resumed, "some mouth rolling in the counter-gutters of the adjacent bar had presumed to drop a coin in The Ark's jukebox, a piece of construction in which American know-how combined with the New World's zeal for ice-cream sundaes had produced an ape-like rainbow, which seemed always to be melting. Not quite content, Yankee science had ingeniously inserted a window in the breast of this banana-split simian, in order for one to observe its ladle-discing digestion in vitro, in which a record is ever-so-gently nudged from a column of the same and slid onto a turntable: it is a kind of infinitely slow spew that takes place, which apparently profoundly satisfied the observer, who probably believes that his own thoughts are similarly engendered, at a much more rapid rate, thanks to the fact that he is alive.

"At any rate," Kip passed a hand over his forehead, his fingertips lightly dabbing at it to conceal its sublimated yawn, "a record was played, or, to be more accurate, a moan was reproduced. Herein, let me inform you," Kip condescended at the top of his voice, "herein is the American genius for abstraction at its zenith. There are words, of course, to the effect that a love has absconded with a body, and that sexual embezzlement proceeds from Cape Hatteras to Cambodia, but that nevertheless the bankruptcy who has remained behind will welcome back, doubtless with an open-thighed banana-split and double-entry psychoanalytic bookkeeping, the poop-gen-italed in faithful. Yes, there are words, words!" Kip still was shouting, as if he, the ringmaster in a blue lounging robe at a thronged circus, were magnifying an announcement, Kip slightly flushed now, faint pink of gray, the freckles like sawdust on his face, his circle leaning toward him avidly, his eyes in blue tights announcing the death-defying leap, the hum of the city outside like a roll on the drums, the dismembered clown of his painting on the nearby wall (his circle had the sensation out of the whirling corner of its eye) wanting to coalesce, to reassemble its pompon buttons of eyes, mouth, navel, and anus, to return to the point prior to the death-defying leap, and to never, never make it, the clown tight in its own throat in Kip's throat, not wanting to venture out of his mouth at all, wanting to stay in the wings of the vocal cords.

"But the words, obviously, obviously are without sense. It is the moan that matters. It is the moan that should be hung in the Museum of Modern Art. It is the moan, absolute, pure, a thoroughly primitive ululation, ladies and gentlemen, that emanates from the factitious jungle of the jukebox, from that ice-cream ape. And so, as Heather and I bent on tripod chin and elbow in the booth opposite each other, as her buttocks sprang up and down in her throat, as her body jounced on the cushion, as her sinusitic blue eyes pingponged from the deaf old skullcaved bastard to the ravaged waitress

Pearl and the drunken redhead — I —."

He stopped. His voice had begun to crawl along creeping-vine whispers. Then: "I think I ..." He stopped again. He was smiling, but the smile was separated into two pieces, both semi-circles on his cheekbones, split, crippled.

"No," he began again, "not that I think. That's an interposition, you understand. The urbane soundproofing. You see, we refine and refine, adding more and more sugar to the strong drink, and stir, the spoon of urbanity stirring endlessly, till we are sweetly mad. Have you really ever seen all the sweet madnesses that walk the metropolitan avenues? So sweet by the necessity of undisturbing pleasures. Good sour male Christ!" Kip whines, "not that I thought then that I wanted her, not that I must tell you that I thought. No. When that abstract moan issued from the jukebox, I wanted that tickertape-titted thing sitting across from me, wanted that Heather, that — " he giggled at the enormity of the name, " — that Heather Sankey."

The Ark tilted.

"I can't be got at," Heather's cactus and steelwool abrading the abstract moan from the jukebox. Gasjets hitting from that deaf old bastard in the opposite booth, surely. That redhead, now, why doesn't she swallow that oilyhaired taunter and his keys; open her belly and swallow him. Wouldn't he be astonished? And the shark cashregister bite of Mike's hand. I won't be an old maid, though, like that thing sitting with that deaf bellower.

The red mitten on Heather's Chippendale nose was ragged and torn.

I'll be damned if Pearl mourns me; nobody will; I'll never give them a chance; people can jump off me, if they like, and fall a hundred storeys, and die, but I'd never jump off them.

Heather hopped around in her seat. "I can't be got at, Kip. I may love fifteen men. I may love none. What are you mad at? You and your languid anger! You love me? Really? How? Why? What's love, Kip?"

"You're loaded," Kip whispered.

"Maybe. But where's your wit, Kip dear? eh?" This, while she lowered her eyelids coyly a moment, then, rewidening them, she rolled them in an oily blue brilliance. "Ha! Definition of a woman: the more a man's with a woman, the more he loses his epigrammatic touch. Eh? Come on, argue, damn it! I used to be a philosophy major."

Tilt went The Ark, tilt! But nobody was sliding from one end of the place to the other, Heather observed, judging this rather odd. There was something flying around, though, she caught out of the trapdoor of her eye: a white moth. In the winter? Impossible. Well, hardly likely. "Do you see a white moth, Kip?"

"No." His head felt cold, balder than ever, while his loins thudded; his ears felt far away from his antelope-like skull, as if kites. His loins thudded, had a sensation of being bitten, and burning.

"Well how do you like New York I like New York a fine city!" the fragment preserved itself in the opposite booth, deaf old man and spinster, to confound the scholars who would discover it on bluewhite cuneiform, bluewhite papyrus, bluewhite microfilm.

"Come on I'll take you home you want to go home," the fragment preserved itself on the counter, drunk handsome redhead and oilyhaired man, a rune to be incanted by yet-to-be-evolved religions.

The cash register was swallowing gas, Pearl helping Mike with the receipts; her great breasts crackled and hissed in grief's frying-pan, for Gale, television-Gale, beautiful Gale. But Pearl could wait on tables, triumphally. She could put things down before people, softly, or with a thump, or shrugging, Mike said, "They ought to keep some of these bills in the Museum of Natural History." "Oh, Mike," Pearl said, squeaky around the eyes, feeling her ankles sinking into her feet, big feet, the suicide of Gale having intruded into the nearly constant thinking about her feet, the corns, the bunions, the feet that carried drinks from the bar, washrags, trays, carried her body, feet she felt each night crouching on her bed, feet hurt or feet good, shoes for feet, archsupports, moleskin for bunions, fingers for feet kneading feet, bending torso down to feet, soaping feet in hot water, she couldn't work without feet, nothing could be without feet, Gale the suicide couldn't be on her feet, oh no, no, no.

The jukebox exhorted the congregation to moan, to put floodlights in the plateglass window of your fifty-storey bungalow and howl that your love come home because, dammit, the floodlights would always be burning in your plateglass window.

"When you're by yourself," Heather taunted, "or with your adoring circle, you're powerful, Kip. But the more you're with me, your skull fades, you get balder, balder!"

"That's happened very rarely, really. And only late tonight. Tonight's an exception."

"The exception would occur more frequently."

"I assure you it — "

"Go on! What makes you think you love me? My god didn't we go to bed with each other originally on the basis that there'd be absolutely nothing else? Wasn't its convenience perfectly established? You liked that,

Kip. You'd had nothing else like it. You said so. I said so. Sex exclusively. I'd phone when I felt like it with you, and you'd phone the same way. No responsibility. We chortled about that, didn't we? We laughed at every other relationship that entertained mutual responsibility." Her powerful calves bulged at her throat, her buttocks bitten by springs.

Lean long Kip with the big belly felt the jukebox moan glue onto the insides of his belly. Look at the floor. What's it like? You understand that you come up from the floor of The Ark, you walk on it. He poked a glance at. it. Nondescript. Bluewhite floating intensity. Thousands of feet. Disembodied feet, scraping, digging heels, leaning on one foot, then the other, up on a toe, turning, faltering, toes splayed to go forward, feet rocking, shuffling, shambling, hesitant, looking for a booth, food, to be waited on, getting up with full bellies in the arches, tapping, waiting for service, irritated, nervous, numb, thank god I'm sitting, let's go, let's get out of here, late, early, on time, hungry, curling, tickled, taut. Too many. They'd rubbed off the identity of the floor, and left only images of feet, feet without floor, feet themselves making the floor, and feet layering on top of feet. What the hell and jesuschrist, there's no solidity in that kind of remembrance. There's no place for your own feet. The Ark had no floor, not the floor Kip wanted, anyhow. And not for his feet. What were his feet? Long, lean and flat, with big bones. And dirty. The rest of his body he'd clean, but often forget to wash his feet, he'd let the dirt accumulate and, perhaps once a month, he'd remember to clean them, and derive great joy therefrom, slowly shaving off the encrusted filth with a nail-file, enjoying watching the shavings of dirt, so plastic they were, so positively alive, springy at the edges of the flesh; would enjoy carving the callouses, down as far as he'd dare, waiting till the skin would be reached, slowly, enjoying the careful prod of the knife. Kip rubbed his toes against each other, rubbed his toes in his loins, and felt a knife carefully prodding.

Heather would like to have caught that white moth she saw flying around — caught it with her mouth, and crunch it in her jaw. It was flying around her eye, she would have sworn. Attracted by the blue candle of her eye, no doubt, she grinned to herself. Or had it flown out of her eye, perhaps, and was it seeking the way back in. Poor white moth. Heather nearly wept, but then, "What's love, Kip? Eh?" Tilt! went The Ark, but not a soul or dish slid anywhere. Ah but the moth, the white moth — it slid! "Come on, Kip!"

"I love you because you're so awfully afraid of not being loved, Heather." His voice was affected, it drawled, pretentious, carried hammy British accents, nasal, pince-nezed. Nevertheless, Heather frowned, deeply, considerable freight on her narrow-gauge forehead; her throat scrawned; her fingers fought each other; her eardrums sensed a light skimming, but it was impossible that the white moth should have got inside. She dratted at her ears anyway, though she saw the moth hovering about the deaf man's booth for a moment. Actually, she admitted to herself, she felt more comfortable with Kip than with Danny, all told. Kip wasn't a Jew. Christ, she must be drunk! And if she could only be as beautiful as that magnificent redheaded lush at the counter. Heather had a picture of that oilyhaired bastard who was urging the girl to let him take her home in his car — a picture of him slicing the redhead up with his twirling keys; Heather wanted him to, now at the counter; slice her up, then lock up the pieces with the very same keys, then present the keys to Heather, of course. Murderess Heather. Accused. Indicted. Brought to court, prosecuted, convicted and — gassed, gassed, gassed. She opened her mouth side.

"Pearl! Is there time for another bourbon?"

Pearl's hand, beringed, amethyst and opal, infinitely semiprecious, rested on the small oblong chef's opening between the restaurant proper and kitchen, to which she had retired with Mike; neither turned toward Heather, but Pearl's ravaged hand called back, "No, honey, it's nearly closing."

"It's nearly closing!" the spinster in the opposite booth yelled at the deaf old man with the sagging canvas topped skull. "I like New York it's a fine city!" he bellowed back. Teeth biting her underlip, the spinster put him into his overcoat as if she were loading a ship. They left.

The handsome drunken redheaded girl at the counter moved, first like a wave surging over the counter, her rich deep breasts overflowing it from her black woolen dress; then her eyes toiled to her evening wrap, her legs and torso hoisting after. The oilyhaired young man, having put his keys in his pocket, helped her on with the wrap, to which she made no sound, no gesture, no glance. He followed her out of The Ark.

And nobody slid, thought Heather. But they couldn't have, now. The Ark was no longer at a tilt.

The powdered intensities of the bluewhite fluorescent lighting dimmed a little. A shoal of shadows had appeared, prowling among the booths. Hyena-shadows, Heather thought, nosing around for a spoor.

Someone had lowered the volume of the jukebox; the wail sounded a little uncertain. As if grief weren't quite sure it should mourn, thought Heather. It's hard to see my white moth now. She squinted, she sprang up a little in her seat, peering, Kip leaned forward to put his knobby-jointed hand to her face, and said, somewhat anxiously, "What is it, Heather? Tell me."

She whipped her face away. Kip's large antelope-like skull looked helplessly scourged, and his skin scarred by the freckles; his scraggly mustache in need of watering.

"I didn't want the deaf old man to go," Heather said.

"But why? Surely you don't know him."

"I wanted him to stay because he couldn't hear me. I'd like anybody to stay that can't hear me. But he was the only one who fitted specifications."

"What about the redhead?"

"Oh, she could hear, Kip. At the bottom of her ocean she could hear me. But the dear old man never. I liked him, Kip dear. He couldn't hear me. Oh!" She oscillated her thin sharpboned head, marionette-like, the faintest makeup of a clowngrin on her lips. Then, secretly, hush-hush, "I could've gone to bed with him, Kip. Yes! And he wouldn't've heard me, even then. I could've made love to him — and he wouldn'tve heard. Isn't that marvellous, Kip?"

Longlipped Kip, slouchlipped Kip for a minute found himself incapable of speech. He scanned her, finally, as he would have a painting, till he could recover.

"I've contrived to rid myself of Victoria and the child," he as last contended.

Heather patted his shoulder. She could see her little white moth circling about her; she followed it in her cheek with the tip of her tongue.

"Now you love me, Kip? Now?"

"Yes."

"Isn't it the actress part of me that you love? The part that performs?"

"No, Heather. Not only that. When we love, we love those elements in a human being that cannot and do not perform, that do not entertain."

"Ah, Kip dear. How sweet." The white moth circled her, she saw, with dizzying rapidity. "But in the expectation that those elements will entertain, that they're potentially performers, and that you will be capable of having them so express themselves. Isn't that right, Kip?"

Doggedly. "No, my dear philosophy major. In the expectation that they will never perform, never entertain."

"You'd want the banal parts of me always to remain banal — is that it?"

"I'm not your instructor in a college class now, Heather." His voice croaked.

"You count the banal elements, Kip, don't you? And make sure they outweigh the brilliant and expressive parts, in the certainty that you — you will never be threatened." Heather frowned, smiled, was angry, felt without weapons and yet fully armored. What was the white moth trying to tell her? "Nor am I afraid of not being loved, Kip," she remarked contemptuously, "so you needn't love me on that score, either, which I don't think you believe for a moment, anyhow."

"But it remained in your mind."

"Oh so do circuses! I wouldn't have your love, dear. See? I've no fear." Her skinny neck jaunted up her chin. "Don't love me," she airily waved her hand, "Stop it!" She rapped smartly on the table.

"There must be many in love with you, Heather," Kip said, quite evenly.

"All for the same reason, that you're fearful of not being loved. Have any of them stopped loving you? If what you said was true, that you're not afraid, then why would so many love you? Surely, Heather, you have no fatalistic beauty; surely you offer none of the more common reasons for loving; surely you're not that superb an actress that men could adore you with admiring love. You're a little less than faithful, a little more than spiteful. Why, then, should so many love you? And love you, Heather, without so much as a single promise of permanence. The one husband you had proved transitory. For you, Heather, men reverse the process: They leave you, and go on loving you."

"Because I choose not to indulge in the concept of permanence. By the way, Kip dear, do you like to play tennis in the wintertime?"

"Why can't you indulge in the concept of permanence, Heather? Does that give you a kind of absolute assurance? that by a process of your constantly changing you will be able to elude your own termination? My dear Heather, you are aging."

Heather lifted a scratched-on eyebrow. The moan from the banana-split jukebox had melted into a pool of simianly remembered sound. One bank of fluorescent lights on the opposite side of The Ark was then extinguished.

"Closing," Pearl called. Heather caught the flash of the waitress's gray hair turning in the kitchen light, itself taking gray.

"Oh no," Heather said flatly. "Not closing." The little white moth still circled. It hadn't entered her yet. "It can't close."

"Really, Heather — !" Kip began.

"No." Heather's fingers, mothlike, touched her hair that had been skimmed blonde. A smile flashed on and off her mouth, on and off. She saw the shoal of shadows had increased, the pack of hyena-shadows multiplied, smelling the spoor. She opened her mouth as wide as she could, like a trap, her teeth rather rounded at the edges, though, and small, much like the pearl buttons on a waistcoat Kip sometimes affected — and, almost automatically, Kip's fingers wandered to his chest, to start an unbuttoning motion, which halted when Heather suddenly clicked her jaw shut, as if she had caught something, because she swallowed, hard, after which appeared a rather wistful, benign expression, and Kip's hands dropped to his lap, enervated. He noted that the springy buttocks in her throat had softened, and that she sat quite still, as she might after a most satisfying meal, and that something within her was safely at rest, but that which must lead to his discomfiture: if she could not bounce, he most certainly could not spring.

"It's so very cold outside," Heather said, quietly. "Still, it will be warmer, later. Love, you see, Kip, dear, is a kind of condescension. I would not want you to stoop part of yourself to me," she spoke sweetly, peacefully. Indeed, Kip thought, she might be masticating a dove. "Love means dropping a part of yourself to another. I certainly wouldn't want to be responsible for causing someone to let part of himself go. I suppose, Kip, you might call me a sort of missionary in reverse: I really save people, particularly men: I save all their parts for themselves, for themselves only."

She rose, then, and her left hand reached for her minkdyed muskrat hanging on the coat-hook, and her next words were delivered in a tone where one felt that its clipped cactus and steel wool qualities had partly canceled each other out in a mordantly misty exit, while her right hand swung an imaginary racket through the shadows of The Ark.

"Naturally, I could have sustained my condescension, continued to drop part of myself to another, according to Heather's definition of love," Kip rested folded arms across bulging belly while he leaned languidly against a window-corner. His long lean flat bigboned feet were crossed and wriggling toward the circle of his admirers. Tonight his feet were shod in slippers of soft black wool, embroidered in scarlet thread suggesting Persian script; inside, he rubbed his toes against each other, and wondered, idly, if his circle could smell their squalor. But flatchested face, creeping-vine features, basso voice, grayhaired lisp, buxom-eyed heavy wool, had it been capable of apprehending stink at all, would have inverted it by the intensity of admiration to a fantastic mellifluence, the rationalization that since this was an area of never-experienced malodorousness it could be as perfectly susceptible to honeyed interpretation.

It is a shame, Kip considered to himself (while his voice began to speak of love), that the sense of smell is not so acutely developed as our others; we would know ourselves and our fellows generally far better were such the case, and certainly find it unnecessary then to utilize in perfumes and oils products of the lower animals. We wash ourselves clean of the remotest self-odors, and then proceed to adorn ourselves with the masks of the lower animals, whose odors do not at all function to conceal. How strange that we should want to attract other human beings through a mask, and the mask of species presumably lesser than ourselves; as if we found it terribly difficult to admit that we must function in the province of attraction, but that, since we must, we exculpate our necessity by filtering it through the glaze of a musk-ox; perhaps, of course (Kip found his reflections on smell continuing to meander through his remarks in love), on the assumption that odor definitively measured a man, we fear that precision; let us measure anything in the world except ourselves. True, some scientists labored diligently in such fields, but we humans, Kip giggled to himself, will frustrate the cyberneticians and the psychologists, by wriggling out in various ways from their measures. Nor need we indeed even consciously frustrate: was there not the principle in physics — possibly itself evolved as the final reflection on the impossibility of self-measurement and consequent on our desire to subvert the ruler — that the ruler altered in relation to the object measured? and that the object itself altered during measurement?

"If dropping part of oneself to another is indeed love," Kip nasally dispensed, his fingers playing now with the small round white teeth of his waistcoat's pearl buttons.

The heat in the apartment building evidently had been turned off by this late hour, and seemed casually to be departing in patches, so that Kip's circle shivered a forearm there, a calf here, a nape of neck elsewhere. But Kip himself apparently was unaffected, though his shoulder rested partly against the icy window.

"But, accepting that for the moment," he went on, "I could have kept on loving Heather. However, in view of her final words, which I shall repeat for you in a few moments — no."

His clown painting gave the illusion of hugging itself.

"No," Kip reiterated, rather strongly. "I found it necessary that I return and — stoop to myself, so to speak. And I wonder if that termination of one's loving another isn't itself a condescension; I wonder if being an independent, self-subsistent entity isn't a kind of ultimate snobbery (which will not alienate you, of course, my admirers," he inclined his head toward the circle momentarily, while lifting sandy and scraggly eyebrows, "from me, because you are bound to me by alienation from yourselves) an illusion that one can replace another by oneself. Especially since I'd loved Heather irresponsibly. How?

"Well, if you love another this, without letting, really, part of yourself go, or, rather, with loaning part of yourself out — how can you return to yourself responsibly?"

Kip, at any rate, as he fiercely rubbed his toes together, could smell their stink, smell it even from the great height of his immense antelope-like skull, at the top of his long lean lech of a body, and that comforted him. It made him, though not for long, positively complacent.

"You've loaned part of yourself out without stipulating an interest-payment, which is irresponsible," he found himself unable to withhold. He wished, in passing, that he could have released his circle, and bade it go, and spoken these reflections to himself; but that would have been utterly impossible. He nearly cried, then, within himself, that these reflections would have been utterly lost upon him should he have voiced them to himself alone. "You had thought it generous, really, not to have demanded interest, but that had been quite selfish, because, without that stipulation, no selfenrichment could ensue. The attitude of non-selfenrichment is an irresponsible self-evaluation. It is a vicious snobbery to feel or think that you cannot be enriched; and an utter isolation."

III

Upon which Kip's voice sank on his chin, and his fat blue eyes quivered; he edged away from the window, where, gradually, the faint surface sheen, common elsewhere, obliterated the smudge of clarity he had left. The circle of his admirers had let its cigarettes burn without puffing, and each mobile of ascending smoke had its source in each open lap, as though incense burned from the clothed groins to signify that the supreme sacrifice had been made: a smouldering fire ate the generative powers of each, oddly evocative of the Spartan tale, where a boy had secreted a vixen on his person, but who could not admit, while it tore away at his vitals, that he felt pain, for such would have demeaned the Spartan demeanor.

"One really cannot come back to oneself, finally, anyhow," Kip barely whispered, his toes no longer wriggling, nor rubbing, and the interlinear thoughts on smell erased. He had shifted to stand beside his painting of the dismembered clown; or, rather, he cowered to one side, its level, perhaps, intolerable. "To think that you can come back totally to yourself is a sentimentality, perhaps worse — a return to a stranger; there, at the mythical feeling of absolute self-subsistent totality, one feels quite estranged, and lives then with a repellent being. You return, really, to a duality, a set, in fact, of multiple strangers, all living in the same body, and crowing that it is now thoroughly independent. But it is actually a snarling, fragmented island, the fragments not recognizing each other at all, a mob at complete variance within itself, impossible to govern amicably — so that — so that — you set about killing the various strangers in yourself, you know — you stalk and kill them, one by one, two by two!" he laughed painfully, "before, you think, your ark can come to rest."

Kip straightened and moved into the center of his circle.

"Stand up!" he adjured, "come on, stand up!"

Overawed and creaking, grayhaired features, creepingvine lisp, basso face and flatchested voice rose unsteadily to their feet.

"But such murder," Kip rasped, denunciatory, "will never set you at rest; for each murdering of the strangers within yourself, each stranger the guilt at having loved irresponsibly — " he gestured scornfully at basso grayhair, creeping face, vice-featured voice and flatchested lisp in turn — "you experience additional awful guilt at having murdered someone you never came to know. Since the most heinous crime is to murder without having learned the identity of the slain elements within oneself: obliteration without understanding. One asks," Kip spreadeagled his long thin arms, long thin blue arms in the blue lounging robe, the ludicrous knobbyjointed fingers splayed, his belly boldly swollen beyond the loosening cord of the robe, so that he seemed a marvelously crapulous scarecrow overstuffed in the most unlikely sphere, his balding blond hair wisping over the large phony weights of ears, "one asks: what has one killed without knowing? An irresponsibility of the grossest nature. Yet, on the other hand ... "

He paused, his voice dropped to a shrug. His circle stared at him in the vacuous remnants of lamed awe. Kip stepped away, waddling toward the apartment door, against which he put his back, as though he feared they might impulsively leave, for which he was not quite ready: your binding to me balds like my hair, he thought, prompted, perhaps by your having suddenly seen my hair. "On the other hand," he nearly pleaded, "is the necessity to love responsibly, that is, to enrich oneself; the indication of the fear to be total? That therefore one will be compelled to fear that one is not; after all, a self-contained unit? — that, if one is thrown back on oneself, there will be the horror of the clear discovery that you are but a half, a moiety? Yes, clichés now, I know — to me, at any rate, certainly to you. But a moment longer, I pray you — to find if after the midnight the Cinderella-cliché will not return to mice gnawing more deeply.

"In the light of what I've said, life then may be a giving of what we do not have, a sort of presentation of an empty symbol, on which is engraved only the hope that the person to whom it has been given will honor it and make it good at her bank, and return it with the fullness it did not originally contain. A gamble, that the empty symbol presented will be the fulfilled symbol returned. All because we must never know, never be conscious — " Kip slowly left the door, while he continued to talk, and shifted over to his painting of the dismembered clown, which he lifted from its hook and gently deposited on the floor, facing it to the wall — "all because we must never be conscious that one is incomplete."

He frowned, faintly, his eyes half shut.

"Well, then," he said to the circle that appeared to be a gray hoop stood on its end, towards which he stretched a finger, as though, like a child, he would roll it with a stick, but, growing up, forbear following, "well, then, perhaps incompleteness, the necessary very partialness of man is his very grandeur. At least," Kip now quite addressed himself alone, softly, his large antelope-like skull hanging forward from his scraggly neck, "at least I discovered that it was not Heather I must love, in the face of her last words ..." he trailed off.

Scoffing, a question came from far far down the room, to which the gray hoop had rolled: "And what were the Saviour's last words?"

Kip's ears grinned, then drooped.

"Rats!" Victoria swirled her lips as she pushed the door to the apartment open, standing there against the door, waiting, in her booming black eyes, the nose an elbow, the teeth pendant large tumblers of graying milk, the voluptuously thin Victoria, in gold evening slippers, large gold hoops of earrings from tiny ears, and a ragged black evening gown; in her arms a sleeping baby.

During Kip's retreat to the window his gray hoop, at the point where he quit the reach of its diameter, straightened into single file and proceeded, silently and without adieux of any kind, through the apartment door, one by one, past Victoria, who once more swirled her lips, ferociously, "Rats! who desert a floating ship! Could there be worse? Rats!" The last left, and Victoria shoved the door shut with a bony shoulder.

For such precious tableaux, Kip had always kept pipe and tobacco in readiness on the low palette-shaped coffee table, to which he hopped, he snatched them, and hopped back to the window, where he engaged in lighting the pipe.

Victoria dumb-waitered the sleeping baby into a deep canvas chair. "In a moment, Kip, I will tell you just how I will tolerate you. Watch the child. I've got to go to the toilet," at which she swirled from the room.

Kip glanced through the window, through the thin sheen, through the tall slats of the skyscrapers, toward the chopped dark stretches of the Hudson River. Incredible! It was quite impossible, surely — he thought his eye caught a white moth hovering just outside the glass. Then he smiled. Of course, it wasn't that cold outside to forbid a flurry of snow. The white moth certainly was no more than an errant snowflake. In a second it was gone. Melted, probably. Or his own eye, in following it, had foreshortened, and could no longer measure the snowflake.

He puffed on his pipe, steadily. He felt that his Adam's apple had dropped nearly to his navel: one could hardly swallow there, he thought. His freckles gleamed faintly on his flesh. The tall blond lean lech of a Kip and his absurdly bulging belly waddled over to his sleeping baby, and bent over it a little — and for the life of him Kip couldn't remember the baby's name, nor — and he turned to look at his painting of the dismembered clown, but it faced the wall — nor could he remember, as he again turned to stare down at his child, his own tongue rustling in his mouth like a dead dry leaf — nor could he remember his baby's sex, but what did vise his memory instead, after he tried to summon tender fingers to touch his child, bringing them forward tentatively, but never quite able to compel them to an actual touching of the child's fair hair, the child's impossibly delicate tinctures of russet and snow as its breath slept slowly — while unable to recall its name or gender, Kip heard in his mind — and then found one hand, while his other held a pipe that had gone out, tearing at and ripping off the rounded white teeth of his waistcoat's pearl buttons, his belly gross and swollen beyond his blue lounging robe — Kip heard the mordantly misty clipped cactus and steelwool uttering the Saviour's last words, sweet Christian Heather's, as her hand had swung an imaginary racket through the shadows of The Ark.

A DEPOSITION OF BEN BERMAN

For the first time in my life I used insulting language, and I want to know if that's enough reason for me to be punished. I said "God damn you" to him. And then I left. You understand, it's not that I want to be punished. But if I committed a crime, then I must take the consequences. If I haven't, then I'll be content to go free, as much as anybody can be content to go free. But before you judge me you've got to hear the whole story. It isn't very long. Whether I committed a crime or not, I think I had good cause to curse him.

My name is Ben Berman. I'm perhaps forty-eight years of age. My mother and I lived in two little rooms over on Eleventh Street, between Avenue A and B, a tenement. I'm telling you this because I think you should know just a little bit about where I'm from, because this too might help you understand why I cursed him. Not that knowing where you're from tells you where you're going. Oh no. That's a lie.

Now I live alone in those two rooms, because a couple of months ago my mother, may she rest in peace, passed away. My mother and I had a pushcart. We made a living selling fruits and vegetables. All over the East Side we sold fruits and vegetables. We had honest scales. We never cheated anybody. Maybe that's why we could never save enough money to open a little store. If my father had lived after we came over to New York from Kiev, maybe he would've cheated and I wouldn't've cursed anybody. But right after he bought the pushcart he got a sneezing-spell. He sneezed and sneezed. This was bad because his heart wasn't too good. The doctors couldn't stop his sneezing. He sneezed himself right into a heart-attack and passed away, may he rest in peace. Oh I know it's funny a man should die from sneezing. It's not a very cultured way for the soul to leave a man's body. It sounds foolish that because something enters your nose your body must be vacated. If he wouldn't've had a weak heart.... Still, who knows how deep the roots of the nose go?

Anyhow, my mother and I took over the pushcart. I helped her when I wasn't going to school. I wasn't very good in school because I would be thinking all the time of my mother and the pushcart and how much she needed my help. She was a little woman with a stumpy body and she wore a cream-colored shawl over her head winter and summer. It wasn't right that she should have to be with the pushcart all by herself even part of the day. I didn't want to study or play with the other children. My whole ambition was to get to the age where I could quit school and help her. This I did.

It's funny. You would think I'd remember a great deal more about her, but I don't. Certainly I remember her patience, that she worked hard, that she never scolded me, that her pushed-together face had lines as long back as I can think, that her eyes were tiny and brown, like mine, that her stumpy body always looked curled over into itself. I think her hair was brown too, like mine, but I couldn't be sure: she wore a wig, and over that the cream-colored shawl, summer and winter, inside and outside the tenement. But this is very little to remember. I should recall her words, but her words were only of prices for tomatoes, and cauliflower, and apples, and celery. There was just one thing I remember her talking about, just to me, over and over: her memory as a little girl of standing on the outskirts of Kiev and watching the Russian counts and countesses whiz by in their troikas. She said they wore black sables, that they were rosy-cheeked and laughing. She said the heads of the horses drawing the troikas were tossing. She said everything was a sight of snow and the steam from the horses' nostrils, and that she could still hear the sound of the troika-bells. Let me tell you she died with that memory on her lips. My father sneezed to death, and my mother died hearing troika-bells: out of those materials her coffin should've been made. That would've made a strange looking coffin, wouldn't it?

When she passed away I gave up the pushcart. 1 knew I had to make a living of some sort, but I didn't know what to do. I didn't want to be reminded of fruits and vegetables. So when an Italian friend of ours, Mr. Marino, who owned the fruit and vegetable stand down the street, offered me a job — I turned it down. It was too late also for me to think of finding a wife. Who would've wanted a peddler of forty-eight? And what did I look like? I ask you. My brown hair was thinning. My brown overcoat with the raglan sleeves was out of shape. I needed a new pair of shoes which I couldn't buy. That, or anything new: the funeral expenses had used up whatever savings we'd had. My brown pants were baggy and creased in the wrong places. Who would want me for a husband? Skinny, balding, Ben Berman with the baggy pants, with his tiny brown eyes, with his shoulders caved in. Still, I realized I had to eat. Mr. Marino said he understood why I couldn't take his offer. But he suggested that maybe I could still peddle. Not fruits and vegetables. But that at least I could pick up a little change peddling something else. It was a week before St. Valentine's Day, he said, and he heard you could pick up a little change peddling Valentine dolls, and maybe, he said, if I could do that successfully I would get a desire to try another selling-line of better merchandise. I shrugged. It was as good as anything else at the moment.

So the whole week before St. Valentine's Day I peddled the dolls. Up and down Avenue A, Avenue B, First Avenue, Second Avenue. They didn't sell very well. Three dollars if you would buy two dolls together. Two dollars if you bought only one doll. And let me tell you, they were very pretty dolls, too. They came in cardboard boxes, the top sections cellophane, so you could see right through to the doll that was either a boy or a girl resting on cotton packing, which was there to take any shock the doll might get in handling — I carried the boxes, you see, a half-dozen under each arm. Besides, the cotton packing made a nice white background, like snow. Each doll had a big red heart strung by ribbon from the neck. I didn't care very much for the boy dolls. But the girl dolls — ah, for those I developed an affection. Blondes and redheads and brunettes with different-colored dresses, but all with the same red heart. The girls looked like they were going to a party. I handled the girls very gently, I can tell you, very carefully. If I'd've had extra cash, I'd've bought one myself, they made that nice a gift. Not that I had anybody I could've given one to. But a girl doll would've made a pretty sight set up on top of the ice-box: I could've thought of my mother liking it, maybe picturing it as a Russian countess riding on a troika through the snow. But enough of that. As I said, they didn't sell too well. People weren't spending money as freely as they did during the war. Perhaps they didn't have it to spend, or spent it only on very necessary things. If that's so, it's bad. When people spend only what's necessary, it means the country is showing signs of getting sick.

Anyhow, I kept on trying, all the way through the day before St. Valentine's Day. I made a poor showing. By the time I reached a little dairy restaurant on Second Avenue near Houston I'd sold only maybe two or three dolls. This was the last place I was going to, absolutely the last, I told myself. I was very tired. I was thinking I didn't want to see any more dolls, or people, or Second Avenue. I didn't want to plead any more with anybody to buy a doll. I was sick of St. Valentine and all the red hearts. And it was late in the day. It was just beginning to get dark and a little flurry of snow was starting, big white flakes that were getting my raglan-sleeve brown overcoat very damp, and I felt wet through the thin soles of my brown shoes. This is the last place I'll try, I told myself.

I straightened up when I went through the door. I didn't look at the floor. My eyes looked straight ahead and the first thing I saw were two signs in the rear of the restaurant, "Men's Room," "Ladies Room," and the sound I heard made me stop right at the cashier's counter. It couldn't be, I thought. And I couldn't look down for a minute. It wasn't Christmas. The snow wasn't packed hard outside on Second Avenue. This was New York, right now. It wasn't the outskirts of Kiev years and years ago. There couldn't be any troikas. But the sound I heard was a faraway one of troika-bells. How could that be? I looked around for a radio, but no radio. And then I saw what it was.

The only customer was shaking a half-empty glass sugar-container, trying to get some of the hardened lumps of sugar through the small metal opening and into his cup of coffee. That shaking of the hardened lumps of sugar against the glass made a sound exactly like the faraway troika-bells. And right at that moment I didn't want to be reminded of my mother. Right at that moment I didn't want to be in mourning.

I put down cardboard boxes by the cashier's counter, which nobody was tending just then, and waited. I couldn't do anything till he would get through shaking the sugar. After a little while he seemed satisfied he had got enough into the coffee, and he stopped. He began to drink his coffee very slow, staring down at the table.

Nobody had noticed me. Two waiters were standing in the back reading newspapers. I decided to put the boxes on an empty table and open them. Perhaps the sugar-shaker would be interested, or the waiters. I said nothing and began to line the boxes on the table for display.

Just then a very important-looking man came out of the kitchen. He must've been important: he wore tortoise-shell glasses, he was fat in the belly, he wasn't less than sixty, he was bald, he had very fat lips that looked like they were always eating something sour, and he walked very fast out of the kitchen. It wasn't a very promising beginning that I had to be reminded of my mother right when I didn't want to be. Otherwise I'm sure the important-looking man wouldn't've frightened me. The minute I saw him I was scared. He must be the proprietor, I thought.

Seeing the waiters frowning over the newspapers, he stopped dead. "You're going to give them a menu of editorials?" he scolded them. "They'll order lox and cream cheese from the State Department?"

The waiters stuck out their lower lips, put their heads to one side, lifted their eyebrows, all as if to say, "With this kind of person who could reason?" They stuffed the newspapers in their pockets and got busy wiping tables already clean, and changing the positions of the bowls of rye-bread and bagels. Also they grumbled. But by then the proprietor was standing by my side looking at me, then at the dolls, and then back at me. He took out a cigar, lit it and chewed and smoked it. I couldn't say a word. All I could do was smile feebly, and run my hand over the cellophane you could see the dolls through.

Like he was ready to throw me out, he said, "Yeh?"

I pointed to the boxes and said, almost in a whisper because my throat was dry, "Dolls. St. Valentine Day dolls. Two dollars if you only buy one. Three dollars if you take two." I tried to open my small brown eyes as wide as I could, to look inviting. At the waiters too, because they had stopped what they were doing. One stood in front of the "Men's Room" door, and the other the "Ladies Room." Both had their arms folded and looked sarcastically at the proprietor and me. The sugar-shaker was marking something down now on a piece of paper, figures maybe, and drinking his coffee; he looked like he didn't see anything in the world but what he was marking down.

"What do I need them for?" the proprietor said, and walked behind the cashier's counter. He chewed on the cigar. It was out but I guess he didn't care. That's how important he was.

I shook my head no. I didn't dare turn around to talk to him. Instead I took out a couple of dolls, the girl ones, and smoothed out their dresses and perched them on top of the boxes.

My suggestion was very quiet while I smoothed down the dresses. Maybe I did wrong making the suggestion like I was talking to the dolls. But with the proprietor I couldn't turn around. I felt that I looked like a scarecrow in my brown raglan overcoat; everything hung from me. I didn't want him to see that if I could help it. And my thin face looked bad too, I knew. I'd shaved that morning but my beard grows fast, you see, and it was twilight and I knew my face already looked a little dirty.

"For the children," I said. Very quietly.

"What children!" I heard him say like he thought I was the dumbest person in the world.

"Your grandchildren maybe," I said. And I tugged a little at the ribbons to make sure the hearts on the dolls were in their right places.

"My little Bettie?" He laughed sarcastically, but I could hear a certain consideration in it. He came around to the table to look over the dolls again. His fat lips were smiling. He crushed his cigar in an ash-tray. It had already been smoked. That showed me even more how important he was. "She already has so many dolls."

"St. Valentine's Day," I reminded him. I shrugged a bit without looking at him, trying to tell him without words, "You know how it is with children on St. Valentine's Day. They have dolls, so one who doesn't will feel left out."

"How much?" and he started to examine them for selection.

Certainly he knew, but I told him again. He picked out two dolls, both girls. He smiled like a king.

"I'll give you two-and-a-half dollars for these two," he said. "One is smaller than the other." He took out the money from his pocket and put it on the table.

"I know one is smaller, but I can't do it. They're all the same price, mister. Three dollars if you're taking two," I said. This time it was a whisper. I wanted to make a sale, but at the regular price. It had to be the regular price. All the years my mother had the pushcart she would let the fruits and vegetables go a thousand times at cost price. The sugar-shaker had reminded me of her. That shouldn't've happened. It had made me frightened of the proprietor but also made me want to not back down from him. For the difference of fifty cents he was making me a nothing and a something all at the same time.

"It cost less to manufacture if it's smaller," he said, angry. As if somebody was threatening to rob him of a thousand dollars, or take his life — he said it that angry. It was crazy, a person has to get that angry for fifty cents. That's crazy.

"You're already getting a discount," I smiled. "For your granddaughter — what's fifty cents?"

He picked up the money from the table. He rolled up the dollar bills and passed them back and forth under his nose, like he was smelling flowers. He didn't seem angry now, just indifferent. "Take it or leave it," he said. He was measuring me, I knew, and enjoying it, I felt.

I passed my hand over one of the doll's hearts. I shouldn't've done that: the material was smooth and soft, and my fingers were rough. And a little scratch was made, but nobody could see it. Not even the manufacturer would notice.

"Two dollars for one, three for two," I chanted. Like a prayer. Sometimes, with money, you have to be a cantor. So that a price shouldn't change, you have to keep on singing it.

The proprietor put the money back in his pocket and went behind the cashier's counter. "For nothing I wouldn't take them," he said in a cold voice. "Who needs them? My Bettie has plenty."

"Two dollars — " I began.

"Don't bother," he said, in a very friendly way, but full of hate. "Just don't bother." And he started making entries in a ledger.

I looked at the waiters. Maybe they would be interested. They turned their backs. One went into the Men's Room. The other filled a glass with water and drank noisily.

I began to pack into the boxes the dolls I had taken out.

The sugar-shaker called out to the waiter drinking water. "Another coffee," and it was brought to him.

Sometimes a man doesn't know how to feel, or even what to feel if he could. Should I have felt angry? or proud? or very tired? or full of victory? or beaten? I didn't know. All I knew then was that I should get the boxes together and leave. And I was all ready to go when that man started to shake the sugar again in the glass container, trying to break up the hard lumps so he could get them through the small metal opening and into his coffee. And again, the sound was like one of far-away troika-bells. The man wouldn't stop. He kept on shaking the container. The lumps of sugar must've been very hard. Up and down, up and down he shook it. The metal opening must've been very very small. I couldn't move. I tried to understand. He had to get the sugar in his coffee. But he could've turned around to the next table and got another glass-container of sugar. That he didn't think of. Or he was too lazy. Or he just had to make this sugar-container give in to his will. But there was no troika. He was such a fool! Such a fool!

"God damn you!" I said to him.

Then I left, the proprietor not even glancing at me, still making entries in the ledger.

It was dark outside, and there was no more snow coming down. I started walking back to our two little rooms over on Eleventh Street, between Avenue A and B. Under each arm I had the half-dozen St. Valentine Day dolls, that I had put together again very carefully, very gently.

So, for the first time in my life I used insulting language. If I committed a crime doing that, I should be punished. I want to know if I committed a crime. Now you can judge me.

I don't think it makes any difference that I said "God damn you" to him under my breath.

SOMETHING TO TELL MOTHER

Behind the frame partition which quadrangulated his small office, the vice-president of the Schneider Mercantile Corporation was speaking on the phone in his guttural and nasal mixture. Norbert Ungemach was authorized to hire and fire; to coordinate the operations of the personnel in the larger outer office; to designate which trucking concerns should handle the Schneider consignments within the city, and which common carriers to destinations out of the state; to run an intermediate check on the firm's books, and to maintain a liaison with the factor, Channing Incorporated, on Fourth Avenue, which in point of law owned the total inventory of Schneider Mercantile until a given item in the stock was invoiced to the consignee; and to troubleshoot any situation which might beset and baffle either the import or the export department in handling the walking dolls, the toy soldiers, the rubber balls, the children's slates and a host of other toys.

It was the British Walking Doll, of course, that made up the firm's biggest volume of sales; and it was Carl Schneider himself, heading the company, who was responsible for having introduced the toy successfully to the American market and made it increasingly attractive to buyers throughout the country.

At the moment, Schneider was charmingly discharging a luncheon engagement with the toy buyer from Gimbels, so that the office he occupied next to Ungemach's was empty but for the occasional presence of his secretary, Anne Glauber, who with superficial protest and desperate pride performed multifarious duties during and beyond her regular hours for an incommensurate salary; it was her feeling that she ought to be grateful for the opportunity to learn the business so intensively, the more so since she had not yet received her final naturalization papers. So that it was not unusual that at six in the evening, her working day officially ended, she could summon up considerable glee licking a large number of stamps for the outgoing mail; there was no doubt that she proved again and again her assertion that she could wet the stamps more rapidly with her tongue than by running them over the glistening little white roller. Ungemach would compassionately shake his large oblong skull with its great, hooked rostrum of a nose, and look down on her with an indulgent smile.

But he was not smiling, paternally or otherwise, as he spoke to the party at the other end of the wire about the firm's former bookkeeper, a Samuel H. I. Ticho, who had resigned a month ago by mutual consent.

"I'm glad ve got rid of him," the vice-president relieved himself with pontifical contempt. "He vas of the old school, you know. He could not accustom himself to the newer ant more expeditious accounting methods ve now have. He vas so slow. Yes. Ant he vas so bad-tempered. If you ask me, he vas simply shtupid. Yes. Shtupid. In my opinion, the initials of Mr Samuel H. I. Ticho perfectly characterized him!"

At which Norbert Ungemach at last expressed laughter in a most interesting manner, that is, by pressing his tongue against the palate, which forced the laughter out of the sides of the mouth and through the nose, making the sounds very much like those produced by a toothless condition. Content, then, with his laughter, vulgarism and scorn, he could no longer assuage his real hunger as he habitually did in the confines of his quadrangle by a sandwich his wife had prepared. It was a rare day when Ungemach rebelled against his budget and set out to dine at a restaurant. Attracting him might have been the fine winter weather that he saw glinting through the window on the thrusting angular patterns of Manhattan. Whatever it was, the far from toothless Ungemach carelessly donned a fedora and hoisted on an overcoat of rough gray-black Irish tweed, curtly informed a grinning Anne that, should Mr Schneider return, she might let him know that he would not be gone too long.

The staff watched him depart.

Peter Zwick dropped his fingers from the Frieden calculator the moment Ungemach was out the door. On so young a man as Peter, it was strange that his skull seemed to have been formed with little benefit of flesh, and that as the years passed the bones looked as if they were tending to displace what scant skin remained. He had large, carious, yellow teeth, a bad breath, and a beak whose nostrils bulged blackly. He blushed easily and as often as Anne did, and went out with as few women as she with men, if indeed either was so bold as to make such arrangements at all.

Not that Peter wasn't personable. His smile captivated his elusively blue eyes as it trespassed his teeth. He had a wit which could even abash Anne, and against which she could not retaliate when it was off-color. More to his credit, he was often genuinely and youthfully merry. He was Frank Carlucci's assistant in the export department. He checked invoices, duty- and freight-rates, and helped figure next season's prices; he corresponded in German and Spanish with prospective customers, prodded manufacturers who sometimes lagged in filling orders Schneider Mercantile garnered, and aided Frank in computing what they would have to order from manufacturers now to supply a probable demand for a group of toys six months hence. The man was fantastic with the Frieden, concentrating on the figures before him on the desk without glancing at the numerals his fingers bounced over on the machine.

He leaned back and thrust a leg over the blotter. "No, really," he said, "I wouldn't believe it."

From the far end of the room, Frank peered up, smiling suspiciously. "What wouldn't you believe?"

"On Ungemach," Peter's grasshopper body swayed back and forth in the chair. "The amazing thing already is how healthy shaved gray cheeks can look on Norbert Ungemach! No really," he urged with gay insincerity, as Frank giggled, "have you ever seen gray flesh look healthy on anybody else?"

In the tiny cubicle adjoining Schneider's spare office, Anne was tickled by Peter's commentary and abruptly shut the book she had taken out to read for her evening Comparative Literature class at NYU, and snatched up her lunch from an open drawer. She didn't care for the book anyhow, either in the original German or the translation. It was Thomas Mann's *The Magic Mountain*, and she forcefully insisted, in tones which suggested that contradiction would signify hopeless inferiority, that that novel was already terribly dated in its description of tuberculosis therapy, and that, furthermore, the author's philosophic pretensions and condescensions were insufferable. She was equally bitter about *Moby Dick*, complaining that the credibility of the entire work was impugned because she had discovered that a tree described as growing in New England did not grow there at all. On her last vacation, when she had taken an auto trip through the area, she had specifically checked for the Melville tree and found it wanting.

On the whole, Anne Glauber preferred chamber music to literature: composers made no factual errors. She was quick to admit that she herself could make one now and then, but the truth of the matter was that when she did she was clever and persistent enough, usually, to focus responsibility elsewhere, which occasioned some irritation and envy in Schneider himself and the rest of the staff, no member of which in the rush of the season could spare the time to detect the origin in Anne's work. But she had made herself invaluable by assuming a heavy workload and frequently committing herself to overtime Saturday mornings, so that her attitude of infallibility was habitually if grudgingly overlooked; and everyone was compelled to admit that, while she could as maliciously as any of the others cackle over one of their weaknesses, she would in many an instance strongly and even frantically defend someone under attack, which nobody expected.

She even quarreled chronically with her boss Schneider, with Ungemach, Peter, Frank and with Bob Hutson, the middle-aged negro who constituted the shipping department and who himself worked a double shift to give his wife and six children a decent home and neighborhood across the river in New Jersey. But, with brows contracting, her face flushing, words thickening, tumbling and trembling, she had just as often, nevertheless, stoutly proclaimed the virtues and the noble sacrifices of each of them in turn. The only one she never opposed, and took issue with only apologetically, was Manuela Soto, the Puerto Rican, who was Frank's secretary, with whom she usually ate her lunch.

Anne waddled over to Manuela, who now was wiping carbon smudges from her fingers, drew up a chair and began eating her sandwich with staccato bites and rapid mastication, and joined the general merriment over Ungemach.

The others took out their lunches too. Henry Gladstone, the new book-keeper, scooped up a small brown bag from a bottom drawer and opened it with niggardly but flashing motions. His fingers twinkled, the brown eyes behind his glasses twinkled, the corners of his mouth twinkled. He had a small round head on a tall soft body with a tuft of potbelly.

Frank Carlucci threw open a considerable area of wax paper to display two enormous meatball sandwiches packed in assorted spices among four slabs of Italian bread. "I shouldn't eat them," he smiled genially in full circle. He oscillated between sweet grins and intolerable frowns. His wavy black hair allowed a full white square face, whose cheeks were plumping. There was muscle on the medium build, but it was slipping into fat. He could hold a rage, but it too often slopped over into complaint. He frequently expressed the wish to be endowed with some of Anne's intermittent iciness, but was wary of what such a quality might cost. More, possibly, than what were already incipient ulcers.

"Why then are you eating them?" Peter inquired innocently. Frank shrugged heavy shoulders. "My wife, you know her." And he directed the explanation toward Henry, who was bound to be ignorant of the situation. "Me and my wife, we believe in a big table. You know the wops. A big table."

"You should see it at dinner," Peter said dryly.

"Yeh," Frank said very seriously. "You should. The table is loaded. Around our house at supper you got to eat. It's an insult to life you don't eat."

"Me, I weesh I could eensult my stomach," Manuela said. "Look at me," she went on, throwing up her hands. "I get beeg and fat," she said hopelessly to Anne, who belittled it. "Ah, you should see my daughter," Manuela turned round to Henry, sorrowfully. "Beeg like a church seence my divorce. Believe me, I could pray. And she just had her fourteen birthday."

"You're a handsome woman, Manuela," Henry said in sarcastic reassurance. There was no need for the sarcasm. At forty, Manuela was not over-ripely preserved. Her legs were finely drawn in their black nylon, and the first ravages on the oval face had wrought rakish shadow. The hair was still superbly and densely jet, with the gray bridges just beginning to show. She might have used less rouge, but it did distract one from the too-heavy down on her upper lip.

Anne, on the other hand, used nothing for distraction whatever: she was devoid of cosmetic, and tended to nullify the ingenuous, diabolically nunlike freckled pleasantry of her features, the snub nose, the keen hazel eyes and the full lips, by drawing back her long hair to cover her ears and then piling it into a bun behind; and further coarsened her early twenties by affecting heavy tweed skirts, and cardigans over too-large sweaters, making her healthy breasts appear ludicrously burdensome; while her woolen stockings, which she defended as eminently practical for the season, only gave her heavy and curveless legs and ankles the look of Percherons.

Certainly it could not be denied that the season was intensely cold this year. It was six weeks before Christmas, and the thermometer had been trysting with the low thirties. No matter how well-heated the lower Madison Avenue building was claimed to be, the offices remained drafty and chill. The Schneider Mercantile employees, however, could not help but keep themselves warm by reason of their activity. The lunch-hour lull was deceptive. The phones and office machines in fifteen minutes would be jangling away.

But it was, after all, very nearly the end of the toy season, the climax of which traditionally came in the summer, when most of the big shipments went out. The staff was largely occupied now with cleaning up the balance, the "splits" as they were called — thirty dozen British Walking Dolls to Rexall's in Boston, twenty dozen to Hecht's in Baltimore, and odds and ends here and there.

It was a time when Schneider might at any hour call for a physical inventory at the warehouse, at which Ungemach or Hutson aided him, to check against Anne's running inventory in the files. It was a time when Schneider, as he was doing today, might clinch a large order for the next season with a large department-store buyer, five hundred dozen, for example, if the item had been selling consistently and well between June and November. It was a time when Schneider would make a transatlantic call to London, to his English manufacturer, as he had done yesterday, and fix a date for a flying visit to the factory, to settle fully what the assembly-line could turn out for the coming season, and to bargain if possible fewer American dollars to pay for the product.

Carl Schneider was highly conscious of the American dollar, and warmly if somewhat bitingly enjoyed it. His three-hundred dollar a week salary and one-hundred dollar a week expense account could hardly maintain the apartment he kept for his wife and baby son just above 60th Street on Central Park West, and the modest luxuries they embraced. The money was not enough. He was fifty now. It had only been a year since he had permitted himself his first marriage — to a cosmetics-buyer of one of the smaller Manhattan department stores. He supported as well an old and tyrannical mother, to whom on the phone he invariably spoke in hushed and reverent tones, in German, the continued mastery of which gave him profound pride. His English was more than adequate. His ear for music was appreciable; and ever since his heart-attack five years ago, when he had been enjoined by his physician to take two afternoons off each week, he had spent one at leisurely games of golf, and the other at afternoon concerts of the Philharmonic.

Periodically, though, he would forego the orchestra, and award his seat to Anne, gruffly dismissing her for the rest of the day, usually when Mitropolos was conducting, explaining that he was not especially inclined to the contemporary, preferring, as he put it, the more solid fare of Beethoven and Brahms.

Anne could speak breathlessly of his generosity on this score. She did not feel the fact that she was his cousin thrice removed had influenced the matter; but she could have thought the fact that Peter was Schneider's nephew might have had some connection with the older man having paid all the hospital and doctor bills three months ago when Peter had inadvertently slipped on a banana peel and broken his kneecap, a painful fracture indeed, and one from which he had not yet fully recovered. It was that leg that he was now resting on his desk blotter.

"How's it feel, Peter?" Frank was solicitous.

"You know what?" Peter thrust his lip out pugnaciously in semicomic intent, "Schneider still thinks I slipped on the banana peel on purpose."

"Ah go on," Anne said.

"That's right, that's right," Frank buttressed immediately. "I overheard him talking to Ungemach. He told him Peter would feel better if some work was brought in to him in the hospital, it would help him convalesce. I'm telling you he was bitter. Who would think of doing a thing like that if he didn't think somebody played him dirty, heh Anne? And I'll say this for Ungemach: he pooh-poohed the whole idea."

Peter was charmed. For the moment he could have laid down a fraction of his life for the vice-president. But his tenuous nobility was snapped.

"It was because Ungemach was afraid of you," Anne squirmed the jeer at him over her shoulder.

"Bah! Afraid of me. What do you know about normal fear?"

"Are you becoming maybe a psychoanalyst, Peter?" She found the masticated bits of sandwich hard to swallow. Manuela tried to quiet her by a warning pressure from her fingers, but Anne was far too alert to compassion to embrace the quality, and she needed it far too much to look on it as honest. If it emanated from someone for whom she had a genuine affection, as she did for Manuela, she ignored it altogether.

"Anne, I hate to do this to you. Don't you think I hate to do this to Anne?" Peter easily induced Frank into a little pack. The export manager licked his mouth into a sweet expectancy.

"We all hate to do things to Anne, don't we?" Frank grew a little chortle toward the girl.

Manuela growled in her gruff voice that they should all shut up.

"Ah, the hot-blooded Castilian!" Frank laughed.

"You know goddamn well I am no Casteelian, I'm Puerto — "

"Where they make lousy rum — "

"All right all right so they make lousy rum. I am not responsible for their lousy rum. I dreenk geen."

"Gin, gin!"

"What did I say? Geen, geen!"

"Ladies and gentlemen, I hate to interrupt you," Peter said, holding up a hand, "but I have something to say to Anne."

"Peter Zwick has the floor," Frank said.

"Anne Glauber couldn't think of me as anything else but a psychoanalyst if she was laying on a couch."

"He's got you there!" Frank roared.

"That's just the trouble — I don't!" Peter concluded and Frank came over to slap him resoundingly on the back.

"But don't worry," Frank turned to the girl, who was pulling her mouth out as widely as she could in a ghastly, angry grin, "Peter did slip on that banana peel on purpose, so he could wear a crutch and really look at himself like he really is."

"Ja, ja," she said, curving her back at them, and dipping her head into the sandwich.

"Peegs, peegs," Manuela wiped her mouth.

"It's about time you got rid of that accent," Frank counseled.

"By the way," Henry Gladstone casually put himself in as Peter took long draws on a cigarette and glanced brightly from time to time at the burrowing Anne, "how long has Norbert Ungemach been in the country?"

Strangely, Frank grew very quiet, very serious. "I'd say about fifteen years. Why?"

Detecting an enmity he could not quite account for, Henry started to stutter, something habitual in his reaction to the possibly hostile, but controlled himself quickly. "Well," he poured out condescension, "for a man who's been in the country fifteen years, the way he still substitutes v's for his w's is a little surprising."

"You think so?" Frank said coldly.

"Why sure it is. It indicates to me — now mind you I can't be absolutely sure — nobody can be absolutely — "

"Nobody," Peter interpolated a viscid sarcasm, airily waving his cigarette.

"That's right," Henry said, stuttering a little, his plump eyes skidding rapidly behind the lids, magnified by the thick spectacles. "It indicates maybe the guy is a little snobbish. Maybe he saves those v's. You know you learn a lot in sociology."

Anne broke into captious howls, "Sociology is one of the most inexact of the sciences."

"Is that so?" Henry stood up. "Well let me tell you something, Anne."

"Tell me, tell me."

"Did you ever notice a negro without a mustache? And if he didn't have a mustache, didn't he have some kind of hair decoration on his face somewhere. A little beard maybe?" He lectured his long arms in his blatantly plaid jacket at her. "But mostly they have mustaches."

"Oh that's nonsense." The others sided with her.

"Well, let me tell you something, do me a favor," Henry was irritated.

"What's the favor, Henry?" Frank's coldness was unrelenting.

"I'll tell you. The next time you're on a subway or bus or along the street, you look at negroes, and then you tell me the next day if you saw just one without a mustache. I'll predict you won't see one without some kind of hair adornment. You want to know how I know?"

"You tell us, Henry," Frank exchanged looks with Peter: this Henry Gladstone somehow was untrustworthy, and simply wasn't one of them.

"I conducted a survey," the bookkeeper was triumphant, "when I was in college, for my sociology class, the inexact science, Anne." But he couldn't dislodge her smirk. "And I made a count of all the negroes I saw and there wasn't one that didn't have a mustache or a beard. How do you like that?"

"If you say so," Peter was already dismissing it.

"Well, that's why I know something about people," Henry insisted, "and I'll say Norbert Ungemach must be a snob if he keeps saying v's for w's. He's either a snob or he just don't know any better!"

"It's his fourth language," Anne said, savagely, waddling back to her little cubicle, and then turning to stand for a moment under the archway.

Henry was a bit rattled. "Fourth language, fourth language — what's that got to do with it?"

And she was remorseless, staccato, sharp. "I said his fourth. German. Then French. Then Spanish. Then English. The places on the way to America, Mr Gladstone. You must forgive him he makes his v for a w. Is English your fourth language, Mr Gladstone?"

He blinked at her. His only reaction was to attempt any kind of disparagement. "Where are my copies of the invoices, Anne?"

"You should know by now I won't have them ready till three o'clock."

"Heh, heh," he laughed nervously, "I guess I can wait. I got this bookkeeping system licked anyway. Nothing to it. Come on over, Anne, I'll show you something of how it works." But she didn't bother to reply, and Henry took out a piece of hard candy to suck on as he returned to his columns of figures, from time to time taking covert glances at the staff as they went back to their respective jobs.

Manuela frowned and cursed over an incredibly lengthy and detailed Spanish bill of lading.

Frank compressed his lips angrily as he listened on the phone to some bastard trucking outfit try to alibi itself out of a tardy shipment, finally switching the call to Peter, bawling that he didn't have time to involve himself with this sonofabitch and ordering his assistant to follow it up and get tough with him. Peter was dismayed that he was interrupted at his Frieden on which he was preparing a table of prices for items at so much per dozen, and irritated with Frank that the trucker had been sloughed off on him, especially since a display of obduracy was not particularly his forte.

Anne positively galloped over to the adding-machine with a yard-wide British manifest and was frenetically transposing pounds sterling into dollars.

The scene amused Henry Gladstone. He cultivated an internal picture: tittering. The people here simply didn't know. They were naive. None of them have the remotest idea that he was here temporarily. He curled his long soft legs under him, and he had the feeling that they were a sort of cushion, and he a sort of potentate contemplating a kingdom whose subjects were ignorant of their monarch. Now he idly turned over a pile of yesterday's invoices as briefly-built Arnold Silverstein, his gray hair briskly curled, snapped the not-quite defrosted door behind him.

Silverstein was the certified public accountant who examined the books monthly. His motions reminded one of a speeded-up mechanical toy, stiff, precise and almost ludicrously invisible.

Everyone commented on the accountant's glamorous Florida tan, which only starched him the more. He made his abbreviated salutations, obtained the necessary ledgers from Henry, and proceeded to inspect them after he sat with the upright morality of a board at the long walnut table at right angles to the tall steel safe, painted a grim green, which stood against the wall.

As far as Henry was concerned, Silverstein was also a fool, because of certain physical culture ideas he might at any time abruptly divulge to anyone he judged in dire need. Indeed, Henry wasn't aware of human beings who weren't fools, except he and his wife. Take this export-import company, for example, he purred to himself. Small staff, all working for outrageously low salaries. Very typical of the trade, especially the medium-sized firms forced to hold a low overhead. As many relatives as he could persuade to work for him, those the president of the corporation preferred. Schneider in an especially fortunate position because they were refugees. Which led him to plead family loyalty and indebtedness since he had been instrumental in extricating them from Germany; so that, furthermore, whenever any one of them thought a salary rise merited, he could indefinitely defer the request.

Peter had told the bookkeeper that in the men's room, about himself and Anne. Peter had made no bones about the fact that he loathed Carl Schneider, but was as yet helpless to do anything about it. He owed Schneider too much: the trip from Germany and now the hospital bills. He wanted to place himself in the downtown district with a private banking house and work on the grain market, which he knew he could master, but he had no capital. Peter still smarted at some of the remarks Schneider had directed toward him, the last one, quite typical, having been made in the men's room at the end of the day when Peter was scrubbing off that damned penetrating purple carbon he had got from typing invoices (copies run off on the ditto machine, a kind of mimeograph), about which he had ironically complained to Schneider as the latter had shaved with an electric razor. Schneider hadn't even done the courteous discourtesy of glancing at him with raised eyebrow; he had simply said flatly into the mirror that Peter ought to come to work in the morning with white gloves. At six in the evening, however, Schneider could be irresistibly urbane, expecting with a pained humor that certainly nobody was going to leave before cleaning up loose ends, though without overtime reimbursement.

Henry felt uproarious. He himself quit the place at precisely five minutes to six. Of course, Schneider had by now on more than one occasion called him into his office for a fatherly talk about company teamwork, "get up and go!" as he had phrased it, stressing that the large clock above the entrance was absolutely non-existent to the rest of the staff.

But Henry had stood his ground, and lied that he had evening courses at Columbia University, to which Schneider had had to surrender, the more readily because Henry was an excellent bookkeeper, as such hard come by. And Henry would go at five minutes to six; nevertheless, to the others, who continued to sweat at desk, ditto-machine, Frieden, adding-machine, typewriter and the outgoing mail — his goodnights were softly if sardonically expressed. He distinctly did not exit like a lion, but bowing his tall soft body he made a swift slink into the hallway and down the elevator.

Once, Henry was pursued by Schneider as he walked toward the Eighth Avenue subway down Broadway, and was finally caught up with, at which point the president greatly deplored Henry having left the others in the lurch, since they had had to pick up chores which should have been more equitably divided, that this was simply not the sporting thing to do, and that, furthermore, he had plans for Henry Gladstone, because he was fine material to take over the import department, with which he, Schneider, simply wasn't satisfied to have the girl Anne Glauber running; he didn't like women in executive positions; in addition, Anne was just not a well girl — she was sick, physically as well as mentally. But the bookkeeper stubbornly kept to his five-of-six, and Schneider, with hurt demeanor, finally accepted as fact that Henry Gladstone did not want to rise to fame in the Schneider

Mercantile Corporation.

Henry made a notation of the last of yesterday's invoices, which had been partially filled in prior to shipment, and then completed when shipment was initiated. He realized that Schneider still had a chance to put away a good bonus after dividends, but any firm which continued to be underwritten by a factor, this Channing — was on dubious financial grounds. It simply meant that it had not yet accumulated sufficient capital to finance its own buying of a product. It was financed to do so by a commercial bank, which is what a factor amounted to. And if the firm was still insecure, so, consequently, must Schneider be himself.

It must be galling to the president, Henry thought most pleasurably, that each order which came into the company had first to be submitted to the factor before shipment could commence. Channing, usually in a 48-hour period, certified or rejected the ordering company as a credit risk. Those it certified, it returned to Schneider Mercantile, which was then permitted to act on the order. As soon as the completed invoices were mailed out to the ordering company, copies were simultaneously dispatched to the factor. When the ordering companies paid their bills to Schneider Mercantile, Henry would make out a check to Channing for the cost of the merchandise the factor had financed plus a commission-percentage Channing had stipulated for the service, about which Schneider could make obscene remarks to express his spleen.

Henry could visualize the president's intense purplish blue eyes, and he pitied the older man's infant son, whose birth had not particularly pleased anyone in the office except the father. It was with considerable foresight that Ungemach wrote insurance during his free time. But the bookkeeper would be quit of the corporation long before any of them.

He despised them. Though Frank and Manuela were otherwise, Henry felt the essential quality of the company Teutonic, projected by Schneider, Ungemach, Peter and Anne, all arrogant in one form or another. They had fled or been ejected from Germany, and yet they were still supremely conscious of their Kultur. Schneider had derided the recent American presidential election. He had been steadfast in his refusal to vote, and grudged the time the others took to exercise the ballot, reminding them that, although the law permitted them a number of hours off to go to the polls, they could quite easily — and quickly, because there would be no queues — vote before nine in the morning or after six at night. With a babylike smile he had once even gone around to each of his employees, curving a kneading hand about their shoulders, to intimate that of course when the state inspector would be coming around the following week to inquire about wage and hour practices that none of them would commit themselves to have ever worked overtime nor admit having been asked to volunteer for such.

Henry Gladstone had his plan of severance from the company worked out, and was fond of reviewing it once to himself at the office, and once during every evening with his wife at home. She was an apprentice dress-designer, and he himself had nearly completed courses in pattern-making, a vocation which gave him the deepest joy he had ever known. Rapidly making the social-security deductions in preparation for tomorrow's payroll, Henry pictured the expressions of balk and hatred on Ungemach and Schneider when they would learn his defection. The bookkeeper in two weeks would have completed his arrangements toward becoming a junior partner in the dressmaking firm his wife worked for. At that point he would make certain that all his bookkeeping chores for Schneider Mercantile would be up to date. It would be a Friday afternoon. He would then leave the office with his usual "So long everybody, have a good weekend," taking the key to the safe with him as he did normally, since he had to open it before the executives arrived for the business of the day. He would go home and write a letter to Carl Schneider, in which he would accuse him of having been penny-pinching, domineering and insulting, and that therefore he, Henry Gladstone, had no further desire to work for the company and was herewith submitting his resignation. He would append the assurance that his books were in order, and could be inspected at any time; and note that he was herein enclosing the keys to the inside door of the safe and the petty-cash box where, he would sardonically add, they could without fear assume that the vouchers were accounted for to the cent. At last he would send the letter to Schneider Mercantile that evening by registered mail, so that it would reach them Saturday morning; through that day and Monday he and his wife had planned not to answer the phone, so as to avoid risking any contact either with Ungemach or Schneider.

"Vhat are you grinning like a baboon for?" Ungemach was peering down at the bookkeeper with an oafishly benign countenance. He actually liked Henry, approving his independence and fine intelligence for trivia.

Henry very nearly spat out the hard candy he was chewing: he had been utterly unconscious of Ungemach's entry. But the vice-president was unaware of the bookkeeper's discomfort because he had his own to unburden. He went past Frank into his quadrangle.

"Has Schneider not come back?"

"I didn't notice, Ungemach," Frank said, totally embroiled in an unsteady pile of order folders. It was a thin whine.

"Vell you needn't get so huffy about it," Ungemach returned with a professionally crinkling smile as he gazed stonily at a photograph of his homely wife Louise tilted glossily away from him, flanked by two positively sabretoothed blond children, both boys, his soul proudly declaimed. But pride careened when his buzzer sounded. "Yes, Louise, I vill get the steaks before I come home. That's correct, Louise." His voice was a very model of indulgent rectitude.

Anne soundlessly chuckled, and communicated heaving shoulders to Manuela across the way, who twisted her mouth.

"Vas there anything else that you vanted?' Ungemach was warmly polite: nobody could have otherwise interpreted it. Evidently, that terminated Louise's desire for the moment. "Tell the boys not to forget their homevork. Yes. Goodby, darling." With apparent calmness, Ungemach worked fresh tobacco into the bowl of his pipe, sauntered to Frank's desk for a match, at last contentedly puffing, while Frank became increasingly nervous.

"Vill the shipment make the boat, do you think?" Ungemach tried to put it cooperatively.

"I think so, Ungemach. For god's sake, I got a hundred things to do. I got to run these new prices off on the ditto and they haven't even been checked yet." Frank gazed worriedly up at the vice-president.

Ungemach called upon Peter, who protested at once that he was again being interrupted at important foreign correspondence. "I can't do three things at once," he frowned.

"It's all right, Peter, it's all right," Ungemach pacified, "I am only asking you to do two things simultaneously." He knocked ashes into Peter's tray.

"Very funny," Peter muttered, and snatched the price lists from Ungemach's friendly hand.

The vice-president looked in on Anne. "Are you sure Schneider vasn't in for a moment vhile I vas out?"

"No."

"Do you perchance have my dictation?"

"I told you it was on your desk."

"You are amazingly fast, Anne."

"Thank you. Will you let me get back to my manifest?"

"I'm sorry. Did I interrupt you?"

"Yes."

"How many errors did the British clerks" — he heavily pronounced it "clarks" — "make this time?"

Anne was suddenly and genuinely happy. "I caught them off five pounds sterling." The nunlike freckled pleasantry of her features tilted up at him with the least amount of the diabolic.

"Good girl," he patted her shoulder, and strolled into his office. He looked out the window at the dulling glints of the sun on the thrusting angular patterns of Manhattan. The enormous towers of the Metropolitan Life Insurance Company were not far off. Only half an hour ago he had skillfully avoided the dense outpour of its office girls into the street on their lunch hour. There had seemed to be thousands upon thousands, not one of which he had been able to translate into a tabulation. Nor could he identify any with the unquestionably human. Ungemach, frankly, did not know what, precisely, they actually were. He could only describe them, helplessly, as office-girls. Yes, they had a definite sex destined for one function and one only. But this, he felt, was impossible — the functional singularity. It was an insult. And he had felt insulted by their outpouring. Grossly and overwhelmingly.

Without realizing their loudness, he flung the words through the partition. "Frank, I met Nathan Brodsky's partner on the street a little vhile ago."

"Yeh?"

"He told me something awful."

"Yeh?"

"This morning Nathan Brodsky had a heart-attack ant passed avay."

Frank got up abruptly to look in on the vice-president. "Is that right?"

Ungemach was serious. "It's a varning."

"Uh-huh." Frank peered at him, anxious.

"It's a varning ve should all think about, so ve should relax, ant not get up too much shteam. It could have happened to any of us in this business."

"You're not kidding," Frank said. The normal whiteness of his face receded into a further pallor. Then he turned to Peter. "What do you think?"

"What do you want me to think while I am checking price-lists? Even Ungemach admits I can do only two things simultaneously," Peter said irascibly, then angled up the two black pits of his nostrils and showed his yellow rotting teeth. "But I tell you what I think anyway, free."

"Tell us, tell us."

"It applies to you, Frank Carlucci."

"How?"

"Export or die!"

Manuela gave a hoarse yell of admiration. Anne came in, hands on her hips, to shake her head at Peter with a grudging grin. Silverstein, starchly laboring, was unmoved. Henry Gladstone, startled, broke into snickers. Ungemach heartily bellowed his toothless-sounding guffaws. And Peter — Peter blushed at his own cleverness. For a moment Frank didn't know whether he wanted to pop the boy on the jaw, or succumb.

He succumbed. And, returning to his desk, laughing, he asked Peter if he'd like to go with him to a Carnegie Hall jazz concert. Next to believing in his "big table," the sexual virtues of his wife and a solid sleep, in that order, he believed in the wonders of as many records of Bessie Smith as he could put his hands on, the prima jazzerina as he called her, and the desirability of getting lost trying to catch Frankie Newton at Village holes. But Peter's reply was ignored when Anne answered an insistent phone and hissed for everyone to be quiet. Then she nodded to Ungemach, who quite consciously let a moment pass before he spoke into the receiver, and just as purposely leaned as far back in his chair as it would go.

"Yes, Carl," Ungemach nodded.

There was total silence in the office.

"Listen, Carl, I don't know precisely vhat Anne's last count vas. It vas in the neighborhood of 126 dozen of the 6-inch valking-dolls, 90 dozen of the 12-inch, ant 48 dozen of the — " He left off, and took a slow draw on his pipe. His features were impassive. "Vell ven do you think you ant Hutson vill be finished?" The great hooked rostrum of his nose momentarily seemed to rest on his massive chin. The large oblong skull was unperturbedly rocklike. "In an hour you say? By the time you return, Carl, Anne vill have made a total of her running inventory. I vouldn't be upset if I vere you. You know me, Schneider: moderation in all things. Yes, yes, I understand how you might feel. Believe me, I am vith you, Carl. Of course, of course." And he hung up.

Anne pulled the oblong cardboard on which she recorded her inventory and slammed the gray steel file drawer shut. Her nose was splotched with red. Wisps of her lifeless brown hair tagged her cheeks as she crowded over her desk thronged with rubber stamps, typewriter, steno pad, pencils, ink erasers, bills of lading, invoices, kleenex, order folders, memo pads covered with abbreviated figuring, a ledger filled with the dates of orders, the companies which had ordered, the quantity, each order with a check against it the day it was filled — and in the heap a German-English dictionary and an American thesaurus. Directly facing her, through the window, were the modest spires of a small church now racked by shadows in the surrendering afternoon.

Fiercely, Manuela wanted to comfort her. "Ah goddamn," she cried suddenly, "anather typo. What do you know. Seex carbons I haf to do over."

Frank glanced at Manuela with concern, only because he wanted to conceal his frown over Anne.

"I weel haf to stay to seven o'clock to feenish thees goddamn invoice," Manuela rasped in anguish. "'You haf nothing weeth your eenventory," she called over to Anne. "Child's play."

But Anne couldn't look up, only mutter an aggrieved "Ja, ja."

Frank gently taunted Manuela. "Your big Puerto Rican importer will wait for you."

"Sure sure," she said, "the question ees can I wait for heem?"

Peter yelled brightly. "Anne, certainly if you've made any mistakes, can't you tell Schneider that to err is human but to forgive only costs a little fine?"

Frank looked disgusted. "It's a real time for humor, Pete."

"Ah you make me sick with all this expectation. It's happened ten thousand times and you're still not used to it," Peter decried. "How long have you worked for Schneider, Frank?"

"Eight years," Frank said glumly.

Ungemach poked out his massive head. "I'm amazed at you, Frank. You are still not acclimated to Carl Schneider?" It was an attempt at levity.

But it was an engulfed and saturnine Frank who answered. "No, no I'm not, Ungemach."

The tall potbelly-tufted Henry Gladstone scowled, banged his petty cash box shut, locked it and started for the door on his way to the men's room. He wanted a five-minute break. The atmosphere was up to his eyes. As he went by Peter he saw the yellow teeth hooking into a soft-voiced query, "What's the matter, Mr Gladstone? All the time I thought you had the belly for it."

"Yeh," the bookkeeper said. "Yeh."

Before he went out the door, he caught a dry smirk from the certified public accountant, Arnold Silverstein, the man with the stiff pale eyes, the stiff soft chin, the neat triangulated head, the gray hair briskly curled, crisply aloof, his sinewy fingers gracefully grasping the slim Parker pen — "the figures, Mr Gladstone, should be neat and clear. You younger men have a habit of scrawling. And with as few erasures as possible. If you are careful, there will be no erasures. You younger men are much too rapid for your own good," as he had tapped his lean gray-socked feet shod in pointed gray suede when he had given the bookkeeper his carefully mellowed advice the first day Henry had worked there. Schneider Mercantile leaned heavily on

Arnold Silverstein, of which he was quite aware. Many firms did similarly, but he bore up under the strain. Florida and the Bahamas helped. And, after all, how much responsibility could be attached to him? — he simply worked with the figures the company supplied. The company might lie, but that was not Silverstein's affair, was it? And the consciousness that it essentially was not, gleamed from his perfect poise.

Go screw your poise, Henry silently cursed him as he walked through the hallway, and screw Peter Zwick with his confidences — it was the last time Henry would listen to him after that crack about his stomach. The bookkeeper decided that the members of the staff, no matter how much in an oblique way they had just seemed to try to palliate what Anne expected to go through — somehow spied on one another and, worse, fed on each other in a kind of miserable glee. Whatever their callousness, Henry felt that they constantly opened their clothes for the tender flesh to be painfully consumed and reconsumed. And Anne, for all her obnoxiousness, impressed him as being the most tender and sensitive of the lot. The fact that she came of a German Catholic father and a Jewish mother, and that as a very young girl she had spent over two years in a Nazi forced labor camp, from which the Americans had liberated her, must have had considerable bearing, but she continued to puzzle him no matter how often and how much she made him feel inferior. Henry Gladstone had, after all, kept up his interest in sociology, and he was happy that he had. He flattered himself that he could observe people with some measure of objectivity. There was a connection, of course — he had more than once patted himself for — between the gratification he derived from pattern-making and the satisfaction from keeping his eye on the social patterns of human behavior.

Funny, he thought, going back to the office through the green-walled and blue granite-floored hallway, how the precisely consecutive doorways always, uncannily, provoked the sense of their having been altered, as if he had never been here before. And then Henry Gladstone's shoulders bowed a little more: he detected a tweedy cologne. Turning a corner, he saw the Schneider Mercantile office door slam; and, tightening his lips, he went in.

"If I were you, Mr Gladstone, I wouldn't take naps in the men's room. For all the literal insistence on the matter, there is little comfort to be had." Carl Schneider delivered the pronouncement mildly but exactly as he stood before Anne. All Henry saw, as his large ears were suffused with red, was Schneider's back, which had not moved an inch. Henry knew that Schneider was wearing a gray pin-stripe, but he had to enlist memory to enforce the knowledge. The bookkeeper's body mumbled back to its ledgers.

"Carl, Carl," Ungemach was easing.

"Oh shut up, Norbert," Schneider regarded the vice-president as he might a slogan. Casually, then, to Anne. "Have you got your count ready on the 12-inch dolls?"

The bulk that was Bob Hutson was flipping his gentle eyes through his shipping records, bending close to Anne, trying to make her notations compatible. Hutson's voice had all but disappeared through the years, and amounted now to a harsh, loud but infinitely tender whisper.

"I have not got it ready, Mr Schneider," Anne snapped.

"You understand, of course, Anne, that Bob and I interrupted our inventory when I discovered a serious discrepancy in Ungemach's approximation of your inventory on the 6-inch dolls and the slates." Schneider's tones were mellifluous. "And I expect a third major error with respect to the 12-inch."

Ungemach bore down: "I'm sure ve can all find vhat the trouble is."

Schneider was patient. "I didn't ask you, Norbert," his lips somewhat pained.

Silverstein glanced up once from his books, immaculately encompassed the fact that Schneider was amongst them, sighed, and once again pursed the figures in his mouth that his eye nipped up from the page.

Schneider tapped next on Peter's desk. Peter was bent practically double over a price-list. "Still on your knees, nephew?"

"One knee, Mr Schneider," he muttered.

"Ah. You have one good knee on which to stand up to me. Isn't that right, Peter?"

"It so happens, Uncle, that because of the accident one leg may turn out to be a little shorter than the other."

"Carl," the vice-president pleaded, "I vish you would come into my office. Really, there is no sense standing out here."

"I'm not a child, Ungemach," Schneider frowned. "I don't understand why you're trying to handle me as if I were."

"I don't think I am in the least implying that you are a child," the vice-president was gratingly unctuous, the nasal and the guttural positively climactic.

"I think you are, Norbert. Don't you think I have a right to know what's going on in my own business?" Wavelets of pouch threatened the deepening purplish blue intensity of Schneider's eyes.

Ungemach denied that anyone had sought to keep clandestine any aspect of the business. The president thanked him acidly and proceeded to knead Peter's shoulder and give him advice in the kindliest of manners.

"You must know, Peter, that the disability which threatens you has often been the long-wanting spur to an individual who has not distinguished himself by vaulting ambition. Your mind may now assume the vault which your knee, almost symbolically, repudiated — so that the accident may have been a happy reflection of the missing constituent in a relatively passive personality." Schneider smiled and lifted a sandy eyebrow at Henry. "There are probably others who could use injuries with equal felicity."

Frank gulped down a snicker.

Anne spoke up, then, sharply and commandingly. "I have the figure, Mr Schneider, if you are interested."

"Of course I'm interested."

"Ninety dozen."

"Oh but that's impossible, Anne. Bob and I counted ninety-seven dozen. Is that correct, Bob?"

"That's right," Hutson vented a hopeless hoarse doom.

"My figure is the correct one," Anne was stubborn.

"Now how could it be?" Schneider wailed softly. "How can you sit there and insist after Bob and I double-checked — that your figure is right while ours is in error? How can you? Please don't let me down."

"I am not letting you down, Mr Schneider." Anne's words came with hideous speed. She stood up, shifting from thick ankle to thick ankle, her hips clumsily undulant. Shafts of grin flickered across her face, her freckles dark against the flushing flesh. She wanted to stop his mouth, close his eyes. Her hideous speed came of desperate adoration. It was inconceivable that what she worshiped could punish her. Inconceivable, yes, and yet necessary — compulsory, even, that her adored should mete out punitive measures. But how could he tell her that she was letting down an object of more than veneration when she would never have dared to do so. And he was insisting that she did and had. "I resent your accusing me of letting you down, Mr Schneider. I have worked for you how many years — ? you are so wonderful at counting so suddenly. Always you have shifted the responsibility for error onto me — "

"Oh that's ridiculous," Schneider said disgustedly. "I've indulged in no such habit. What kind of sadist do you take me for?" He stared at her, hatred high on his lip. "You'd better calm down, Anne, if you know what's good for you."

"I know very well what's good for me. I know very well. Yes, yes."

"I wonder. Indeed, I wonder."

"You need not." Her voice fluttered, full of scudding fleeciness. "I will tell you certainly I do not like admitting I have made mistakes, but you Mr Schneider, you find it difficult to bring your own out into the open I have found. Not that you have made very many. No. You have not. But to listen to you, you are a god — you — " She halted, shaking her head, her throat working. She pressed her knuckles against her nostrils, to shut out the odor of the tweed.

Ungemach towered over them as from across the room Henry's round soft head lifted up like a turtle's from the flat rocks of the ledgers to zero the three people in.

"Carl," the vice-president pressed out his special brand of sobriety for all difficult circumstances, "there is a lot of vork to be done — "

"You're interrupting yourself, Ungemach. Nobody else is involved. Simply Anne. Can't you understand that? It's very simple. Only Anne — "

"Vill you please keep your voice down — "

"Goddamn it, Norbert, I organized this company. Are you implying I don't have the right to discipline any of my employees if I see fit? Furthermore, my voice is my own. My anger is my own, and if I deem it necessary to express, I will express it."

"Let him be angry," Anne directed her venom at Ungemach. "I don't care. I am not afraid of it." She thrust her head at Schneider. "I don't wilt under your anger."

"No, I'm sure you don't." Schneider wanted to strike her down, and Anne might have welcomed it. It might have put an end to the words. She was sure that in a crisis she was better than he with words. But she didn't necessarily want to be. It was unseemly that she be superior to Schneider in any way. Outrageously wrong. She could have struck herself down.

"Schneider, really, do you intend to crucify a girl for a difference of seven dozen dolls?" Ungemach inclined his massive torso toward him.

Schneider found him the essence of nausea. "Oh for christ's sake I'm not crucifying anybody." Then, impassively, to Anne. "Is the afternoon mail on my desk?"

In low tones, Anne said it was.

"Thank you." He was most courtly. He turned slowly, went into his office and gently closed the door.

The rest of them went about their work, depressed. Hutson told Anne he was sorry, which she curtly dismissed, and then he pleaded that he had to get back to the warehouse, which the girl never even heard. Miserably, he rolled his bulk out of the office. Manuela swiftly bent over Frank.

"I could keel heem," she whispered.

"Wait, you'll see. Another hour," Frank promised her with a set mouth in his full white square face, "and he'll melt you. You'll love him."

"I weel not love heem. Ever again." And she wearily returned to her invoice. Peter shook his head in thorough agreement.

Carl Schneider opened the letter on the top of the pile with a swift slit. He read it standing. He had no desire to sit. He permitted himself, however, to lean against the point of his desk and, rhythmically, as he read, pressed his hip against it, enjoying its not quite painful prod. His hip, after all, was well padded. First, by his gray pin-stripe singlebreasted suit (before, going off to England, he would attire himself in a Scotch tweed sports coat, probably of a large mutedly colored check design; his trousers would be charcoal gray; his shoes, rich brown Scotch grain); second, by his fine blue nylon shorts; and, last, by his plump pink flesh. At fifty, Carl Schneider was rotund in a most socially acceptable manner; he did not protrude anywhere more than was esthetically mandatory. And if Ungemach was a uniquely healthy gray after shaving, Schneider was a conventionally healthy roseate after he blew softly through the electric razorhead. True, his blond silken curls were balding, but evenly. His nose was unobtrusively wrought; his chin was determined, but carefully so, that it should not have too obvious a point. His lips nearly overflowed their pretty bounds, but missed a pout, their curves judiciously controlled by the man's irony whenever he could manage it. Still, he would have been offensively handsome had not the deepset purplish blue eyes spurned it. He was a little taller than Anne, with good broad shoulders and stocky hips. He stopped prodding his hip as a baffled laughter with a sort of gentle savagery behind rose from his throat. In the twenty odd years he had risen from the position of a shipping clerk at Macy's to be a head buyer, and in the succeeding decade in which he had organized his own export-import firm, he had never encountered the kind of business letter he had just finished reading.

"Ungemach!"

In a moment, clattering his pipe down on the ashtray, the vice-president was at Schneider's door.

"Carl, you must calm down," Ungemach humbled his herculean shoulders.

The clashing purplish blue eyes ignored the plea. Schneider went out into the main office as he rapped the letter smartly. Everyone looked up, including Arnold Silverstein.

"I am going to read you," said Schneider, "an excerpt from a letter of cancellation." The baffled laughter with its soft savagery again gently stumbled from his throat. His eyes startled everyone in turn except Silverstein, whose concentration on his task was apparently immovable; Schneider's eyes seemed devoid of his body, and of all but their color and the kind of glitter seen only on the most expensive crystal, as Peter had once remarked to Frank — "a kind, also," Peter had gone on, "of decapitated incandescence, if that is possible." A guillotine incessantly descending to cut through glass necks. As if all the necks Schneider wanted to sever he saw as glass. More: as if the necks must be glass that no blood spill. And there seemed no blood in the man's eyes, but rather a present-arms array of glass splinters in a blinding purplish blue. Anne felt her stomach bloated and loathsome, and she reviled herself for eating so much of an insubstantial diet — greens and non-fattening bread.

"This letter," gloated Schneider now, "is from the president of a midwestern firm, in Wisconsin, as a matter of fact, that state graced by the noble utterances of its late junior senator, Joseph McCarthy."

Anne had to chuckle in quick absolute admiration for Schneider's theatrics.

"Pay attention, Anne," he told her, not unkindly.

"Of course."

"I quote now from the letter," Schneider said smoothly as he held it up, and then adjusted a prodding finger to each consecutive word. "'I must, without regret, let me strongly accentuate, cancel our order in view of the worsening international situation. I knew, of course, that the British Walking Doll that you import is manufactured in England. However, little did I know of the intent of Great Britain to increase its trade with Red Russia and to continue its commerce, if possible, with Red China. I, sir, for one, refuse to permit our company to traffic in goods made by a nation which refuses to cut off its trade — and, please understand, increases it — with a country which we see by the paper threatens us more and more on every side. Why should we buy goods from England which indirectly will aid our greatest enemy — Atheistic Russia? Therefore, this cancellation. And if the Schneider Mercantile Corporation, permit me to say, had any sense of national security and a little patriotism, it would at this instant cease doing business with England.'"

Schneider glared at Ungemach, who looked at him helplessly. "Vell you know, Carl — " he began to deprecate, but Schneider cut him off:

"Can't I trust anybody, Ungemach?"

"I may be shtupid, Carl, but I can't see vhat that letter has to do vith — "

"Anne knows! Anne Glauber knows!" Schneider whipped.

"I know nothing of that company's political opinions, Mr Schneider. How can you — "

"Naturally, Miss Glauber, I expected that."

Anne rose behind her crowded desk, trembling. "I don't follow you. What are you trying to make out … " She came forward to stand directly in front of him.

Frank Carlucci gripped his pencil. Peter was terrified, his long grass-hopper body sticking to the wall. Manuela moaned that if she had no four-teen-year-old daughter she would leave, now. Henry crouched, watching, like an elongated plaid-jacketed brown spider, over his ledgers.

"You heard her, Ungemach," Schneider shrilled, "she says she knows nothing. Obviously I can't trust her. I would like to know who I can if not my own trusted employees? I pay her to keep an accurate inventory, one that will tally with mine when I make the physical one at — "

The immaculate Silverstein interrupted, his pale eyes stiff, his soft chin stiff, the gray hair briskly curled. He shook an admonitory finger at Schnei-der. " You've got to relax, Carl — "

"What the hell are you talking about, Silverstein? I pay you to look at my books — " Schneider shouted.

"No no no," Silverstein shook his head, "you don't understand. This is the sort of situation in which you've got to take yourself in hand and con-sciously relax. And let me tell you — "

"I'm not in the least interested — "

"Of course you're not," Silverstein. briskly but paternally reproved as he stood up straight, lean and short in his pointed gray shoes, "but you should be. After all, I'm older, I've been through the worst, let me tell you. What you should do," he advised as Schneider gazed at him in disbelief and amazement, and as some of the others giggled nervously, Anne herself feel-ing that the whole scene was impossible but that she was torturedly rooted to the spot — "what you should do right now is sit down in a straightbacked chair, Carl, and draw back your shoulders as far as they'll go and hold them that way, hold them, you understand, while expanding your chest as much as you can — hold your shoulders thus for a full five minutes. Believe me," he concluded triumphantly, "you will feel like a new man!"

"Will you shut up?" Schneider screamed.

"Certainly," the accountant shrugged, and pointed his neat triangu-lated skull at the long table, behind which he sat once again, his slim foun-tain-pen superbly poised as he obliterated the office completely from mind and took the beautiful numerals in the open book in hand.

"You've made me look like a fool, Anne," Schneider mentally clawed at the climax he was in danger of losing, a climax his whole body simply could not afford to lose. "You've made me out a fool before Bob Hutson. Not only him. I had a buyer who was waiting for the information, Miss Glauber. What could I tell him? What accurate figure could I base my judgment on to negotiate with the man? You've made me out an idiot with him as well. My own organization," he was close to tears, his voice whined and dragged and whimpered as he turned to Ungemach, "I can't even depend on that."

Anne stood perfectly still. Her long hair straggled over her childish neck. Altogether, her body appeared ludicrously burdensome, unable to shift or move a muscle, and her keen hazel eyes had dulled. Her arms hung stupidly.

Ungemach tried, gently, to steer Schneider into his office. "At heart it's a good organization, Carl," he said. "All of us vunce in a vhile are bound to make some errors, ant ve mustn't — "

But Schneider wheeled on Anne and seized her right arm. She gaped. He grinned, showing his even and flawlessly white teeth. Then he turned up the palm of her hand so that the inside of her wrist was visible.

"Mr Schneider," she whispered.

"I have asked you to be more familiar, Anne. Have I not asked you?" he said, sweetly.

"Yes."

"Then you must remember to call me Carl. Here in America we are very democratic. This is not Germany. You understand that, do you not?"

"Yes."

"Then I should have thought by this time you would have also got rid of these blue numbers on your wrist from the labor-camp. You must get them taken off somehow before you can be a good, naturalized American citizen. Why haven't you got rid of them by now, Anne?" And for the second time, he screamed. "I don't like to see them here in my office!"

He elevated her arm slightly and moved aside, so that everyone could see. His pretty mouth was tight, his face blanched, his purplish blue eyes chattering with brilliant light.

She tried to say something. Nothing came. And then her eyelids stumbled over the fattening tears that heaved up. She sucked a sob, wrenched her hand away and half-ran, half-waddled out of the office on her stolid, curveless legs in their heavy woolen stockings.

Schneider then looked quite annoyed, but nothing more. "What's the matter with her?" he asked nobody in particular.

Ungemach undertook to reply with scathing disdain. "You should go out ant cool off, Schneider. You should be ashamed of yourself, yes — ashamed." He turned his back.

Still only with annoyance, Schneider countered that this was one of the few firms in a strictly seasonal business that kept its employees on the payroll the whole year round. "And who, may I ask, is responsible? I pay the stockholders fewer dividends to keep my staff employed every day of the year. Is this the sort of thanks I get? Jesus Christ. It's disgusting, disgusting, disgusting, indescribably disgusting." And, with the expression of a god betrayed, he snatched up coat and hat and slammed the door after him on his way to the elevator.

Silverstein never bothered to glance either at Anne or Schneider as each had passed his table: his frown at the figures before him remained unperturbed. It was to be doubted that the accountant's frown had ever been perturbed; as a matter of fact, it enhanced the crisp serenity of his features.

A few moments later the certified public accountant advised Ungemach that the firm was in relatively sound shape, that higher dividends could be anticipated, and that its outstanding debts were being retired in an orderly and altogether respectable fashion. But Ungemach only nodded absently; and Silverstein, starching his shoulders, slid a slim briefcase under his arm and slipped out on his pointed gray suedes.

"Nathan Brodsky, eh?" Peter said.

"Yeh," Frank said.

"I'm relaxing," Henry said, brightly.

"Yeh," Frank grunted, frowning intolerably. He slowly rubbed his scalp through the wavy black hair.

Manuela took out a sizable bottle of cheap perfume and doused herself. "I hate tweed," she loudly proclaimed.

A melancholy Ungemach peeped out. "All right, people, that vill be enough."

"Yes sir! yes sir! yes sir!" Peter cried.

Ungemach buried himself at the bottom of the *Times* page devoted to the arrivals and departures of steamships.

It was very quiet when Carl Schneider, ten minutes before six, reappeared. He was smiling sweetly, the very picture of unaggrieved innocence, and his observation to Henry was impeccably bland: "Not working overtime, are you?" Nor did his question to Anne hint reproach: "Channing get the invoice copies?" When she assured him, dryly, that she herself had taken them to the factor's, Schneider grinned broadly and propped himself up on Manuela's desk. Then he tilted his head back, folded his arms over his chest and charged his voice with the rich tones of perfectly-understood memory, speaking as if he would have committed the most heinous of crimes had he not at this point taken his entire staff into the warmest confidence. He had a story to tell them, he said. The invoices which had been sent over to Channing had just reminded him of it, and it was a very good one, he promised.

It was already dark outside, and the light inside the office was a peculiar blend of yellow from the overheads and blue from the fluorescents. It was chill, and growing colder. Frank, though he wore woolen underwear, rolled down his shirtsleeves and put on his jacket. Anne buttoned her cardigan and huddled, shivering, between her shoulders, looking like a lost peasant. Manuela rubbed her hands. Peter squirmed into a sleeveless scarlet pullover. Henry buttoned his black vest with flashing niggardly motions. Ungemach drew more deeply on his pipe, and leaned against a partition, studiously listening.

The modest spires of the church beyond Anne's window, the girl saw, were blacker than the sky. When she would leave here, she would have to take the subway all the way to the Bronx; it was a long ride, and there was only her mother at the other end, and she had nothing to tell her living Jewish mother, as she habitually thought of her, for Anne's Catholic father had been murdered in Germany.

Schneider was full of a quiet rubicund glee. He seemed barbered and powdered and tweeded and seductively clean from tip to toe. "Yes," he said, his cheeks chuckling, "I think it's a good story, and true," he waggishly insisted, his legs dangling like a boy's from a riverbank, revealing the mauve garters that kept his socks translucent and taut. "For the purpose of the tale, let's call the man the experience happened to — Meyer. He turned out to be a fraud. There really wasn't very much to his experience, so none of you need fear you'll be late for your dinners, for your 'big table.'" he merrily directed a glance at Frank.

"Nah, it'll be all right," Frank shrugged.

When Anne heard Schneider mention "fraud," she began to heed every word. Perhaps the story of a fraud might be something she could tell her mother, her living Jewish mother. And she stopped shivering.

A BACK COVER

On the back cover of a paperback there is a still shot of a celebrated Hollywood star dressed for the role of a European general, beribboned, debonair,
mustached, visibly virile and, with a successfully festering smile, about to
seat himself at a diminutive circular restaurant table. For purposes of at
least geographic accuracy the nation to which his uniform adverts should be
noted, but the studio which costumes him insists on the license of creative
imagination, so that research goes aborted. No such license is accorded the
brief creature who hovers under the general with napkin and tray: anywhere on the Continent he is quickly identifiable as a waiter belonging to no
country but who may be with respect to his nasal structure either Syrian, or
Italian, or Jewish, depending on one's tentative tolerance. Since the star has
been already unnecessarily named on the front cover, it would have been
insulting to name him on the rear. And, of course, so far as the actor who
portrays the waiter is concerned, he cannot but regard it as inevitable that
on the back cover insult must yield to total anonymity.

Diana Fried keeps the paperback suitably dogeared, mostly out of
respect for the screenplay within, an anti-Communist tract which the Catholic Church recommends for viewing by the entire family. Mrs Fried's con-
sists of her husband, Karl, the waiter on the back cover; Jennifer McBurney,
a onetime practical nurse; and one black dachshund and three cats

Oh, dear, you didn't come back in time to let them out and now look
what they've done, oh dear, the cats, I think I'm going to faint:

Tom Horgan, a letter from his wife in hand, waits patiently; the flesh
under his eyes resembles a pair of baggy khaki shorts (I've shipped all the
furniture to your California address, and I'm following with the children)

I'm not at all sure we should let the animals see the film, what do
you think? Karl Fried addresses his wife, his German accent having been
blended by considerable hauteur with a severely functional English enunci-
ation.

Both Diana and Karl are Christian Scientists

through the open door of the KARL FRIED ACTING STUDIO can

be heard through the fatty summer night the thick slabs of the nearby Methodist churchbell piling up one by tongue-slavering one the putrescent thrills of the clapper enunciating in the thickest caricature of a holy accent

EIGHT O'CLOCK. At 1432¼ Passim Place, Hollywood, the upstairs apartment, where the living quarters of the Frieds blend in the front room with a tiny raised platform suggesting a stage, on which are focussed two small spotlights of the type one sees in department store windows glaring on the mannikins. There is no curtain. In front of the raised platform (it must be insisted that somehow this is not a stage) are a number of hard wooden chairs taken up by the students who are divided into two classes, the beginners and the advanced, though working actors can be found as well in the former. A week after Karl Fried dies, Martin Rattner addresses the roomful of actors and actresses, all of whom at one time or another have been students of Karl Fried;

(at the Munich State Theatre, Germany, plays leading roles

a wiry Hamlet

a wiry Lear

a wiry Macbeth

a wiry Falstaff half English half liar half fat half thin half German half Jewish half Cyrano;

Karl Fried is but half-conscious of his nose: he but half catches it in a sideglance at the mirror, a snatch here and a snatch there, he never breathes fully or stertorously, he catches at the air through his nose, catches at a smell, the nose partly in shadow though the nostrils own such holes that the Methodist bells could be hung there and announce the hour, announce Karl Fried; indeed, the sounds come ringing through his nostrils. Looking at him, one can see the time being announced; he is stunned, he is encased; he is stockstill under the hammering; he does not yield; you never see him in a blur, though he may be looking at you through a blur, as if you may be vibrating, and through the vibrations he can see a perfectly transfixed image beyond); a word concerning Martin Rattner:

He is Jeremiah Ratner's brother; their father beloved upon the Yiddish Stage, a cultural anomaly once limited to perhaps six blocks at the lower end of Manhattan's Second Avenue. Jeremiah is an internationally-acclaimed player; Martin's ability is known only to the trade, but it is as steadily employed, principally in the movies and television; the two brothers resemble each other remarkably, but Martin is a decade older, more shrunken; less polished, more sweaty: he would never consider carrying a naked statuette of an ex-wife with him to his dressing-room, as Jeremiah does, caressing it in front of strangers who come to pay their respects; Martin, indeed, might think of caressing a live naked woman before strangers, and entertain the idea at some length; Karl Fried might think of the possibility momentarily, and dismiss it; in a ribald moment, Karl might evoke the whole image in the air itself, but satirically only, and end the matter by tickling the evocation out of the spectator's brain, make it flee and possibly trip over itself as it runs down a stairway, falling as Karl looks down from a landing and shaking his head as if to say, Too bad, too bad

Anyhow: a little more on Karl's nose:

the nostrils in their constant flare disclose big black hairy holes. In a dream one night Karl conceives them as a woman's black breasts whose nipples are clumps of black hair.

Martin Rattner's pushed cluttered shining face, as though things are growing there: cheek-roots, eyebrow-roots, chin-roots, a crushed ear on either side of the crewcut skull with its matted short gray hairs. Underneath, shockingly, an expensively soft cream openthroated shirt, a softly-gleaming gray gabardine suit. Unbelievable. There's no gabardine body, no tailored belly; one can demand the small thick shoulders. Shockingly, again, gray hairy hands thrust from the gabardine cuffs

and the tough Second Avenue speech nothing more than a role everyone half-believes, except Karl Fried

Look we're all here tonight to help Diana. That's the main object. Now I'll be honest with allaya. I can take over one class. I aint got the time, but for that I can make time, one class. I can do it for a month and the first student who don't pay out he goes, for that I won't have no patience because Diana needs the money, Karl left no insurance, I understand Stan Remming'll take care of those details, is that right Stan?

Stan swiftly snips away at each corner of his mouth to cut a flitsmile as he tips his body away from Martin Rattner and ducks his head over the listening ex-students toward the rear door in which the grief-pasted Diana Fried stands, handkerchief wadded in doublefist, double-fisted face, pugilistic breasts and the face of a piglet-eyed pug, a figure for the gulps in Karl Fried's bed, Karl having a large Adam's apple, the hooknose motif repeated in the throat, gulping Diana, curt angular snake gulping, you can see her wadded throughout his body as he swallows her in massive chunks on the sheets as a midnight snack while he studies tomorrow's Matinee Theatre script, Diana quite happy that she's being gulped in the interests of the acting art, feeling his big yellow front teeth biting into her, she shakes like a thick jelly, is Karl at the trough or is she? Difficult to tell, but clearly sex is feeding time, feeding time, and Karl throws her a wriggling fish for which Diana is gruntingly grateful;

but she makes an obvious show of Karl's memory being too overwhelmingly provocative, death is feeding time too and she smells the food and she exits, her throat working, her belly heaving, weeping for pure hunger.

The ex-students are embarrassed. There is some confusion of sentiment here. Are we for Karl or Diana?

Though I walk into the valley of the shadow of death one of his ex-students, a tall thin girl, whom Karl would never consider teaching unless he judges her viable, reads the psalm and botches it not because she's overcome with emotion but because she simply doesn't know how to handle Elizabethan prosody; stumbling, familiar only with the rhetoric of naturalism, the American toughtalk now called upon to terminate this paying of respects, the poor girl reads the poem as if it is couched in some alien exotic tongue, as indeed it is for her television-oriented syllables, she knows Karl will flay her for her shoddy diction.

Worse, there's no creative imagination in what you're doing, he smiles his scorn upon her, and traps the class behind with rapping grins, slashing at them with his scintillant glares. You have no idea what the poet means. What does it mean to walk into the valley of the shadow of death, eh? he insists. In your own words of course, he glances back at the class over his shoulder. Take your time. Think about it. The bible rattles in her hands as she compresses her mouth, the tall thin girl with the whitespots on her cheekbones from which the blood has blurted. He takes several hypotenuses, a geometrician in his scoots across the floor

to a love scene on the small raised platform he pays concentrated attention. The black dachshund jumps onto Diana's lap behind him. Diana caresses the dog while she smiles on the love scene, she laughs at one point and Karl turns on his wife furiously, Shhh! sshh! he sibilants enragedly at her. Diana giggles. Sssh! Quiet! he manages to impart a howl to his whisper. On the small raised platform the actor who currently believes in Zen Buddhism kisses the actress. Karl Fried fastens concentration on the two as if to leech them, as if the two are incredible. A love scene is probably the most difficult kind of scene to do con-vin-cing-ly. He parts the syllables. He's entranced by the two on the platform. Is it possible? Are they? What is it that they are doing? There's no doubt there's an element of humor in a particular exchange the two have, tickling his wife behind him. She must laugh. Here he is attempting to understand what they're doing, and his wife laughs. There's no humor in Karl Fried's attempt to understand. It might be possible that his wife is laughing at him because he's trying to understand. That tends to break up the scene; more importantly, to break up the Karl Fried scene, he who watches. Diana is amused by his watching, and she can't tolerate it, she remains undigested behind him while he gulps what is before him. Karl tickles her in her throat: she is consuming him, and it tickles. He has smiled at the humorous element on the platform, while Diana laughs. Laughs, she implies, to make Karl laugh, because Karl is not permitted to smile, there's a hypocrisy in his smile, she believes, in that very quiet indulgence. He is not to be indulgent, she won't have it, she won't have the two people on the platform, nor the man in front of her as she fondles the black dachshund who resembles Karl, the dog with the long sad nose, the large sad floppy ears, the long sad low-axised underslung body, the long sad eyes which are Karl's counterparts except that Karl's have black holes, the flareblaring black pits of nostrils have sunk into the man's eyes, tunnels with black hairy sides into which the man's sights go tumbling down, each sight striving to catch on to a hair, but the hairs are slippery with mucous (as you see in Karl's eyes, mucid, glistening), so that the sight's hold slips, falls further down, till sight is lost sight of but undeniably keeps falling, there's no end to the fall, and constantly Karl knows this so that his perception is a vertigo having no bottom, he can never hear the end of the sight, the unmistakable thud, never, only the sound of wind made by the falling — and it is Diana's laughter which intrudes upon the falling sound, for it is possible that in that very moment of her laughter a sight might reach its thud and he will not have heard it, the possible one time Diana has drowned out, unforgivable he looks at her, for which there's no possible apology.

A pummeled prehistoric sofa resembling a dachshund runs perpendicular to the hard chairs in the studio; lumpy and lachrymose sofa. Above which, on the wall: a photo of Greta Garbo, curling at the edges, fadingly inscribed To my dearest friend, Karl. There is something bitter to Greta Garbo's face, hard and bitter; something of an implied sneer at the mouth, a faint sniffing disgust around the eyes and nostrils. Not that the perfection is marred, but that the mar is perfected, made extraordinarily beautiful, a breathtaking mar in itself, a glaze, nature at its most triumphant in making the flaw a matter of ravishing artistry, Karl must shrug his adoration of Garbo's achievement whenever she is mentioned, he will not even deign to analyze the marvel of her,

in the compass of the American fraternal and sorority orders the presence of an imported Swedish actress whose shoulders have been absorbed by her cheekbones, whose face is an anglicized african mask (the whole face as seen through a profile, as though one must painfully crane one's neck around the corner, the Picasso loan from the Egyptian bas-reliefs, Karl remarks that the Spanish artist has been greatly influenced by the Egyptians, a characteristic nobody seems to have noted, Karl says rather arrogantly, I have seen the Young Woman Regarding Herself In The Egyptian Mirrors, which were also constructed in miniature pyramids, in which the great Pharaohs were interred, who knew well that the preservation of the race lay in the woman's pyramidal mirror constructed upon a desert guarded by sphinxes as She goes on eternally chattering

chattering

chattering)

devoid of function, becoming then a museum piece to be viewed for an admission-price accompanied by rapidly moving slides while somebody lectures the plot in the dark, the chatter of a face guarded by silence —

Garbo's acrid insistence on her loneliness a taunting of the American public confessional

You understand that acting must be a kind of taunting of the audience, but you must hold them in check, they must not charge at you, you must persuade them they taunt themselves and must then turn from themselves to worship you

there is nothing new about acting as a form of religious observance; you are after all taking the roles of gods and goddesses performing in perfect control their own destiny, comic or tragic. Gods have always taunted men and deceived them into thinking they taunted themselves and must therefore turn to the gods to love

there is nothing new about men wanting other men to believe they are gods

who are terribly lonely, male or female; therefore:

Garbo, striding

imperiously, or

compassionately, or, best of all,

grandly dying. How ultimately satisfying to see one's god die. The secret of the greatness of Greta Garbo is that she had made her audience see her as Christ, and how one wishes to lay one's hands greedily on Christ, eh? To break in upon his rigorous intimacy: How does a God live by herself? What does she do? How does she divinely rise in the morning and go to sleep at night god

DAMN the audience, Karl Fried nearly spits at the mirror as he shaves. When have gods not hated men? Martin Rattner says I'll be honest withya like I was always honest with Karl, I aint gonna teach like he did, it aint I didn't respect his method like you refer to it, I respect it but I got my own way, I think I recognize a coupla faces here who were in my classes before, I think they'll tellya I got results

Hot as hell, Karl Fried shakes his bead at his students and scratches his back with the Chinese backscratcher. Shirtless, he hypotenuses amongst them, his skinny hairy chickenbreastedness sweating, as he rapidly beats the air with a fan in front of his face. We're getting an air-conditioner here in a few days. It's ridiculous to come from a hot working day to a hot studio at night, nobody can do his best under such conditions, nobody

The class watches his naked torso, its skimpy frailty, feeling that its hair should be plucked and readied for the broiler.

(... results ... $$$$ ...)

Restlessly Karl darts back and forth among the students, scratching his back, waving the backscratcher as a baton, a rumble in his throat when a student on the platform complains of the difficulty of achievement, so he turns his back to the platform and sotto voce addresses nobody in particular, Difficult, the horse rears in his throat; Difficult, the contempt in tight abandon under his breath, When they will actually realize the difficulty, of what it is to be an actor. He snorts. A row of footlights burns under his eyes, and Karl Fried is thrown into the blackest shadow,

never mind the script, it is your business to do a good acting job. However bad the writing, however short the rehearsal time, you can bring art to your role. There is no excuse for doing otherwise, you understand? Of course television is a business and only a business, but as actors you can still bring creative imagination to what you are doing onstage

Abruptly, he has a naked torso; abruptly, he detects repulsion in his students' eyes at his trivial torso; the naked frailty is too much for them; he must endure the heat, he must be tortured by it, and he dons a thin shirt to everyone's relief but his own; ugliness is too much for the American, after all, especially that of the body, the frame

once, walking along Vista Street with Diana on a smogless spring day, the Wilshire business district and the Baldwin Hills in the prickly distance, and the Venice oil derricks further beyond overlooking the Pacific, Diana begins to malign a house they pass for its use of garish color (Diana tells the story herself in memory of Karl Fried's sense of the beautiful), but Karl instantly rebukes her. He asks her to look around at the other houses, what does she see? She admits they are quite drab.

Exactly! Karl nods once, sharply. The people who live in the garish house feel a need for beauty and they try to express it. Badly, to be sure. But they are not vulgar in the sense that they feel the need; these garish colors are their idea of the beautiful; those who live in the drab houses feel no such need, and they are the vulgar and ugly ones

Diana and Karl often take walks around Hollywood's residential districts, an illmatched pair, she with the body of the famous Lipschultz floating nude and the porcine narrow squeaking eyes and face; he shorter by half a head, toddling by her waddling. A rare sight, rarer by virtue of the fact that hardly anyone is to be seen walking in these areas; it is very nearly a sin to be without a car. Not that the Frieds do not own one; they do, a British-made crimson Goliath. Which Karl hates to drive, it demands too much of him, he does it only because Diana insists she be relieved of some of it. She must do a great deal of it as a companion to a child-actor whom she drives back and forth to the studios, and waits on while the boy is on set, for which she is of course recompensed, for Karl's income is not so great that she can afford to turn down additional. His agent blithely informs him on the phone he bad a job offer for Karl this morning, but turned it down. Why, Karl inquires. Because the producer will not meet our price. I would have liked the job anyhow, and it would have been 400 dollars. Our price is five hundred and fifty, the agent replies; your status will be affected, as you know, if you accept any role for less. But I could use the 400 dollars, Karl protests, that's 400 dollars lost. Your price will steadily go down if you begin to accept less, the agent patiently points out.

You have got to be a good deal of a child to want to be an actor, Karl tells his class. Is it not childlike to want to be in such a profession? in which your meals are not assured, your rent is long overdue, your wardrobe is in tatters, in which you must turn down jobs if your price is not met...

He feeds Stan Remming, a young indigent actor. Also Jimmy Roe till he quits, enraged because Karl tells him before the whole class that while Jimmy is richly talented he has no discipline and will amount to nothing till he gains it

I can't tell you what I owe him, Jimmy says to Franny Mister at the edge of the Morocco Apartments swimming-pool on Hayworth Avenue, a long brilliant blue rectangle. When did you hear it?

Stan Remming just called me, the gobletbodied whorlblonded girl says.

You know I just can't believe he's dead, Jimmy complains.

Yeh, Franny nods dolorously.

I just can't believe it. You're sure, now.

Uh-huh. The girl stares at the brilliant blue rectangle of the pool. Flawless. The middle of summer and the blue pool is flawless. The long blue rectangle of the sky above is flawless. The adjacent apartment house is a sort of New Orleans type, with outside porches running the length of each storey, and open stairways landscaped down the sides, something like the set for A Streetcar Named Desire. The Morocco Apartments have a whitewashed quality under the noon sun. Whitewashed and flawless here we are, Franny thinks. I believe Karl is a spirit watching us. He just can't be dead, he just can't be

You know I was starving when he took me in, Jimmy says, his face like a gnarled clown's of Irish and Italian parentage, a little piglike too, more elongated, however, than Diana's, more twistedly knobby. Did you know that, Franny?

She shakes her head no. There is a living mass in her throat that grows and grows but won't move up or down. Nobody's swimming in the pool

I met him at the airport once with Diana, Jimmy says in incredulous tones, and he suddenly bent in two, and when I tried to help him he just straightened up and told me to forget about it, that he was just tired, he never went to a doctor, you know that, Franny?

Yes.

Because he was a Christian Scientist. Can you believe that? Jimmy looks at her, lower lip pendulous. It's his own fault, I know that, Jimmy assures himself sadly, sadly looking after the girl as she abruptly moves off, she's got to get into her apartment before her ugly sobs come out, like gusts of gut spurting to thrust up and out that living mass in her throat, before she'll be compelled to answer how Karl Fried died, thinking with fantastic horror how Karl Fried tells the class A man dies as he lives, in the way that he lives thus he dies, no other way, which is why so many death scenes are so false, they do not convince you. Franny doesn't understand how he can talk so glibly about death at all, because she avoids the subject like the plague.

Franny?

Yes.

This is Diana. You haven't phoned since you left the class so I thought I'd phone you. Dear, how are you?

Franny giggles. Things are still tight moneywise.

Oh I'm sorry, dear. I know how it is. Someday we must have lunch and you will tell me why you had to leave the class, won't you?

Yes. Let's do that.

I'm also calling about Bob Terrance. I'm calling everybody I know. It's true, dear, that I'm hardly on speaking terms with Bob anymore, but he's such a terribly gifted performer I feel I ought to do something for him and I'm calling everybody I know. And I know your husband knows Bill Marchant and I want Bob to meet Bill, I think he might give him an introduction to a few producers.

But Gregg only met him once and hardly talked with him.

Oh I thought he knew him better than that.

No.

Well you understand I wanted so much for Bob to get started. I've been on the phone for an hour.

I guess I can't help you, Diana.

Oh, dear, I am sorry. You will remember we are to have lunch. Please call me, dear.

Oh, yes.

Jimmy.

Yes, Karl. Jimmy Roe's Italo-Irish pug-pinocchio face quite blithely arrogant, seamed, sere for all its rich creasings on its long torso and the abruptly short legs on the platform (would you believe it Cagney the great Cagney came up to me after the scene and said Jimmy Roe? I gulped. I could hardly answer. Yes, Mr Cagney. Caught you on tv last night, Jimmy. You did, Mr Cagney? ((I must've sounded like an idiot, I didn't know what to say)) Yeh. Good acting job, Jimmy. It's pretty great of you to say so Mr Cagney. No, no, don't say that, Jimmy, don't say that! A good job's a good job and I believe an actor ought to be praised for it. And off Cagney walks. My mouth was open. I just stood there, I was blushing), the young man who says he can't stand being in a play because it means doing the same role over and over again and he can't stand that so that's why he prefers movie and tv acting, there's something new all the time, I don't understand how actors do plays, I just don't, his eyes in chinks, the class silent.

Did the scene call for cursing? Karl anchors the small toyboat of a smile at either lipcorner, but grim gusts blowing from his bald black eyes.

The scene didn't but I did, Jimmy avers superiorly, snottily. I felt it that way.

Did you? Karl aims at the class. Was anybody else here in the class convinced by Jimmy's necessity? Skeptical murmurs.

I felt it that way, Karl, Jimmy's is a jagged whine.

Cursing does not shock me, Jimmy.

I know that.

I am only shocked where there is no necessity for shock.

I felt the necessity.

But no one else here did. How do you account for that? Tell us in your own words. Think about it.

I don't have to think about it. If I feel like cursing, I'm going to curse.

No, I am afraid you will not.

I'm sorry I've got to disagree.

Oh, disagree, by all means. We allow anyone to disagree, do we not? Karl grips the entire class with the black smile coursing over his white face. But there has not been a single scene, Jimmy, which we have heard without your cursing. Do you always feel you must curse, Jimmy?

I don't think so

But you always do. You must know by now that this is not a class in psychoanalytic group therapy. For that you go elsewhere, and there you can curse to your heart's content, and everyone there will believe you. But I do not believe you. I am not your doctor, Jimmy.

I know that, Jimmy is surly.

No you do not know that. I will have to ask you to refrain from cursing henceforth.

Now look here, Karl, if I feel like cursing I'm

Big long gnarled pinocchio toes in the rubber sandals at the Morocco Apartments swimmingpool, I can't believe he's gone, Franny. I'm going to

Franny?

Yes?

This is Stan Remming, I have something very unpleasant to tell you

What what what

is the matter with this room? Along which the black dachshund sniffs, radically differentiated from the room with the small raised

Look what Diana gave me, Bob Terrance says to Tom Horgan waiting for Bob to turn out the light so he can go to sleep in the big double bed, Bob holding up a shapeless mustard-yellow longsleeved sweater. The baggy khaki shorts under Tom's eyes are baggier than ever as he lies abed, his hair balding, his thin sparsely-settled mustache already asleep for the night.

Well Tom you're certainly welcome to stay here as long as you like, Diana tells him, really it's not that I can't see what she wants but I'm just too damn tired for that sort of thing, as Tom recounts it,

You don't have to pay any rent, Diana assures him.

That's a warm-looking sweater, Bob. It used to be Karl's.

On the back cover.

You think I should wear it?

Of a paperback.

Sure. You're sleeping in his bed.

That's right.

There is a still shot.

You're sleeping with his wife.

Of a celebrated Hollywood star.

There's something wrong. If he'd been a celebrated Hollywood star, that is. But he wasn't.

Dressed for the role of a European general.

Not in a shapeless mustard-yellow longsleeved sweater. I really don't know what's inside.

Turn it inside out.

I can't.

Try.

It won't turn inside out. You know, if its shapeless enough right side out...

Karl says put it on and then turn yourself inside out. That's acting

My whole trouble as a human being is that I have never been able to love, Karl Fried addresses the class. I have been married three times, and I have not loved any of my wives. Diana will tell you that this is true, is it not so?

Diana grins at the dachshund in her lap. Yes.

I envy any of you who is able to love, Karl says.

Franny Mister is stupefied at her teacher's admission. No, but it is not an admission. It is very nearly a triumphal announcement, a signal of unique status for Karl Fried, especially with Diana present with a dog in her lap. Karl does not insult Diana; rather, it is the other way around, in that since she consents to marry Karl without his loving her then she is humiliating him. Worse, it's mortification in the extreme. Doggedly: I will love a man who does not love me; I will live with a man who does not live with me; I will sleep with a man who does not sleep with me; I will know a man who does not and cannot know me. Quite an experience, Franny Mister admits to herself. A unique experience, Diana feels to herself, strokes it, puts her fingers in the dog's mouth about it, roughs up the dog, rolls the dog over on his belly, is the dog male or female? That doesn't matter, since he or she or it doesn't love her, sex is no object, sex is rather subject, something for Diana alone, well it's all clear Franny Mister thinks, because what Diana is doing is masturbating, she is able to experience her supreme gratification of being able cardinally to love herself because Karl cannot love her. Marvelous. Her heart's desire. She isn't really gulped down by Karl, not in the truthful sense: she is using him for jawwork, he's her medium, his yellow teeth are the fingers she cannot use upon herself for the end wish of onanism, while she knows all along that Karl despises her as she reaches for her own joy, that's why she seems and is so apart from him, which everybody recognizes, theirs is no relationship, simply a geographical propinquity. So they each practice sex for themselves. But Karl Fried isn't masturbating. His sex-objects are simply anonymous

Insult must yield to total anonymity.

Karl Fried must have the strange strange belief, Franny Mister thinks, of being able to impart ecstasy to the anonymous. He is par example, then, an Actor. Let not the anonymous identify itself, or he won't give out with ecstasy, because: if an object is already identified, what should it want of Karl Fried? Because it will already have achieved the next-to-most magnificent goal, that of self-identification. But being Fried-ecstatic in anonymity is the greatest goal, but that's something an object can't know until it receives the Fried-ecstatic. Fried will then have transcended the self-identification. What, then, he is doing for Diana is to provide her, so to speak, with Ecstasy Anonymous got through her masturbation via Karl the medium, he therefore performing a double role, medium and giver, impossible for her to realize his double role, naturally, otherwise the doubleness would become single. Maybe, Franny Mister thinks, his greatest acting is reserved for his wives and mistresses; maybe it's just possible he misses being a Great Actor onstage because he's achieved it Privately, with No Audience. Very arcane, indeed. Very recondite. So that if Karl Fried commits suicide, then ... Franny Mister won't permit herself to go further. To go further, she thinks, would stop her from ever being a Mother again, she has one eight-year-old daughter. Does Karl Fried have children? No. But he, and Diana, do take in stray objects.

The onetime practical nurse Jennifer McBurney for instance who one night after Jimmy Roe gives a specially dynamic piece of improvisation on the small raised platform shyly approaches him...

Jimmy...

Yes, Jennifer who has glistening lavender eyes of shimmering lustre.

Tom, Diana says, looking at the balding wisping player of debonair slightly addled roles, the fey uncle, the somewhat distrait father in the Diplomatic Service, the French elderly lover, the tarnished bon vivant, the kindly humorous Doctor who Franny Mister has told Diana about because he's been staying with Charlie Morgan his wife and child in their small Beverly Hills apartment on the wrong side of the Hills without the pastel estates and the anal-shaped swimmingpools having just come from New York to try cracking television in Hollywood because tv in NY has all but vanished, and it's simply too crowded in the Morgan establishment though Charlie never protests but his wife becomes increasingly irascible about the matter, Charlie's a great big ex-Marine with a soupy heart, so it's really necessary Tom get to move, so Franny acquaints Diana with the picture especially since Karl is dead and Diana says certainly he can move right in but then she's not sure and then she's sure and keeps vacillating, uttering things like What will my neighbors think what with Karl just dead, oh let him move right in but he's got to do certain things if he does live here, I've got to tell him about the cats and the dog because he's got to walk the dog and see the cats get properly fed, and Look here, Jennifer says she's been wanting to move ANYHOW and she will once Tom comes in

Oh I feel so BADLY about Jennifer, Diana insists Franny have coffee with her after class Diana's trying to keep going with Karl's students but they have now shrunk to four, she's not the teacher Karl is though she once taught before and did a good deal of acting in Children's Theatres,

acting in children's theatres, Gregg snorts

and you know what, Gregg?

What?

Well I think she's just plain sadistic, Franny tells her husband.

Why is that?

Well like how she insists I keep doing that kissing scene with that fairy. It's just not right Diana keeps saying. Do it again. Again, again. And the fairy's awfully embarrassed, and so am I. Sure Karl used to insist, but he wasn't sadistic, and he'd never do it with a kissing sequence

oh

not

a

kissing

sequence

well ... And Diana does. Standing there. Watching. The fairy blushing. And I'm blushing, Gregg.

Jennifer went to visit her daughter in Denver and got a heart attack there and died and I feel so awful, Franny, as though I ejected her to send her to her death, I think I'm going to faint Franny

No you're not.

I feel very badly. Come with me to the bathroom.

That goddamn bitch, Franny tells her husband. I don't want to get involved with her, I won't, I won't stay after hours, I won't listen to her, SHE'S not sick, I told her to put her head down between her knees, she didn't faint of shimmering lavender lustre,

Jimmy, Jennifer whispers. The lavender eyes brilliantly pulsating in her soft white deadfleshed tiny heartshaped face with a million lines all underneath the skin, you can detect them, as though everything is crumpling underneath and simply making shadows of the buckling on the surface, the neck mushroomstemmed and mushroomfleshed, dying whitely in the dark, the blood coming up only as a kind of shy ladies' perfume from the weakened dispenser beneath in the toilet of the body,

You were very brilliant, Jennifer whispers, and we've simply got to do something for you. You should be very famous, and we've got to see to it, and we shall. You are a great artist, Jimmy. Do you know I used to play piano? Oh yes, very well indeed, but my parents seemed to discourage it, and artists shouldn't be discouraged, Jennifer now speaks aloud, aloud by god, a ladylike anger in her voice, her whiteflesh abruptly firming, the lines of her years momentarily emerging to the surface where they should be, out in the open. Then,

she turns away, swiftly, nodding with purposeful vigor

I TRY to get her to come along with me to do the shopping, Diana says, but Jennifer insists on staying in the car, she just won't venture out, and she's so wonderful, she does all the cooking and ironing and washing and she gets so IRRITATED when I don't come home on time

to Franny on the phone, No I don't know where Diana is.

Do you expect her soon?

Well I certainly hope so, Jennifer tartly replies. I've got her supper ready and it's going to be just unpalatable if she doesn't come home soon

The dachshund sniffs around the living quarters of the Fried apartment at 1432¼ Passim Place, Hollywood

The brief creature who hovers under the general.

Karl Fried wears black sharply-pointed shoes, scuffed. In Belsen, while bleeding thinly during a beating by his Nazi captors, his blood a pale pink, Karl manages to act a smile in front of the swastika uniforms, behind whom is a mass of unseeing men, behind whom is a mass of unseeing buildings, above which is a thin sun casting nondescript shadow on the scuffed pointed torso of Karl Fried wearing black pointed ribs as he acts a smile, acts it most unwillingly because his yellow teeth keep sucking the insides of his lips, the teeth don't want to be shown. they're terribly shy because not only are they yellow but they're big and most unesthetic for Karl's face and they like to keep hidden in corners, but Karl forces them out, it's about time they stopped being virgins anyhow, a concentration-camp is hardly the place for virginity, especially that of teeth he tells himself as his black hairy torso with the thistle nipples is strapped and unstrapped successively by a stinging tickle

a tickling stingle

making the nipples want to giggle

but that giggle never even reaches his larynx because it's stopped by the strapping at the base of the throat; starts again, and then is cringed back to circle around the nipples; but his mind can get hold of the giggle around the nipples, and his mind, you see, can understand and observe the grins of the Nazis, can, you see, partake of those grins for his smile-act, thereby in the faculty of using humor as it exists externally and as it exists in the cells of his nipples internally which are defending themselves by going round and round and round trying to become dizzy

he can push a concentration of both into his lips, because he is attempting to force-feed himself, and whisper to the lovely scent of the Germans bending over him,

I'm only half a Jew, you see, gentlemen, (smiling, smiling, smiling) so, after all, it's very logical that you can only half kill me.

lovely scent,

the dachshund is sniffing for in the livingroom with its long pointed black-shoe scuffed nose, Karl Fried swears the perfume the Nazis used he would delicately dab himself with for the rest of his life (smiling, smiling, smiling):

THAT smile-act Karl never rids himself of; THAT smile permeates each smile he does thereafter, whether real or acting, you can only half kill me

HALF a spirit at least of Karl Fried must be hovering about, Franny Mister believes

under the low bamboo table used as a sofa or couch, pillows scattered on it, hard to the rump, but Karl manages to curl up on it, the brief creature, a misshapen boy very nearly, with the big adult skull, the body a barelegged fishingboy creature;

a round low table in the center of the room for magazines and the like. Against one wall a combination hi-fi recordplayer, FM and AM radio, in pale blond wood like the bamboo, like the table, like the bookcase against the opposite wall, in which book collection, mainly plays, there is the curious thick volume Emil Ludwig's *The Nile*. A great writer, Karl says. The decor is hard wood, blond wood, bamboo discomfort, straightbacked chairs, one must sit up straight or curl or lie down flat; impossible to slump. One must be spartan or acrobat. Karl is a spartan acrobat. Once outside the Mister apartment, on taking leave, he delicately flips himself into an overstuffed sofa in the hallway, pillowing head in crooked elbow, looks up slyly, says,

Scheherazade, thousand and second night

Diana squirts giggles into the hallway, her porky features kneading themselves instantly into knobs, nodes, lumps, clumps and clusters

Stan Remming takes rollcall;

walks Diana and the dachshund;

feeds the cats;

sets the raised platform for an improvisation;

gives instruction when the Master must be at rehearsal;

cleans the ashtrays;

serves coffee from the anteroom, on the wall of which hangs a board with nails on which hang clean coffeecups over a washstand, the room also used for various costumes and a clothes-dummy which Diana uses for designing her own dresses and fitting them;

keeps weekly accounts, which student is paying and which in arrears; whispers to students in arrears;

wears but one suit of clothing, shiny serge; his shirt-cuffs ragged; his black shoes pointed and scuffed; his black hair slicked; his face freshlyshaven; bassvoiced; five feet ten, thin, thinfaced but romantic-lead type but hair nicked here and there by gray; flitsmiled, flitmovemented; big basso-assured voice, but a wisp of a thing underneath the skin, but leaves the KARL FRIED ACTING STUDIO a month after Karl's death, Very VERY ungrateful of Stan, Diana says, I'm terribly disappointed in him, dear. There is a bust of Beethoven in the livingroom, but Diana who buys most of the records plays American jazz, the kind with the thumpiest beat, Isn't it just marvelous she shrills, I just want to do all kinds of things when I listen to it, don't YOU? Karl carries the grocerybags as they emerge from the supermarket on Sunset Boulevard and walk to their red Goliath

the dachshund wobbles from one set of shoes to another in the livingroom, the mawkish big black eyes lachrymosely peering up at the legs, the torso, the face, the damn dog

mewing, really,

mewing like a cat with a deep voice, mewing in its dull grief, paddywobbling about, stubtail ticktocking, hardly lifting its paws, fat with loyalty, overstuffed with it, trying somehow to vomit it out in a lump on the floor get out GET OUT Diana shrills at Tom Horgan, because the TWO of you can't stay, not you and Bob both, and Bob's going to be here so you find yourself another place I'm not going to have you and your wife and your child and your belongings here

Now you just stay as long as you need to, Tom, Diana tells him, pouch-voiced, fatvoiced, adenoidally overstuffed, the adenoids like monstrous bulging sofas under and over her squeakdeep eyes

padding about, the dachshund is an old decrepit man as the three cats peer at him from vantage points around the hard blond hifi room, one of them perched on the bookcase above Emil Ludwig's *The Nile*, one rakishly lifting an ear on the table, one hunched on the windowsill Franny what do you think of this magnificent piece of driftwood Bob found for me at the beach the other day, doesn't it have marvelous shapes, like a piece of sculpture

I'm sorry I don't agree with you, Franny, Karl demurs, on the contrary I found Kim Stanley's performance in the Odets play very mannered, very mannered indeed, I could not watch it

on Friday noon Karl is seen on the television screen playing the role of a Moroccan physician; he leers and he practically hisses, he bows and he scrapes, he drips obsequiousness and bares his teeth as he fans the Mediterranean heat away in the stifling office, the overcorrupt doctor, discontent with his sub-villainy he Iagos it, so that, in the oblation of his acting, decanted once into the hard ethos of a Lessing and the iridescent miscellany of an atonal Shakespeare, to the plucked artificial fowl frying on the sight of American housewife in the midst of vacuum-cleaner and Draino — Karl Fried becomes nothing more on the screen than an amputee going door-to-door for magazine subscriptions and holding out his super-pathetic shining hook from the prosthetic arm,

half-alive,

half-Jew,

half-artist; and, therefore, half a liar to his acting students, and half-laughing at them for believing him.

Greta Garbo seems rather sour.

Yes.

Reaching the United States, the account goes on, Karl Fried teaches an acting class in Erwin Piscator's Dramatic Workshop in New York, at which Charlie Morgan, ex-Marine, ex-childactor, a complex and tender hulk of a man, is a student. In one production, Karl Fried is momentarily overenamored of an exit he must make, and overstays his leave, infuriating Charlie to the extent that he wreaks instant revenge by upstaging and totally obliterating Karl from the audience and infuriating the brief creature in turn. Karl's first wife has died in a concentration-camp. Diana meets him in New York as he is pondering divorce from his second wife, a sickly, nagging thing who ceases complaint only when he is bed with her

Belonging to no country.

Diana is in a state of constant shame because she's his second wife's best friend, her guilt instantly assuaged the moment Karl divorces her best friend and marries Diana.

He then is the recipient of an offer from a major Hollywood studio to do a supporting role in an anti-Communist picture. He accepts and takes the gamble, for there are no further commitments, but he believes that once in Hollywood other roles will be offered him as a matter of course.

This does not occur. Both he and Diana, finding their savings depleted, obtain jobs on the assemblyline of an aircraft factory. They live in a tiny apartment at Hermosa Beach, a small slum on the outskirts of Los Angeles.

Diana, in dryeyed memory, says: There were days we didn't eat. One night, she says, we had only a potato before we were to be paid the next day. I boiled it and we ate it and we drank the water I boiled it in.

Anywhere on the Continent he is quickly identifiable as a waiter.

Nights, Karl Fried works the production line. Days, he makes the rounds of agents.

He begins to do small roles. The Munich State Theatre:

Ariel.

Puck

Of course on the overstuffed sofa in the hallway outside the Mister apartment he is

at last able to open an acting studio at 1432¼ Passim Place, Hollywood, the street-level apartment underneath resounding with the torments of voice students raw-assed from going up and down scales

you understand, he addresses the tall lanternjawed blondhaired thirtytwo year old professional actor, Wolfe Shields, you actually understand what it means to be a Zen Buddhist, do you?

I think so, Karl, Wolfe mixes his lips on the raised platform.

Karl smacks his open palm with the Chinese backscratcher, his violently black eyes itching on their shining whites, his Nazi smile hooking the students as he glances at them.

Very well, then, Wolfe, suppose you tell us. I believe it will be appropriate.

Well, I think the first thing, Karl, Wolfe's jaw dangles in his neck, a tall blond man fishing from a high bank

Yes yes the first thing, tell us.

Shysmiling, Wolfe clears his throat, very gently making a passing remark, Well I shall, Karl, if you'll desist a moment

Karl throws up his hands.

Well the first thing is that it involves considerable discipline

Discipline! Karl pucks up his mouth at the class.

Yes, and introspection, Wolfe diffidently suggests. And it is said that after years and years of discipline and introspection that — ah — it will very suddenly come to you —

What will? Karl sharply intrudes. What will suddenly come to you?

Now I'm getting to that, Wolfe gently protests on the small raised platform, the students licking the sight of the hypotenusing Karl and Wolfe shambling, hunching, straightening, chindangling, throatclearing all in one and same spot. It's supposed to be indescribable, you see, Wolfe licks his lips and hitches up his finely-cut jacket. You're supposed to suddenly understand what's indescribable — it's the bit that says — now forgive me if I sound a little pretentious, I don't mean to — after all, students have spent years studying Zen —

Karl's hooknose makes nicks on the air. Yes. Yes.

I mean you're supposed to suddenly know the principle at — I guess you might call it the root of the universe.

I see. Now. How did the Zen monks teach their students discipline and introspection? Can you tell us that? Vitally important, don't you think, Wolfe?

Oh, yes, yes. Wolfe clasps his hands in front of him. Well, they — they sort of make fun of their students.

Fun?

Yes. The monks, I believe, would deride them — derision would be the accurate term, I suppose.

Well, then, Karl shrugs, laughing shortly, nodding at the class who then laugh shortly, you must tell us what makes you think you wish to be an actor.

Is that quite fair, Karl? Wolfe is very gentlemanly, very correct, very polite, his trousers are very pressed, his tie is very straight even in the sweltering heat of the fatty summer night, very six feet two and a half inches tall

I am not in love

No neither am I

What do you think a Zen monk would have replied to your question of fairness, eh Wolfe?

Wolfe Shields grins swiftly, beautifully, correct charm; then stifles the grin, twinkles an eye

I don't think it's funny, Wolfe, do you? Do you, really? Karl sounds unbelievingly offended.

Oh no, Karl. It's simply I didn't see you quite in the role of a Zen Monk, you know.

All right! Karl dazzlingly condescends the mot. But but but, Wolfe, you might think of me in such a role —

He had you there, Karl, Diana vulgarly guffaws.

Please keep quiet, Karl viciously raps at her.

Diana folds her lips, looks down, strokes the dachshund.

So. Karl pulls hypotenuses from the room, backscratching, batoning it. So, will you tell us why you think you wish to be an actor? Karl turns black nostrils on the tall blond man.

Wolfe Shields has great lowering bones over his eyes, and a heavy jaw, but he responds without rancor. His is an enormously larger body than Karl Fried's, and he must give his teacher a head start. Wolfe can stand there, a hulk, reinforced concrete, while a rabbit with black pistols scurries here and there. The big bone must be gnawed at, else there's no point to Wolfe's size. And it is to Wolfe's perceptive advantage to see Karl in the role of a monk; Karl is giving Wolfe credit for such a perception, after all; it is a compliment to Wolfe, and he begins to treasure a small smile about his own mouth. He can see Karl as a medicine-man, a priest, can see him with his little bones frothing about his skin; a lascivious monk who carries his genitals as a skull-and-crossbones; can see him as a pirate pacing a miniature deck, and ordering all the mice of the ship to walk the plank! Wolfe is never over-heated, after all, on the hottest night, while Karl is drenched in sweat and getting whiter and whiter by the second, his immense hooked nose making the air a part of the earth, nosing along it, there must be a clue somewhere to the death of the man. The murderer must not go unpunished: he must be made manifest: root out the destroyer, Karl Fried will not permit him to remain concealed; and insofar as each man nourishes a murderer in himself, he must be discovered, else we become hollowed out. Karl Fried seems terribly hollowed out, Wolfe thinks. Karl has not been successful, and must feel that since he himself is betrayed he then must help others not to betray themselves: his whole body is an act of warning; the backscratcher a constant admonition; his angular turns about the room the annunciation of peril. I wish to be an actor, Wolfe says, so that I shall never forget who I am, so that I shall always remember myself.

That is much too vague, Karl says crossly.

Well in each of our roles, Karl, we have got to use ourselves, so that we never forget who we are.

How do you know you are using yourself? Tell me that, Wolfe. Think about it a minute. Tell us in your own words. Pah. it is hot. Diana, you will make sure about the air-conditioner tomorrow.

Yes, Karl. Diana has a secret code she uses for herself, but it is a babble she herself does not understand, but feels comfortable mumbling it.

I don't know if I am using myself, Karl, but the audience will know, and will tell me. Yes, yes that's it — the words are cluttering his lips now. I wish to be an actor because the audience will point up to the stage and say, yes, yes, he's the man who's disloyal to his friend, who's the fraudulent hero to his son, who's the thief of the crown jewels — the audience will love me for the role I best play, so that I can go about onstage constantly absolved while constantly guilty. I wish to be an actor for the sake of whatever hidden human I am can go about in the sharpest light and be adored for it —

Is the actor then a narcissist who looks into the reflecting pool of the audience? Is he a beggar who asks alms of an audience? Do you wish to be an actor to pick up whatever images an audience is willing to part with?

Well —

Well indeed! The brief creature all but flings himself on Wolfe Shields. Suppose an audience isn't willing to part with a single image of an evening? Will you cry for mercy? If you do, that is being a very bad actor indeed. You understand that, do you not?

Oh, yes.

Then you really don't know why you want to be an actor.

I'm somewhat confused at this juncture, Karl.

Good good good! Karl is elated with Wolfe. It's very rich to be confused. You have taken an important step. Most of us never get to the point of admitting how confused we are. We try to solve rather than dissolve. Have you ever attempted crushing everything within you into a kind of juice rather than crystallizing? No, of course you have not. Ah, juices … I think it is time for a break, eh Stan?

Flitheaded Stan Remming sticks out a basso smile, Yes it is.

But before we break, I have a question for the class. What is beautiful about a blind man crossing the street? With vast superiority Karl looks over the students. Franny Mister trembles: she knows, she knows, and the whorlblonded girl trembles her face up at Karl Fried —

Ah, of course, I might have known, Karl all but pats her on the head from afar. Well, what is it?

Franny does not play with herself, but the words hardly manage to come up for air in the hurt love she bears for Karl Fried, this half-Jew Christian Scientist who hopes to cure Diana Fried's very existence in this little studio with its raised platform surrounded by the gigantic Hollywood sound stages silkily awarding Karl Fried the part of a waiter

so that research goes aborted

Franny can feel the dissolving juices she wishes to warn him, but the paradox locks up her throat

Come, come, Franny, you had your face up! Karl gently admonishes her, pleased by his wit.

Oh, Franny flushes. Well, she swallows. What's beautiful about a blind man crossing the street? Well, why — the fact that he's crossing the street!

A red Goliath is parked in the underground garage of the Morocco Apartments on Hayworth Avenue. This means that Diana Fried is taking voice lessons from Franny Mister on Saturday morning. Yes, dear, I have only 400 dollars in the bank and I really shouldn't go to New York, but my friends have invited me, and I think I should, don't you? for Christmas. Christmas. I do need a vacation, Franny, don't you think. It'll help me forget. I'm in terrible financial straits and I shouldn't spend the money. I don't know where I'm going to get new students, you must be sure to attend Monday night, Franny, it's terribly important, I'm having a few new prospects come in, and incidentally if you know of anyone wanting to rent the studio for showcase performances I do wish you'd have them consult me, does your husband really want Charlie Morgan to direct his play, oh yes of course your husband can have the studio anytime he wants, well now I'm not so sure I was speaking to my friends last night and they advised me so I've thought twice well the cigarette butts you know the cast has got to clean up whatever dirt they, no I've simply got to make some money now and my friends say that a production wouldn't help me much, now look all I wasn't is that when the production is advertised that they mention the studio in connection with, oh I'm terribly sorry Gregg I shouldn't have led you to think

Karl Fried tells Franny Your husband writes very beautiful and powerful plays but they're not what I'm looking for I want to do a play now that has hope in it

hope

hope

hope Diana's father a thin spike of a man sits in the livingroom of the Fried apartment, quire British. Well, you know, I did try to give up smoking when my wife died of cancer, but a year after her death I resumed

the dachshund sniffs blackbowleyed at his pointed black shoes, I suppose he's inquiring after Karl, Diana's father says

hope

Are you feeling a little better, Diana.

Yes.

Wouldn't you rather lie down a bit more? Jennifer worriedly inquires.

I can't lie down anymore, Jennifer. Please don't ask me. It's very sweet of you to come, Franny.

you tell Charlie Morgan I want to talk to Tom on the phone. Tom

Yes?

You can pack your bags and come over right away

the Methodist churchbell on the sweet young thing of a braless morning, a morning cool and bluegray at the temples, no thick sandwichsound, but a bareheaded prayer, the mists braless slipping through the palmfringed streets, a morning no more than nine years old getting up very early at seven a.m. to go out and find friends to play, other nine-year-olds, look what he wrote in my copybook, a low guitar of a giggle through the resilient streets, the day just beginning to draw cool braless breath, the sounds of the Methodist churchbell a trickle of a childlike bell over a shopdoor as the early customer ventures out on the new street

seven o'clock in the morning

that's all

no more

not very impressive

just seven

quite early

don't tense

seven for a nine-year-old who suddenly sits up in bed

no that's not how he, Franny tenses, that's impossible, that's not how he said, con-vin-cing-ly, I'd never had believed

no

well and yet, so: a hurt love for somebody not quite grown up is that the way he

Karl Fried opens his eyes to Diana lightly sleeping, black pointed eyes, as he lies abed at seven a.m., Diana instantly awake, his shoes are pinching him, says, I'm not feeling well.

Before Diana can rise, Karl sits abruptly up, thin black pointed ribs with their hands up, his heart with both nipples pointed straight in at it, the circles of the German's whip tightening in ever-smaller circles around the tiny red vessel, Karl's eyes wide

wide

wide, blind man crossing the street. His hands grope for the mustard-yellow shapeless sweater. Dumbly, Diana turns to get it for him when, disappointed, the actor slumps over.

What about the other half of you? the Nazi answers Karl Fried.

Beautiful.

ON SUCH SUNDAYS

Luther hadn't rubbed his eyes once through the rear windows, but Anita hadn't been garrulous, either, and had rested a wonderfully unresponsive hand on his for some time. Her mother, Fay Maimon, was sitting up front with her second husband, Jack, who drove his new car quite soberly, enjoying the low, rich hum of the engine, like felt slippers around his feet.

Spring had begun to turn out on the rather sober countryside, which took a carefully prepared swell now and again and settled its declivities with just such a consort bearing. The earth hereabouts seemed to have led a well-ordered life: when the trees verged on becoming too thick, a field appeared; when the fields too open, a brook hustled out from under a modest highway bridge to scurry across and parry the monotony; or a white farmhouse, as if by the most courteous of magicians, came to.

Everywhere the tentative green sprang a nearly imperceptible down on the declining blue light, and a light damp, common to the late afternoons of the season.

The agreeableness of the atmosphere disposed Luther to scan the blonde down on Anita's cheeks with a sensation bordering on affection. She dismissed it with the dimmest shrug, and turned her face away.

"Well you know how it is, Anita," a smile scrambled on the faintly twisted, overhanging boughs of his lips, "it's only been a very short while since I ate that very good meal, and it's settling in my eyes now."

But she chose, instead, to yawn in the direction she was looking.

"Jack, that reminds me," Mrs. Maimon said. She was satisfied by way of the rear-view mirror that her diet had at last nipped her to vie with the beautifully groomed loneliness of her daughter's recumbent tall figure.

"What," Jack grunted.

"We didn't eat before we left town. Let's stop at the next diner." Her marcelled chin saw inversion, in profile, on her set gray hair, shining. Mrs. Maimon's long sharp fingernails, against the light, rested icicles on her husband's shoulder. Her voice, in timbre, swiftly inserted the physician's quills into sinuses.

"What for? Another twenty minutes we'll be home. I'm doing fifty steady. There isn't a decent diner around anyhow. How hungry could you be?'"

Fay capitulated, noting the indicator curve to fifty-five. She laughed merrily as she twisted to Luther, "You're the first man I've seen Anita with shorter than her, like Jack and me, and the first time I liked anybody the first time meeting them. The food's settling in your eyes, hah? He's a funny guy, this Luther, hah?" she demanded of Anita.

Luther slouched even more comfortably. Of their own accord, Anita's legs crossed to assume a perfect pose.

"Oh, very," Anita said.

Fay Maimon leaned intimately for a moment against her husband. "Jack's funny too sometimes. A man is shorter than a woman, he should be funnier. Look look!" she suddenly pointed, "a baby horse!" The stiffened colt that had been nibbling grass in the pasture gazed after the receding car till it was gone, and Fay after the colt till it was gone. "Such a baby," Mrs. Maimon muttered, slumping. Stiffening, she plucked a fresh pack of cigarettes from the dashboard compartment, jaggedly tore an opening but lit one with perfectly steady fingers; her fine, unpretentious sapphire licked by a small flame perpendicular to the concrete line of the highway; the patrol of the darkening, still quite far away, had breathed in the east. "Want a smoke," she urged Jack.

"I can do without them, Fay," he said, kindly. He had heard, really, only the sounds of the serene sundering of the air by the car, and the secure contained continuous combustions in the engine, to which he was a kind of filling-station on such Sundays, especially when there was so little traffic.

Fay Maimon rested her back against the door, slung an arm across the seat and inhaled deeply. "You think Anita should go so much to college, Luther? Postgraduate she says."

Anita ran the hand that had been resting on Luther's up her own profile, practiced, a sheer face that had been often scaled, and indifferently, rather, to peril; and then a long strand of finger through her lank blonde strands. "Mother."

Remaining at pale peace with himself, Luther grinned. "Sure it's all right, Mrs. Maimon. I write advertising copy myself. Your daughter's studying history. Same thing."

"She got a divorce so she had to go back to college," Mrs. Maimon said, friend to friend.

"Believe me," Anita at last privileged Luther, "I'm here. Beside you."

"I saw her ex-husband," Luther said to Mrs. Maimon, cheerfully. "Last night."

"How did Melvin look?" Mrs. Maimon said.

"Like he wouldn't make it," Luther folded his arms behind his neck, stretching luxuriously.

"Maybe," Jack said, "he didn't have too much to go on."

"Finally you're listening," Mrs. Maimon managed to her husband between her violent coughing laughter. She squirted an index finger underneath his knee. Jack lifted the powerful basin of his chin and bulged hairy knuckles on the wheel, a car flipping dangerously close in the opposite direction through his coin-slit vision; in the box of his belly an empty anger rang, burning.

"Not when I'm driving, Fay," he said. She whirled into silence, a wire in a crimson frock. Jack muttered something into the rear-view mirror.

Anita was white, so much that it nearly stained the edges of her black dress; her fingers whimpered slowly against Luther, who made no sign of response, reflecting that her pallor would never have reached that extremity from the near-collision had she not shown him last night, in black and white, the diary of her fifty-three brief affairs, which had moved him to maneuver the incompetent Melvin to spend the rest of the evening with her. Luther had discovered that he could excite Anita's pity toward the pitiful at the times he understood she was unable to foresee the inexorable consequence.

The car had the gentlest kind of sway. Jack had stepped it up to sixty. He experienced for the first time the discomfort of a light beating upon his ankles, and could derive no pleasure from the onset of the twilight, even though it was disposing itself in a dull banana tone on the highway ahead and a deep green eye shade from a group of evergreens behind, quite as conservatively as the landscape itself. Nor could it be said when, while the car approached a long, very reasonable curve which rose over a knoll, where an aluminum diner had not long ago been built, and whose crackling blue neons and gray marine shimmer could now be seen, a double line of railroad tracks gradually sheared in from the south, and whose slate continuous slivers paralleled the road after Mr. Maimon had driven round the curve — that any visual discord had occurred.

"Jack wasn't that trainwreck a couple days ago?"

"Up ahead a mile maybe."

"Where? I don't see."

"You can't. It's behind a lot of trees."

"They didn't clean it all up yet?" Mrs. Maimon properly condemnatory. "It's too soon."

Anita's fingers had whimpered against Luther; now they trembled; he gave the girl a disgusted look, and his body curled with his face into the corner.

"Jack." Mrs. Maimon stuffed the cigarette into the ashtray.

"Yeh."

Fay snapped the ashtray back into its recess; a puff of smoke escaped, and no more. She ran a finger, something like a tongue, over her sapphire, at which she stared hungrily, her eyes widening as the light in the gem was dying, as she spoke. "Stop a couple minutes."

"What for?"

"I never saw a trainwreck. Let's go look. I read in the paper — " she broke off.

Luther's sneer shinnied off the faintly twisted boughs of his lips; they slacked, overhanging. His eyelids frowned at Anita, and the girl opened hers, at him, as if her sight found it hard to breathe.

Jack Maimon was slowing down the car. Casually, "What did you read, Fay?" A small smile edged over his big round chin.

Mrs. Maimon ran all the words together. "After the wreck it said in the paper some fires started and somebody that saw it all said some of the pieces of people popped." She paused, then, and looked straight at her husband. "Like toast." She made her mouth a circle, sat up in the seat and arched her back like an astonished mannequin.

Jack swerved the car off the road, the tires crunching on the gravel, and brought it to a halt. They had stopped by an astonishingly dense area of trees, which had chopped off the railroad tracks. Mr. Maimon leaned across Fay and jerked the door open, the hairy knuckles of his hand coming to rest, waiting, under her belly.

"So let's look," he said, as though she could never again answer him.

It was not her daughter she addressed, but Luther. "You coming with?"

"No," he replied, softly.

"So you don't mind waiting a little. After all you and Anita ate already not so long ago."

"Sure, Mrs. Maimon." Luther bent forward eagerly. "But it's getting dark, you should take a flashlight." He sought Anita over his shoulder. "'Don't you think they'll look better with a flashlight?"

"Perfectly."

Jack Maimon shook his head heavily and slowly at Luther, like a great eraser over a blackboard, after he and Fay had squirmed out of the front seat to stand on the gravel. "It won't be that dark," he said, his body bunching beneath his wife's.

"You don't think so."

"Not me. I don't think so."

From the sprawling gray depths of the car's back seat, Anita and Luther watched Mr. and Mrs. Maimon take each other's hand, looking quite young from behind, as they swung into the trees, where they were soon lost sight of. Luther took hold of Anita's hand, lightly kneading her fingers. Her gray eyes, on a level with his, in myriads coming out of caves brushed all over him.

"We wouldn't have to look younger from behind, would we?" Anita said.

ESSAYS

SOME AUTOBIOGRAPHICAL WORDS

To start with, the autobiographer is a born solipsist, an event in my circumstance that took place at Philadelphia; of a father whose extensive memory of the Talmud could and did admonish me on the relative finality of humanity and art; and of a mother who was satisfied that I could have some winnings based on a childhood of babble, lox and love. I developed, logically, into a healthy concentric, but acquired an English teacher who frowned me into a German treatise on prosody which I mused on during chemistry, whose docent was equable simply to my *doppelganger's* presence in class. The balance of adolescence hung on innumerable coffees at a downtown Philadelphia cafeteria, since demolished, where I had been preceded by some aging contributors to *transition*. Thus cased, I dozed through a semester of dramaturgy at Columbia University under Hatcher Hughes; caught four years of the Air Corps during World War II; and brought myself into a valuable rough at the Dramatic Workshop in New York, to which Erwin Piscator had condescended, a man whose intimacy with the theatre in all its norms and abnorms I have nowhere seen equaled. Survival called and, irresistibly, I found havens in radio monitoring, export-import; and researching for Standard Oil of New Jersey. After three off-Broadway productions of my plays, Columbia Pictures nudged me into staff-screenwriting; but I have since nudged off into freelance television, in which the burdens are sometimes shared by my actress-singer wife, Lynn Marquize, and my ten-year-old daughter. All of us now live modestly in Hollywood, not really too difficult a feat if one believes in the relative finality of humanity and art.

Four major projects in poetry and one in fiction presently engage my work; each is thoroughly committed to metaphor as a mode, and paradox as a fulfillment, of the author's desire to display phenomena at their least vulnerable, which is to say at their most commonplace; their unruly pluralism, then, resolves into a ridiculed unified field theory contained in the sensuous proof of experience through the word.

The poetry projects are: *The Diary of Matthew Parson, M'sieu Mishiga, The Letters of Great Ape,* and the *Art of the Sonnet.*

The *Parson* work is essentially what its title implies: the construction of the personality of an ordained American minister ruminating upon religious attitudes not confined to any one sect, and exercising upon them a wit at some expense to dogma; and altogether at the expense of himself. Since the assumption is made that religious attitudes are a legitimate concern of ontology, a search is conducted as to their reality in the context of the contemporary American scene.

M'sieu Mishiga predicates a psychiatrically non-classifiable lunacy on the part of its hero; with this operating attribute, the major principles of sanity, as our zeitgeist has them, are put to test and protest.

In *The Letters of Great Ape*, however, satirical provocation is founded on a somewhat less than human note. The conceit is posited that literacy tests have been more than ably negotiated on the lower animal level, and that a superior member of this class, at some residential distance from his superior genus but provisionally accepted therein, expresses himself at length in correspondence with typical representatives of the human society, whose replies the author sees fit to withhold. Once again, from another vantage, the effort is made to crack the substance of the self-made image and to expose the ruthless comedy of the living parallax.

These biographical masques belong to a plan which I inaugurated in *The Diary of Dr. Eric Zeno* and continued in *The Diary of Alexander Patience* and *Professor Bold*; wherein, successively, the errant ganglia of a Western Christian psychoanalyst, a self-confessed but unreliable stoic, and a somewhat rococo academician are brought to book.

A considerably older design involves the *Art of the Sonnet* series, with eighty-four sonnets completed. Within the fourteen-line frame I am attempting to explore prosodic innovation without violating the organic necessity of the poet's metaphorical obligations.

The work in fiction provisionally entitled *Now*, has for its initiating and autonomous section the volume *Ice Never F.* It has always seemed to me that the offense in depth cannot be avoided if the artist means to cope both with the evolution of the novel form and his fundamental astonishment at the multiplicity of being. In this instance the offense in depth is a specifc strategy employed to educate a protagonist in the ramifications of the paradoxes of apparently commonplace phenomena. Logically, then, at any given point, the characteristics of the protagonist can assume those of any other created personality in the novel, or groups of personalities, just as theirs can take on his. With equal validity, the chronologic age of the characters are subject to a behavioral age in a given experience, so that at no stage is there a time specification. We are then engrossed by the created present, and cannot be accused of historical distortion. In such a created present, the experiences of a given number of characters (whose locale is that of Philadelphia), impinging one upon the other singly and by groups, their experiences in the milieu of conventional time-sequence transpiring at widely separate intervals in their lives, are in parallel and interlocking analogic action by reason of emotional, intellectual and social congruencies.

On the completion of the novel, I will resume (given sufficient phylogenetic grace) the dramaturgic incursions into American historical mythmen, of which *Gray* is the fillip. I will be deeply touched if the American theatre shall at last find itself temperamentally equipoised to mount them.

THE UBIQUITOUS SYMBOL

POETRY, some informal remarks on my method and intent

The reader scanning the bulk of my verse should never look for a linearly developed idea; nor should he attempt to make *prose* sense out of it. Analogically, no one can paraphrase a painting or sonata; the best one can do is describe sketchily the plastic methods utilized.

My verse must be read as one looks at a painting or listens to music; I seek to make the reader capitulate to the world of my images. Prose contains the logic of time in terms of tenses; the time of my poetry is contained in the efflorescence of images, a logic of constantly flowering surrealist paradox. My intent is quite simple: to transmit thru image the paradoxes of experienced phenomena. The understanding of it, then, does not occur on the rational-intellectual level, but on the *feeling* level.

The image will contain the paradox of the experienced phenomenon; but it will go further: it will try to convert the experienced phenomenon into an experience itself. For me, symbols in poetry do not simply connote reality: my intent is to make the symbols pieces of reality themselves. If a group of words can be made to so function, and an image struck to evoke the correspondence in the reader's mind, an experience has been created.

I seek to suffuse my poetry with a sense of drama. I cannot understand a point of view which omits a constant play of tensions; to exclude tensions is to exclude art and to make for a product which will slide past the reader as an indifferent record of a value-system making negligible contact — seen in the reams of stanzas by authors who give the impression that they have never participated in any conflict whatsoever; such an impression is fatal to the product itself, characterized by the hackneyed metaphor, a standby of creative impotence pleading that it must be simple. Simplicity, certainly, or simpleness, is all that's available, a fetish for people fearful of the complex — people whose *idée fixe* is that everything must be explained.

Nor do I adhere to the conventional formulation that the dramatic must be resolved. Merely because I may leave you hanging does not require that you must feel lynched, or that even a more modest strain is involved. Not at all. Enjoy yourself: there is a certain marvel, I think we may admit, in suspension without the preconception of a rope. I feel under no obligation to tie you up, or to settle everything for you. One might inquire as to who legislated the esthetic statutes of symmetry and resolution and as to when their misshapen salons will stand forward to validate their subjective notions.

Too often the reader will apply traditional prose criteria to verse. Let him read my poetry with the same approach that he would bring to experience as it occurs to him on the street, in his bedroom, on his voyages, in his eating and drinking, in his relationships with other people. In the case of my poetry, the metaphor *is* the experience, is the phenomenon. What immediately occurs to me, before all else, when I write a poem, is a given paradox identified by metaphor. The metaphor, for me, in the event of the poem, is one of its experiences.

Too much verse is written *about* phenomena; too much in the arts generally is created *about* phenomena. My intent is to make the phenomenon itself one of symbols. As much as possible, I rule out making the phenomenon of "about." Analogically: That a given substance becomes differentiable from other substances, its constituents form relationships and behaviors of those relationships which render its events distinctive from the events of other substances (whatever the method, though the method itself contributes to the substance's distinction); but in the formation of that distinctiveness, certainly, the elements of other substances are utilized. To form the substance of an image, I too will seek to utilize other substances to make the distinctive relationships and their behaviors of an *image-substance*. Most poets fashion an *about-substance*, which has, I think, a considerably lesser impact on perception.

Since, as yet, we really know very little more about substances than their having come into being, it would follow that though we experience them, we do not necessarily understand them. Must we understand them in order to react strongly? Of course not. One could adduce hundreds of phenomena to which we powerfully react but which resist our analytic faculties. It is sheer nonsense, therefore, to say that art must be lucid. Art is not a science, though many contemporary artists believe they must knuckle under to scientific criteria, which is simply another way of saying that they are unable to create persuasive art. The greatest art is not distinguishable as such by its lucidity; on the contrary, it is often puzzling and downright irritating. Many a mediocrity possesses the lucidity to fashion a corpse undeniably transparent.

On the more general problem of the difficulty of understanding certain works of art, I would venture that the difficulty may stem from the possible fact that the congeries of symbols in the work of art could have their sources distinctively in the unconscious evolution of the artist's whole organism, integral with the evolution of the species itself. Symbols, of course, are conscious phenomena; but if they are permeated with the force of the act of evolution, of which even in the Darwinian sense we have but scant comprehension (and that, mind you, relevant to the past with possibly vague extrapolations), then a good deal of time may have to elapse before we can identify the attributes in the symbols of the evolutionary act, which makes for a contemporary difficulty of understanding a work of art thus involved.

What I am saying could, of course, be held to be a defense of impenetrability; I do not mean it as such, and I hope it will be clarified if I remark that the perceiver of an art's substances must sense the event of a phenomenon; otherwise the art has no merit, and has failed.

I may be taken to task for phenomenalizing symbols. Langner presumes symbolization the specializing mark of our species. But the definition of the process of symbolization must perforce be extended. Communication by selection, and the alterations on the objects communicated with, by virtue of the act of communication itself and the connotative values of symbols, comprise a process transpiring in all nature. We often maintain that in order for symbolization to take place there must be a human consciousness. But we discover increasingly that types of consciousness are not indigenous to man. I mention this only to contest the assertion that symbols cannot be phenomena. I can only observe that, since all being is phenomena, I do not see how we can be so presumptuous as to excuse symbols from a rather ubiquitous world.

THE CLASSIC OFFENDER

We now no longer can say with any precision what the nature of precision is. Further, the more we comprehend of phenomena the more we understand that precision as we understood it has no existential analogue outside of the phenomenon of its semantic. It follows, then, that any value system based on precision — and we are here concerned with its applicability to creative literature, specifically poetry — becomes quixotic. The idea that we cannot construct without knowing what we are constructing is one of unrelieved absurdity.

The American poet and, indeed, his confrere wherever, because he has been led by various combinations of circumstance to believe that economy of means, cultivation of an impersonal style — in itself a contradiction in terms — and exact calculation of metrical, lineal, stanzaic and typographical means to convey precisely the desired emotion or insight constitute the attributes of exceptional prosody, has turned at the expense of whatever talent may be his to putting forth neat musics which he seriously discusses under numerous guises: neo-classical architectonics, esthetics of rational control, and polarized ambiguities. The American poet is structuring; he is systematizing a series of balances; he is disciplining his free-associating — another stunning contradiction in terms; he is fabricating meaningful suspensions; he is manipulating tensions by precisely placed stresses.

Reacting subserviently on the one hand to the arrogance of the so-called exact sciences that insist all disciplines — in which art is sneeringly included — perform according to clarity, measurement and laboratory demonstration while at the same time the sciences are yielding to the grave modification involved in the formulation of Probability; and reacting on the other to the fiats of political juntas that the arts and sciences must orient toward the basic needs of a given society however arbitrarily defined — the American poet points proudly to his verse as a product of American know-how. He is, unfortunately, unaware that he is conforming to censorious scientific and political attitudes based on Eighteenth Century rationalist convictions, a perfect example of which, adulterated by certain Anglican-Royalist confusions, was the work of T. S. Eliot; with charming naivete, he attempted to yoke selected fractions of the stream of consciousness to classical metrics as modified by later Miltonic counterpoint and eclectic Poundian ellipsis, this bastard entity sprayed at the finish with Victorian insecticide guaranteed to immobilize the preceding century's occasional vulgarities, and insuring against too virulent an infection by the Twentieth Century's surrealists; the poetic insect-killer further fortified for condescending counter-irritant by choice exhumations from the French symbolists; and, wherever lucidity was jeopardized, a prose explication could be had at the back of the poem.

It may, then, fairly be stated that what we understand to be the classical mode is now both comically antiquated and exhausted. The severe limitations of that mode force an artist to echo descriptions of phenomena already catalogued, and to reiterate observed states of mind. Properly speaking, classicism belongs to the secondary stages of art, and in its time attained to the limited splendor of which it was capable. But if the articles of its faith, for example, had been certified by the Elizabethans, the literature of the drama could never have known a Lear, and the magnificent contortions of a Donne would never have come into being. Had Dostoyevsky obeyed the Aristotelian scheme, Karamazov would have come out a Greek Orthodox Oedipus.

One would think it would be quite unnecessary to repeat those facts; but again and again the neo-classicists manage to make out a catastrophic case against themselves in tedium and eventual unreadability for all their vaunted clarities and unities, while rendering themselves decoratively acceptable in the juvenile world, the collegiate institutions and the prestige pulps, the latter connoting themselves the guardians of the esthetic trust. Today we are treated to the superb circus of the dead critical mind granting the same superlatives to a vapidly restrained Salinger that the same mind once granted quite ex post facto to the later work of Henry James for all its stylistic elegance reeling in the brilliant savagery of the exploration of the non-rational to violate canon after canon of even the most Euripidean of classical extensions; the same mind unwilling to admit the statistic that the majority of readers who glow over a Salinger are the chronologically and chronically adolescent. In the same manner, in response to the classical deadbeats, author and critic alike, the mass of the untrained and the imperceptive turn in relief to the single-track simplicities of a Hemingway as against the convoluted and often incomprehensible narrations of a Faulkner. It is no error that the giants of modern literature, with the exception of Mann, received no Nobel awards — Tolstoi, Kafka, Proust, James, Joyce;

one has to be a minor non-rationalist, such as Faulkner, to qualify.

Only, then, by cultivating the non-rational may we illuminate those areas of phenomena and human sensoria, behavior and motivation that by their dynamic morphologies mock and mutilate the pathos of precision; while the continuing evolution of all categories of energy and matter can only be grasped by the Shakespeare-Dostoyevsky luxuriance, profusion and frequent unintelligibility of symbol and sense.

LETTER TO THE EDITOR: BEAT POETRY

Editor's note: In the July 19, 1961, New York Times, *James Dickey (later U.S. Poet Laureate and author of* Deliverance*) reviewed two new collections by poets associated with the Beat movement: Allen Ginsberg's* Kaddish and Other Poems *and Charles Olson's* The Maximus Poems. *Dickey "took them down," and generally made light of their literary movement as a whole. In later Letters to the Editor, writers Selden Rodman and John J. Gill took Dickey to task, defending the poets and their works. Gil Orlovitz's following response to the original review and subsequent letters was published on September 23, 1961.*

To the Editor:

I was considerably startled to hear from interested friends that *The New York Times Sunday Book Review*, abetted by Mr. James Dickey, had committed the rather large social error of having lowered the sociologic dignity of the Beatlings by publishing a reaction — in the form of a review — to the youthful diaries of Mr. Allen Ginsberg; specifically, I believe, an entry labeled "Kaddish," the Hebrew liturgy for the dead.

It had been my understanding, gained from periodicals of some political standing, and from literary quarterlies that try to maintain a rough screening process, that the Beatlings had been finally recognized as an American group phenomenon meriting analysis and concern from a behavioral standpoint, and that their recordings of their actions to the milieu could be studied for certain historical insights. But *The New York Times* apparently reached a judgment that took issue with the Beatlings' sociologic dignity, and wished to reduce their societal importance by rendering the Beatlings answerable to precise esthetic poses, one of which has been, as we know, their frugal incursions into the craft of verse, also called poetry, which American society of course connotes as possessing far less dignity than, for instance, the sounds in an auto body shop.

I must courteously, therefore, take *The New York Times* to task for having confused categories of thought, in the wake of which I note, in Letters to the Editor that some very sensitive people have got quite incensed at Mr. Dickey who, after all, was only grading papers as *The Times* editor must have asked him to do. Mr. Dickey was not mentioning any names, but it seems obvious that he was comparing Mr. Ginsberg's stanzas to what Mr. Dickey supposed poetry to be as evinced, I presume we would all agree, in Sophocles, or Shakespeare, or Donne, or Corbière, or Mallarmé or, perhaps, Emily Dickinson at her best. "Kaddish," it would seem, contained no metaphors more recent than, say, Apollinaire.

But such an implied vintage was quite unsatisfactory to Mr. John J. Gill and altogether repellent to Mr. Selden Rodman who proceeded to support the reporter of "Kaddish" by revealing to us that the Prophet himself, Walt Kahlil Whitman, had been very similarly received early in his free-flowing day, and by no less personage than Henry James. Now, I have no wish to defend the sociologic status of one of our greatest Civil War Epicenes, but I do feel that Mr. Rodman should be reminded, gently, that those who read Whitman for poetic content may be counted with the lilacs that last bloomed in their dooryards. We have yet to see demonstrated, in the whole of the Whitman arsenal soufflé, images on the level of the few poets mentioned above; we have yet to see quoted a penetration of any depth by the quiverer to the body electric. Certainly, as computer of primitive democratic yardage, Whitman cannot be denied — and I see I am finally, willy-nilly, rising to affirm the sociologic salience of the Nurse to the States Beside Themselves.

Mr. Rodman, then, with Mr. Gill and *The New York Times*, should be held strictly accountable for having disturbed the resting place of Walt Whitman, even though accomplished by implication only; and the more castigated for having disturbed the resting place of the Beatlings, since their inhumation has been so fresh.

Gil Orlovitz
New York

POEMS

PORTRAIT

She premiered the souls
of others, made one mad birthday
of strange red rubies
from some human's dull coals.

Her body, tongue and eyes
announcer, screen and spotlight
for a new show, a grand show, a purple show
of a creature never heard of:
some Man in his man's disguise!

THIRD ELEGY

What passion is the direction? Whose flesh is the going?
                              What straining
of the squinting eye is the coming?

After all, even though
your senses have edited the processions and published in the rain
the long shining triangle of tracks with the triangle's bottom
                              never
completed and always dropped into the endless backing up
of your perception (that's the shattering of the lie
right there!) — even though — after all, isn't the compass
(go on, now, turn your blood and flesh around in a complete
circle right on that point of earth which by your turning
will be scooped out slowly and steadily for a depth enough
of grave) —

isn't the compass people and things gazing at you from each
degree of the three-hundred-and-sixty, converging on you, and are
not each of them stared at also, by the you-degree
in its turn?

Why then do you ask destinations? And why
do you ask beginnings?

Have you not noticed that we have put
up our tents with an infinite variety of poles, and staked them
                              down
with many kinds of ephemeral anchors?

Our core
is a whirling one, and men find the great whoredom with energy
in being thrown off into the natural nomadry.

Have you not seen
the silver earrings that are the planets —
dangling from gypsy space?

BRIEF ME ON GOD

For god's sake brief me on god.
Not the roil Red Sea, nor Aaron's rod,
not pasture of miracle where we graze,
when want freezes in a maw of glaze,
not the cracked statuary of apocalypses,
nor coronas of beauty in body eclipses.

For god's sake brief me quick.
The vital surface is madly slick,
ignition's wild to spark holocaust
at eternity's chassis beneath man's exhaust,
time's a gamin five-fingered at nose,
mortalities taunt from lynching rows.

For god's sake brief me on god.
Grandeur is curt under the sod,
humanity's grid-lines snarl in space
to balls of star who have lost face,
tell me what savior, tell me what form
in the midnight express to multiple swarm.

For god's sake telegraph him.
Give me a zag of his graph through the limb
of my terror plumbing the dark,
or tell me true, tell me with laughter
as you howl from infinity's rafter —
god is grafter, god is grafter!

TO ST. R

I have caught love a-nap,
she is spring without longing,
gold beyond tap.
I will lie with her sleeping,
that love shall not wake,
for without slumber
she must decline
by the well of our slake.

I have caught love a-nap,
all golding and greening,
and ever is mine
while knowing me not;
we must dread full meeting,
all merging is fleeting
though I've caught love a-nap
from fertility's cheating.

Goodnight, goodnight,
my green and golden sight,
I will shut my eye
for love's napping immortality!

MEMO TO ST. R

Love, coffinlined and satined with your browngold hair,
endeaths me, nails me away from the pallbearers who
would carry me naked to breath's shallow grave. What priest
would pray me here, sprinkle me holy, shove Christ
against me with a dirty shovel? None. Swell!

Your lopsided torque of gut and torso,
the shimmertaut strangle of your skull's auburn ropes,
your fingerghosts arch up a million little rising gods of sweat
commanding me to suck up their goatish stench. Oh jesus
I have not tongues enough to caucus your flesh, hive
it in me, the shivering honey curdling the ripping
teeth. I suffocate in the coffin,
got to to spasm in the passionwind,
else the marathon round your bodytrack stops. I
am the star of love's
olympics:
sprint to the belly, polevault over frenzy's rod,
broadjump of mouth from mouth to groin, hurdle and race and dive
                                                        and wrestle.
We are the parallelbars for gymnastic love's
headstand, flipover and strut.

You burning bitch
of a woman — we're insane in a padded cell
of stars!

NINTH ELEGY

And what of us as blades?

The knife-thrower at the carnival outlines the spectator's
rage, murder, freedom, whip and swoon with each stab
of the cast. And what astonishment of shame they gape when
        they see
that his daggers quiver in the total shape of man or woman,
though he had made them his target all the time. "It is a wonder
        we were
not killed, but at least we found, in his jealousy, that he envied
        us our being,
and proved it!" The knife-throwers are gods, and take us out of
        dust,
which is why we pray to them, and ask for peril.

But what
of us as blades?

As: moving through man's colossal marketplace
of cutlery we sharpen ourselves on each other till our cutting-edges
consume our bodies and in turn keen so thin that we
are sliced through to death.

Those of us, that is, that are blades.

And as point of the blade?

What if it were all a Damoclean universe?
Is it not a stupendous game to point out that we have a vast
and immortal and unchangeable lust to remain paralysed beneath
the suspended godhead of the father's murderous sword?

We
are at blade-points with each other!

A FURTHER INSTRUCTION OF HAMLET TO HIS PLAYERS

Death neither is assumable, nor actable, nor aped:
so, make it a fantasy. That is, if you would stage
it, have your actress chiffon her gestures when
she scenes it.

Now consider. The soldier who
applauds his breast in a most curious clenching manner
as bullets take up lodging for his night
there, falls, I tell you, like a king tripping over
his foot-stool, at which his clown chortles and giggles,
the jaw growing the mouth into bigger and bigger
gaping howls until great cartwheels of laughter
come tumbling out. Would you thus ruin the play?
wreck the actress' career?

Take care. Grace death
with grace. Festoon it with sighs, the wrist in limp
parabola, the eyelid laboring up the curve
of eyeball, the chaste form chaise-lounged and negligeed
for death's ravishment.

Bullnecked hatred you know,
and love's scream in the pasture you yourself
have diaphrammed, and pity, and exultation,
and you have hurled the heavy discus of anger:
all these have sweated in your body's grapplement
that you may sweat them out again upon

the stage; but these moistures do not fever
death's brow, for death is the command
performance of the body unrelivable.

How then is it assumable, or actable, or aped?
Make it, then, a fantasy chiffon. You cannot
dub death in.

FOR GEORGE WASHINGTON

Remember how the nurses walked underwater,
with only their caps showing?
Remember how the oars paid only glances to the ice-floes?
At Trenton the Reds would be fought.
The nurses were gracious:
they let the boat pass;
waiting till they would tend the sickbed of history again.

But I doubt if you knew them.
They wore green teeth to encourage their patients,
and smiled openly when you posed in the boat for the children,
a cherry-tree in your hand,
the infant hatchet-man.

I cannot tell a lie clucked wooden teeth over the Reds later,
and the nurses ironed their caps looking into the mirrored ceiling of
        the Delaware,
unable to cry or laugh.
This winter the Delaware is frozen over between Trenton and New Hope.
What shall I write on that postcard?
and to whom shall I send it?
That I cannot tell a lie surveys no problem except
the cherry-tree on which ghosts are lynched, and what
avail to cut it down.
That no boats pass.
And that all of us, in training to be nurses, stand on the riverbed,
at starch attention, icecap to icecap, in universal sisterhood at last.

And take the copper penny
of the western sun, to mail the message to the East.

ON A MODIFICATION

sullen sifting of the waters,
liquid boulder under thigh,
lift my nervework, roll it seaweed
toward the shrug of ocean brow.
outward, outward, far from shoring,

down the dune of drifting comber
swift my body till it foam
white eyeletry for hook of star,
ring for fingered light and wind,

ceremonial, though I be
sheer and landless,

death waits with no virginity.

LINES ON LAWNS

row-houses
grim upright pianos
where slim green lawns
try to practice

anon
dog pedagogue jogs up
critiques a sniff
and in keeping with chartreuse pupils
shakes a blending stick
at a bald interpretation
in the grace-notes of grass

"you are discharged!"
cry a matron and a sire
for matrons and sires stand on pavements

children
are the political prisoners
of parents
who live in row-houses

now
the slim green lawns
try to practice alone
within fences
and make the dull errors

of unseeded passages
children
who otherwise
would go to the dogs

MUG MANHATTANS SWINGING DOORS

spaghetti fog
springs knives like eels
streetcorners slouch
in satin blouses

skyline rabbis
read river scrolls
by bridges torahs
throw in the toll

truckwheel brogue
oils the manholes
for up the republic
saint and slob

aspirin castanets
skyscraper high heels
atomic shine
for a dime

mug manhattans swinging doors
all come on the mayflower
springdom come
youre all on the house
for a risky hour

HYMN

fivethirty a.m.
the electricgenerator
started off like an immortal scream
whelped in low key and smothered in thin snot
and exploded into a sickbelly throwup of fiery
eels   and there was my woman   my love
outside the window where god in the alleyway
went infinitely upstairs in a striped prisonsuit
of irondrunken firescapesteps   but
there was my woman   my love
outside the window with her crackling hands
on my oily neck blubbering   Dont let me die
dont let me die   dont let me die
but her legs and crotchair and hips were gone
and her entrails hanging out her torso
twisted clubs from an inverted golfbag
and I bawled   I hate machines   I hate machines
they make a hole in one
too gaddam easy

SOLVENT, A PLUME EVOKE, SHE

solvent, a plume evoke, she
indian, impassive called a smile,
jollybean skip a rope aplay, she
mutterhum, papoose a shrug, single-file

her motion stole, a north note, she,
licorice eyes, hips in her eyes
diamond baton, crept at a cat, she,
whittled up the small mew to her size,

nose ah pantaloon, oh tragic sly,
live knick-knacks or suicide, she,
tophatted ghost, noodle on the fly,
south toot, feathered my love-sneeze, she.

THE DIARY OF DR. ERIC ZENO: ONE

A cat. A child teasing a shadow. A Minnesota license-plate.

I heard a joke: a psychoanalyst was asked how he kept so
    spruce.
"Who listens?" he replied.

I wouldn't put a dime on Criteria in the Seventh.

After five years of psychoanalysis,
a patient adjusted to suicide.

A striped Shade, that rolled up in fright
at the approach of detectives, in the depths of darkest
    America.

Whatever else I never knew about her hours,
I knew on summer afternoons she made love
in an airconditioned movie,
high on the balcony,
smoking.
A smoky girl, with dusk in green eyes.

A mirror breaking in a child.

THE DIARY OF DR. ERIC ZENO: FIVE

There is but one purpose in life:
its possibility.

Keep the muscles tight as lovers.
Retreat into reality.
Do not let the meter run too long
when you take a trip in macabre.
There are no dedications worth the slab.

Before the earth explodes,
do not hide too far:
you have a right to be included
in the light from this star.

If you marry, man or woman,
let him be Ben Franklin:
for, in addition to his many saws,
he has a lightning rod.

What is least ideal
is most probable:
the Rhodes White Scholar Class
suffering the mass.

Excuse me, there's a patient here.
But, please remember, that only after treatment
do we know exactly who the doctor was,
as yet not quite clear.

ON THE WONDER OF WHAT IS

the traces of suddeness in the crunch of schoolboy sunlight
    on the blueboard air, as a bird, with black chalk, draws
    a teacher escaping;
the whores who become the four wheels of an automobile
    speeding,
        hat low on the forehead, to the world burning up at the
        north and south poles;
the scarecrow politicians stuck in the wheatfield of men;
the woman anybody used to love tossing as waves of welt in
    his faces;
the rain that brings the surfaces out from under;
the television-antennae marking the graves of roofs;
the idiot leading the genius around by the tail;
the foolish trap the hour-hand sets for the minute;
the mother who is her child's only sun;
the fresh bedsheets that are cartilage after she and I;
the stone spotlights of the pyramids focussing on the spindle-
    shanked egos of pharaohs, as the sphinxes pasture on the
    dune-flanks of tourist prosceniums.

birth drinks, unstatuesque, at trinket-basso minds.

WHAT MAXIM IS A SILENCER

i charged the woman
massaging my nose
she crouched like a mother
of dynamos

and electric evergreens
chirped on my spine
for chinese characters
papering wine

from spiral nebulae
hung ebony brides
singing wire oh wherefore
wind the tides

round turbines of thigh
and quicksand of ear
children sank
to find megaphones near

christs plugged in blizzards
of torpid lamb
alternating current
sweet jigglejam

to anteater graph
and circuit clown
thermostatic boils
lanced by a frown

of what was there
to lure scums wiggle
dumbfounded i heard
angel radar giggle

intercept god
in the sinuosphere
mother please hurry
father wormed my gear

fast wound her finger
marimba krypton grew
nuggets of nerve
scarlet gongs sneezed achoo

where is he where is he
the stars my snuff
hey god virus x
couldnt call his fluff

couldnt trace her either
though i smell her loss
a rolling dynamo
gathers no moss

ADDRESS TO THE UNION

is it that the citizens fear death because their lives
    have gone so distantly
We have become the idolaters of masks so that the visitors
    may not know how far we have wandered from home
this the tragedy of the uprooted who have remained on
    their own territories
to have pulled up stakes and stay fixed shatters the very
    hope of love

we inquire as to when the ministers in their pulpits with
    the other American Laughing Liars
will report I was talking with God only last Sunday and
    he told me angels are income-tax deductible
a new parlorgame called Lets Pretend Whos Different
sex practically a bullfight lets see how close the horns
    can get without touching and then

whom the gods would destroy they first make bored
like wait whitman said thou shalt not covet thy neighbors
    navel to drill for oil
what they forgot to yell was ALL MEN HAVE THE RIGHT
    TO BE CREATED UNEQUAL THATS democracy

the infamous boredom that will have us export psycho-
    analytic couches
the docile boredom that puts fairy gandhis onstage danc-
    ing their pouting loincloths
capital and labor sitting together before a VD set singing
    The last Time I Saw Paresis
I say its a great country so lets have more of
applepicking time in the rural snotholes

that crackerbarrel wit around the old country potbellied
    whore
picture magazines sporting that slick gloss taken right off
    the readers eye
the executive landscapes of the metropolises
he threw a forward pass right down where she said you
    gotta see my nipplewriting on the wall

hell this countrys outa this world
we got two cars in every mirage
abe lincolns on the mound
georgie washingtons backing him up
its tommie to jimmie to al
the fans are standing for the seventh inning retch
it aint anybodys ballgame
its the united states of americas

its chewinggum tangled in your neighbors nervelice
its the inside plumbing that counts baby
its the blues going out like the white of your eye
its the cowmoo inside a diesel train
the fourth of july in popcorn blood
its the glory of the marines boy they'll fight with their
    backs to the nuthouse wall
its oakridge mother dear where the atoms at night come
    out like fireflies
its the supermarket american brain you cant beat it
its babys drool snapped in kodachrome
paul bunyan suffering from corns
and I guess its those strange men the cactus cripples limp-
    ing across the southwestern deserts
and the little towns on sunday mornings with their steep
    curbs like stiff high celluloid collars

and I guess theres really no other place but the USA
    we can go to on saturday nights
because a few people will be dredging the delaware
a few people noticing how the small animals play dice
    with the moonlight

a few madmen putting stethoscopes to the bats who will
    fly in the wrong windows
a few people smiling at how many honeymooners will
    look over niagara falls without trembling
a nuclear physicist who no matter how much lead and con-
    crete he puts between himself and his wife will sustain
    the effects of radiation the moment she gives birth to
    their child

if only there werent so many phony wrestlers.

THE ROOSTER

the rooster crows in my belly
an old hangout for the billiard cues of the morning
and table-hopping hail hail the ganglias all here
after sunset like a mouthwash last yesterlight
and the white tails of the gorillas on television
and that liberal politician stumping for twilight supremacy
down by that old
        shill
        stream
As I buttonholed the Ancient Auctioneer
how goes America going
          going

after the thunderbird pooped out over the canyon
when he clovered her cleavage
and she pleaded like an electric organ in the rain
the moon greased out of the ten commandments a make-
        up too late
what about the negative feedback of death
what about magnetism striking as a poisonous snake
or a hoop of jazzedup wire
snarling up communications over the Morse Pole
after the statesmen belched ionized yeast
and the physics convention approved the musical
        selection
        Quartet
        For
        Four
        Mesons

in an expanding economy they do not matter

the rooster will take us on a guided missile tour
we are knellbent for automation
the minister prays Our Lord Who Art in Heaven judge
         us not by our actions
but fractions
the skullskinner intones judge us not by our transgressions
but analytic sessions
the physicist says christ anybody can have a halo wheres
         the hesitance
when we can boast electronic resonance

you think anybodyll look for the pinprick in an expanding
         economy

look easy and you will see
a cad and a ford in every nebulae
that no comettail you lost
but gods custombuilt Buicks exhaust
Americas producing for the Infinite
Holy Ghost Mongerers for the Universe
Export or Die
theres a report we got a parimutuel for the flying angels
constipation
will be solved by
                  automation

Miss Wall Street does a dance of the seven tickertapes
mathematicians enter the bullring to lock equations
in the circus the economists show off their Trained Graphs
the specialists hide from the specialists
the whores organize their first Vertical Union
to which madames
         pimps and
         cops must belong
waddya mean youre contemptuous of the Middle Class
    theyre the
         National
         Compromise

going
going

(its like some sort of abdominal bell)
the historians yang and yin
says its not too late to get out
and not too late to get in
hole hole the gongs all here
like some sort of abdominal bell
shes a Supermarket Baby with all the skimmings
mate doth look for automate
male finds femalleable
we dont die we reincarnate
this goes for everybody but the lower animal orders
those down-at-the-heel aristocrats who simply wont take
        in boarders

its already noon and I'm still expanding
I'm a Paul Bunyan Giveaway
schizophrenia for lonely dolts
manic nuts for shy bolts
paranoia for those who say nobody has followed them
telescopes by god for those who say we've hollowed them
hail to the architects whove eliminated the five-oclock
        shadow
we function beardless from the cradle to the nave
free sexual irrigation for the ascetic
and thorns to bower the apoplectic
the cardiacs will look like roses
in this Promised Land without a Moses

hail to the farmers and their cows
in swimmingpools of milk and honey
hail to parity granaries of money
the worker with his fake-home pay
and the sociological gangster parentally rejected
steals his fathers in property quite protected

alls fair in an expanding economy

alls fair in love and boredom
the heavyweight champ
is still damp
       behind his fears

the opera star endorses beers
the homerun king belts one into the stratofears
rich as a churchmouse the saying goes
the deacon leaves cheese between the foes
the cathedral is built in stunted gothic
this is america
       their very own
I'm going to the bank to get a loan
get a loan
       little dogie
       get a loan
       going
       going

get a loan to
       integrate the negro in the south
       with white hoof-&-mouth
       a new perfume
       for the bladderroom
       pouting purses
       for wetnurses
       democratic steel
          for teething kings
          david-slings
             for the delinquent
             juvenile
       and giant breweries
       spiking castoroil with luminal
waddya mean whats the international policy
we got an expanding economy

we're counting cosmic rays in the bank
crow
   rooster
     crow
we got cocacola in labrador
thats what you call getting your mouth in the door
crow
   rooster
     crow
we'll have skyscrapers in the ionosfear
every suicide'll live a charged particle here
crow
   rooster
     crow
we're putting extra-sensory-perception on the production-
   line
get rid of that goose
our economys on the loose
we'll advertise a hermit for snob-appeal
we'll get every hunchbacked shoulder behind the com-
   monweal
crow
   rooster
     crow

pile all your energies into the new Golden Calf
                   THE ELECTRONOLAUGH
                   THE COMPUTER
                   WITH THE SMILING TOMORROW
all the great comics willed their bodies to it
the graveyard with the future in it
WHEN IT LAUGHS IT DISPLAYS URANIUM-FILLED
       TOMBSTONES
the bones
     of contemporary saints
CROW
   ROOSTER
     CROW

  going

                        going

Forest Lawn?

            NO!

                        ELECTRONOLAUGH!

THE LETTERS OF GREAT APE: I

(To his son, Edward Ape,
Rattan-on-Hudson. May 6, 1958)

My Dear Edward: Let me warn you,
we Apes were never meant for the military.
Of course, with your generic camouflage,
I can see the hidden logic
of a violent outcome, and a certain
social acceptance; citizenship, perhaps,
conferred by the human group who call
us static revolutionaries —
reacting, as you may say, to
our innate Reserve Officer status.
But, I beg you, remember that even
when we swung our sorties tree
to tree, we kept our heads by tails,
balancing what went before with what
might come to be, whilst our cousins,
who seem a little awkward at
reunion and insist on too much small
talk, too habitually scan
themselves in hairless mirrors, confusing
nakedness with destiny. I fear
that war, my son, is fought above
the forest now in the rootless candor
of atoms making childish faces
at each other, and men confessing
to their caricatures. And while, my son,
it is true that men ask pity
of all the animals, pity cannot

make the human problems the apes'.
There is some merit, after all,
in surviving as the son of the Great
Ape, rather than risking your all
on a throw of snobbery, which got us where
we are, I do admit, but no
further: aristocracy nullifies
assumptions. I should be griefstricken
to lose you as you are; but fathers
are utterly damned if they must lose
sons to what they're not. Will
you think on this a little? a little
more on me? and much more
on your youth, of which there is
so much, I know, you hardly know
where to begin to age. — Will
you be bringing guests for Merry
Linkmas? All of us miss you at
the Thirsting Pool where, happily,
we never learned to look down
at ourselves, but only drink our absences.
Study diligently: we are not given
many scholarships. Aff'c't'ly, Your Father.

THE LETTERS OF GREAT APE: 2

My Dear Cousin: We Apes cannot exhibit
this year: we have taken to a Walden (blameless,
and thus anonymous) for sabbatical, there to
    determine
how far our fur will fly — where the resemblance
stops. We too have dignity, and a rainbow
at the other end. We are somewhat piqued
(one of your natural selections) that you have not
exhibited in human return such abstract
craft of the Unconscious as you may deem
worthy of our non-verbal logic.
As for us, we have no laws governing
Esthetic Anthropology: we have come
to you, whereas you cannot seem to come
to us a mere half way — all the while
you antidote on rotifers and decapitated
electrons: do you really prefer the primitive
probability-waves of non-Euclidean
gore? In all semantic innocence, Cousin,
we are hurt. We may rebel against
the Income-Tax, and have it paid by one of
our Detranscendentalists waving the Categorical
Pejorative. Forgive my long levities:
they protect the tender briefs of skin at the winter
Pond — full of vulgar torsos twirling
naked-toed on the ice. I think it very
possible no Ape will ever exhibit to Man
again. I think it time you keep your basic
drives quite secret, without the comic rationalizations
from your cousins: it will be very hard
to swing human laughter in a treeless world.

Besides, you have enough to show yourselves:
machines and engines with every kind of open
drive to shrink your surface areas — so that
at last you will find yourself exactly
where you are, which will demand the boldest
front conceivable. By then, of course, we
may no longer be present to bring
up your rear, for you will have evolved altogether
in the round. I counsel caution, then: a rolling
ball can gather no space, and will slip
through the feet of its own catch-as-catch-can
God. You will lose loneliness, Cousin,
as befits a species unconscious of itself;
therein the greatest danger: unable to advertise.
Still, if we change our minds, we will
give them to you, a salvation by
a quarter you never anticipated;
we bodies do not need much mind
to survive, but you may require all of ours —
exhibited in your frame, an animal compromise.
Till then, if such be so, Cousin, walk
upright in our paths, adjusting to
our shadows without fear: they also serve
who crouch behind. — After You, Your Cousin.

SUNBURNT THE BATHER

sunburnt the bather she bade
the limb foreclose the fluency
the blue eye underground
by blonde shade and iamb of wave

wherever form indicted by the wind
she loosed torrents of stillness
nipplenerved and ruddybrown
mouthclue to the cloven world

that rippling down the golden void
she shoaled round the bone
in the faint foam of the moonspine morning
lofted the hearts shoulders to the sea

NOT

not the commander grinning through the periscopic
 bowel,
not the butterfly masses sucking pyramids
 they wormed,
not god with his totem earth, not the devil with
 red suspenders,
not the sweating angel, not the potpourri ape,
nor a moment to be lost, not a love that giggles
 ghastly
over green gall and greasy ghosts, not the woman
engineered from a mans squib, not my life
nor yours nor the hairshirt of history,
not the slimemould chewing gum, not the hairpin
 penis
for a monsveneris permanent wave, not the epileptic
 clown,
not the jolly specialist addressing the whole convention,
not bathing beauties springing leaks, not the foam-
 titted sea,
not the storm with the heart of a haggle, not jezebel
 jelly,
not jesus jerking off, not mohammet with his coeds,
not confucius with scotch&soda in the mens club at
 dusk,
not while theres time, not the housefly taking baths
 in eyes,
not the weathervane tattooed on my windpipe, not
 moses
cracking his knuckles as the thoushaltnots bored
 him,

not the Old Testicle nor the New Testicle nor the
      Hypocrypha,
not the hydrostatics of spit, not the dynamics of
      gored mirrors,
not magnetism laying an egg, not the condoms
of executives from saudi arabia to death valley
with prickly heat on the grass roots of profit and
      loss,
not gothic spiders, not arthritic architecture, not the
      matadors
in hysterical capes corkscrewing through the mu-
      seum of bulls,
not while theres a stone unturned, not for a minute,
not that you know, not that theres anything to hide,
not for anything, not for all the jade in china,
not for the reason you think, not the old men
with their tomahawk memories, not the old masters
urging purring electricity to lap at the milk,
not atlas with his base on balls, not the smiling
little boys with their equation-mustaches, not the
      revolutionaries
stroking the convulsives into catalepsy, not the
      financiers
pissing silvergray numeralhairs into steel urinals,
not the artists riding their paranoid nags to sacrifice,
not the general astride his hydrogen fart,
not squashed insects dreaming of bubbling light,
not the north and south poles in their vast owls of ice,
not black and white and yellow tungstens of hate,
not the bunomastodontidae of industry
with the openhearth tusk and whanging gut
and their salesmens suburban fury, not the nerve low
      on radar,
not the children wading in the waters of their
      mothers and fathers,
not my love my woman with the tiny blue trumpets in
      her eyes,
not the people waiting in their stalls to be saddled

with bright
jockeys, not the spirituals or the blues on the four-
footed tremors,
not the moviestars posing on the drums of stills,
not the twilight my darling my love pausing in my
throat,
not the friends impacted wisdomteeth at grief and
death,
not the sandpipers tacking dartburs along the shore,
not the last of the suns snowballs at the moon,
not the kitchenwall copperware chiming the sizes of
home,
not the tv comic thinning under the spotlights bald-
spot.
not the sprocketwheels in the deaf mans ear tugging
at his eye,
not the tears trapped in the wilds like small game,
not the woman intent on calisthenics in the coffin
to lose weight, no, no, not anything like that,
not while theres time, not while theres time, not
while theres time.

THERE IS A MAN I DO NOT KNOW

There is a man I do not know, whom I must strike
with my fists, in the pleasure of the strange,
in the guiltlessness of the blind,
that all his features may be gone, I think, and unidentifiable
for any of my later sobrieties.

He is the man who never resisted.
His shape has the soft power of a vacuum;
no matter how often I beat him
in the full standing congress of my rage, his
blood never bleeds, he
never looks up, he
never speaks.

I could not tell you if he is blond or black,
fat or lean, or how he fills any craft of questionnaires,
for he is there only as I bring down my
shrieking knuckles
on his knowing unknowingness.

I see, now, that I may never meet him when I am quiet,
when in a deep graceful fear I think I might
have to blackmail my responsibilites,
to stop him from acting against me.

In time, possibly,
I shall look for a way of asking him to appear,
when he shall not be in terror that I shall strike him, nor
stroke him, either.

WESLEY THORNE

The money leaped with an aging shriek
from the largesse of contempt
to account overdrawn. The wrinkled throats of
        dollars would sneak
down another alleyway of another week.

Now that could make a torso-murder.
A perfect crime. Famous Americans: Washington, Lincoln,
        Hamilton torn
to bits and stuffed into the valises of the wind,
shipped to old mints of an old spring,
winter curators might find.
The weapon, his fingers, could never be serially
        traced:
he would have filed down the nails, manicured homicide,
checkbook chaste.
And the murderer of money identifiable only with the
        mass.

But such violences
could merely be the vain ventriloquy of dummy desire.
He would pat his wallet, the second heart,
and jingle his coins in the pocket next
to sex, adulthood's newest charms, that neither
        bauble might be vexed.

Were not all figures on American currency male?
Was this not proof
American womanhood could never stay aloof
before negotiable, sustained virility? that into
        deflated impotence could at no time fail.

He could stoke his belly; he could walk new shoes;
he could listen to classic comfort to the St. Louis
    Blues.

Still, the insurance-premiums would have to be met,
    and met, and met,
the endless enemies to fill out one's existence:
there were so few friends
without scissors in the coupon-clipping set.
The payments on the car
in the nation of garaged equality:
stamped steel frames
simonized by hormone-creams.
The monthly rent
for washbowl, spindle chair and jostling jollity;
camphor, soap, bacon, and vermouth,
landscape by Mouthwash, wife by Douche.
The monetary menstruation of every truth:
what ad, in fullpage gore, girls, grinning brickwork
    white,
sacrificing bosoms to tractors,
mother's booze to actors,
julietting in panties and bra
to romeos in plaid and rah-rah,
could supply his green cramps
spelled backwards?

All his nerves seemed tongue-out to dry,
bank-teller birds plucking at the crumbs in low
    denominations
on each taut insolvency.
How like a canvas bag the gray slack sky —
for the more fortunate depositors.
Never mind the sun. Nor the moon, an obstinate,
    obsolete mechanism
to raise and lower tides,
and the apologies of old lovers to young brides.
Never mind the sun. Nor the dandelion burning in
    effigy,

nor the slanted young shoots of rain, nor the white
    shooting-gallery of cloud
from blue balustrade.
Never mind the sun. Here in his humdrum dome
    sufficient
planetarium of expenditure,
the interest falling due south of overhead —
could not bankrupt nature ruin man?
Never mind the sun.

There was the silver, the nickle, the copper and
    the gold
phosphorescent in the chlorophyll feces of his dark.
Here he could huddle, scratching at the brambles on
    rose-faced
idiocy, and wipe himself with emerald certificates.
The silver, the nickel, the copper and the gold
would impose upon a single individual's anxiety
noble federal reserve. Till the species of specie
would move among his fellow stubs as he signed,
blank, bent check, checkbook-chaste, mumbling,
"Come, fill me out.
Come, endorse me.
Endorse me and fill me out,"
to be murdered, not murdering, by the aging thugs
    of mortgages
in the alleyway of next week, next week, next week,
splashing, as they foreclosed,
great Shiva-showers of genes
from the puddles of the silver, the nickle, the
    copper and the gold,
that only an American monk, puttering with a
    Creditor God
amongst the peas in a monastery-garden,
could possibly have foretold.

INDEX (8)

from the island aquamarine
her eyelashes the combers the sunburnt breakers

I am deaf to the seashell at his ear
blind to the knives of noon between his teeth
but who shall walk with me when the truth comes
in without love's familiar infamies

the wind hollowed her cheekbones
shook bronze bracelet breast and breast
beneath her belly the sacrificial network caught
thoughts of children their heads on chins

shuddering at the planets those coldcream jars
the fauna these perfume bottles drinking
at the mirror's edge
and the flower Beget-me-not from the diaphragm moon
he shall not have me anymore
but then who can
I have not said anymore to him but that women
took Christs down
oh God how they prefer their arms about the cross
        and thieves
let me laugh
let me laugh at their mistletoe martyrdoms

naked she bit the sea's green apples
plunging at the white salt fruit

naked her horses on the foaming vines

INDEX (3RD SERIES): 2

I have felt the weight of myself but separately
I have felt the weight of others but collectively
I have felt the weight of others and myself only an idea
I have felt the weight of my woman and myself a rising rock
I have felt the weight of love a weight in the process of making itself
    known a weight in forever varying degrees and of becoming weight
    more as becoming less and less as becoming more
I have felt the crotch of things
crotch like a crocodile
the crystal crotch
and the crotch humming an idle air
and now and then the crotch I could not bear
and I have blown nipples at a clock
as a foetus I can recall being a buoy-marker over my mother
as a foetus I recall I displaced the weight of my mother
as a foetus I recall I bore the diminishing weight of my mother
I drew forth the thin green sap of snot like a sick rubberband and
    crocheted it with my fingernail
I rested and was like the world
crumbles
crevices
courtesies
a butterfly dared me to fuck it
I was seduced by the weddings of the magnetic lines of force
I attracted myself by my nakedness
I went round myself and found myself grateful on all sides
there was a dream of such significance that could not dream it
there were circles under her thighs they had been up all night
I had held her applestick buttocks and sucked at them like a child while
    I walked through the puckered streets

there had been the massive bannisters that had blown bugles
the arthritic clocks
and against the current the swimmer swollen with weight
I felt myself dragged by an ant
my prick chased after pollen with a butterfly net
I caught my death of sail and coughed white rigging after white rigging
    after white rigging
I was a mass of necks twisting and basking on blazing rocks
a shy monolith
a baby pyramid
I have felt the earth topple up screaming and running witless away from
    the pursuit of foundations
burials
burials
burials
I have felt the mud flung at my spoiled teeth laughed to death at my
    indigestion
feel cried the woman done her labor
I put down my hand
feel cried the woman
I put down my hand
what is it that you feel she said
your hair like a damp autumn fire and your cunt split like the red sea
    the jews passed through I said
were the egyptians all drowned she said
I put down my hand
not a single egyptian there she said
nothing I said
I have felt slickness spill through my fingers
I have felt sand with its nerves grating and on edge
I have let a hooked nerve reel out from the spinal rod into the snapping
    waters
and I have felt age as if a mass explosion were a bird
and youth a delicate maniac
down narrow streets the sun slipped on bananapeels
the polevaulters goosed by whistles
the virgins vowed vengeance at the maternity-wards
on the perceptive rested the burden of spoof

the cracks squinted along like lizards
the eyelids skidded into gutters
in the city the empty cages marched as the newest conquerors
the cannon put on rouge and shrieked like fags
the flags of all nations swing their hips as their flagpoles minced
no greater weight than the wind shifting
no lesser than idols worshipless
the falling into slumber farewell and confession and the acquisition
    of weight so steadily it becomes a weightlessness
the burning of weight may be defined as motion
the flame declining in the corner of her eye
the new prometheus returns the stolen fire to the gods
the sole of the foot is tickled as a bell
laughter the usurer exacting the highest rates of interest
walking like a slice of melon
dancing like a stammering echo
rolling like looking over your shoulder with your tongue steeped in
    your armpit
floating like the belly drawn over your head as a tortoise-shell
the touch of hammocks like sleepwalkers
webs like moccasined prickles
the summer was the inside of winter
the cats were the gloss of light arched under your palms
the hearts were oxen
icicles were toy soldiers
the hollows had it in for things
the clowns had balloons on their cheeks
the machines looked over their shoulders at the men behind
turn the machines into salt if you can
each night before bedtime we sprinkle the streets with jitter
the groin craves audience with the pope
a pack of niches roams the spaciousness
the signs swore theyd revenge themselves on their meanings
the instant the bladders tried to relieve themselves against the walls
    dissolved
remember patience as a ghetto
and I remember the stainedglass jews gassed with their stainedglass
    bowels and beards

I remember the stainedglass jews huddling after they had let christ out
and I remember their austere god who would let no one invade his privacy
who greased the cross for christ
I remember the feel of a murderer whittling from birth
and guns displayed on velvet
and stretching tall as a circus centerpole ah the acrobats who skimp
    on mass
and the slack wire wiretalkers tooting my mouth amidst the hissing
    jets of my trusting terrors
and the beckoning girlish mountains of the empty swaying trapezes
and the slipping on faces at the going away
and the clutter of heartbeats at someone coming
take a jigger of clitoris mix one part dervish
take a scissor to a nipple and paste on your mouth
a dash of sweat
and a dab of dig
and the feel of the thing is the salmon of prick up the shuddering
    spillway of her skiing brawn
I remember the slingshouldered strides through the icy dusks
and the great graceful taper to the warless weary
we are the weighers of the shimmer of feel
the hand with the muscle of cloud
the sinew that struck the lean shaft down the lonely bellow the crowd stills
we are the millers of move
the windmill bones round the daft dike
the deft sowers of stun
stick sweet pikes through the stone seed
and wrestle the young lad god over ditches of martyrdom and the
    tinkling goats of blood
feel the cowlick hangmans rope over mans forehead
and the spikewings south from his sperm
we are the weighers of the milling shimmer
hangers-on at the poolroom clouds
and the hands and the hands that start the selfwinding toy shadows
    that wobble a smile from the children in the sun

of the flora and fauna of scream, of
the cyclone cravat god got to be a colorblind corpse in
the rumors spreading like wildwire,
bleeding vines ...
shellshock shines
out
goddamn the eyes are hootloose goddamn smut squashed electrons;
    goddamn whistle
after that webtoed resonance come back
where the fat
is the chat
is who was that woman I seen you with last night that was no woman that
    was my
life.
sponges
are doorknobs;
advertise — the apartment has wall-to-wall fungusing now
where do you think he is that old salesman of door-to-door thunder ...
and: that sign of the whisper he
made across his lips
with the finger of
lightning
well lemme tell you the sinews lurchswerve around the corners of
    that awful neck like a tenton trailortruck no
I don't know
about discrimination down south
but I do know the baleful bias from his everycolored mouth; so
come — all — ye — grinners.
stuff gods jockstrap down his throat,
accuse him
of communism

cosmic imperialism
                    now we got it, boy
                    now we're on the track
                    we're after him hot, boy
gods the big security-crack thats it
hes a security-risk
he aint fit
for civil
service —
SEND GOD BACK WHERE HE CAME FROM
AINT HE A KIKE?
except if hes a sort of middleclass failure, a sort of poor
doohickey-eyed slob that writes insurance.
in which case, I'm
gunning for cover, I'm
putting my flesh in slothballs, I'm
putting an ad in the paper Gil isnt responsible for any of his gods debts, I'm
out to tie tincans to the tornados tail
let the flora and fauna of scream
scamper through adams apple, lets see
if you can untie the gordian knot of the waters hack through with what
        proud prow?
bend down and let the starlight goose you if you will,
turn the tables of the elements, frisk
the flotsam of yourself
stickemup by jetsam aircraft, honor
by the hophead owl, the historian
doesnt know his past from a hole in the ground, the physicist'll
be the unification of us all
the agglomerated phylogeny of the crystallised ball into which an
old witch will look playing hooky
from her nooky thats her
broom, son thats her
floozie-flue, son thats her
moo-cue from the sacred cow of the world, son dont let her
down, son she'll stick her
doze into anybodys business
jesus the bitch has a running doze: there wouldnt be any trouble
if somebody could cure the common cold

ON THE NATURE OF SUICIDE

take my word for it
the morning I saw the pterodactyls flying tight
    formation with the jets
nobody had a limb to go out on
the aerial museum dropped my egghead
featuring jesus in a leather jacket and a black
    belt
well all right how would you like to ride the cross
    like it was a motorcycle
what kind of choice is it when the pilots got to
    watch the windshield wiper flipping like a
    striptease over the sweating television set
take my word for it
that was when I stuffed myself into a culdesac
    condom
and holding my nose drowned myself in a pool of
    stagnant sperm
hygienic to the last I took no chances of contamina-
    tion
and here I am

blowing jellybeans into balloons
Im not really
whats happening really is that somebody just hit a
    fly ball
and it hurts like hell
and like the idealist I am and let me tell you that
    really takes idealism
Im zipping down my pants to catch the damn thing
and if that isnt suicide I dont know what is

except that if nothing is where I expect something to
        be
then Im going to look like one helluva misty monster
        hanging only one for christmas

but as I say here I am
the only problem being that the alarmclocks keep
        ringing me to wake up
there isnt a living soul around to believe that death
        provides the most brilliant perceptions
because the truth can go right through anything
of course it keeps going and you can kill yourself
        trying to keep up with it
and alarmclocks are giving me a sheerache
Im losing all my electrons
a dead man is about to go mad
it isnt fair
wholl give me postmortal therapy
and if anybody could what good would it do because
        Ive a terrible block
a total resistance to life
the solution is to capture the alarmclocks
and wind them and wind them and wind them
till you break their pretty little necks
and they spew out their mortal coils
because suicide just wont work till you murder
        everything around you

so here I am murdering
my mother and father because they had some nerve
all my relatives as part of the nervous conspiracy
adam and eve because they had a snakecharming act
my landlord because he demanded rent for something
        he already owned
the college president because he passed out sheepskins
        to people
the president of the united states because he
        flinched at character assassination and this

was the next best thing
karl marx because I couldnt stand his suffering from
        carbuncles on his ass as he cursed the
        aristocrass
sigmund freud because he dreamed about it all the
        time anyway
albert einstein because he believed in the ultimate
        simplification
adolph hitler because I was damned if Id let him
        commit suicide
napoleon bonaparte because he retreated from moscow
archimedes because no man is indisplaceable
stalin because he never took a bath
erlich because what did syphilis ever do to him
mendel because he did it in a garden with peas
some early renaissance artist because he gave me
        the perspective to do it in
the bank president because it was all his vault

when the corpses were knocking about like so many
        farts in a picklebarrel

Between the palm trees rattling their venetian slats
in a wind giving no quarter by being from none,
and a fraternal order quarter moon left
by a secret society, I cannot openly pray
tonight; and I will not rely on Sunday sermons
for the week. I have no Adversary of my own.
Evils are rented, leased and temporarily
installed; and Good a vague promissory to pay.
I begged both architect and congregation
that spaces be left in the church for gargoyles;
outside the church, then, I said, if you must
be traditional; — it was no on both mounts:
there can exist no trophies of anonymity,
And, having something of a craggy
face, I held my tongue. One must hold
something. If not dearly; cheaply; if not
cheaply: merely; if not merely; sleepily;
if not sleepily: then dumbly, by God, for speechless
possession must count to a Saint Chances of
this world, to whom scientists bear but a countdown
          rosary,
I inquired: rather than wine, why not a cup
of liquid oxygen? Rather than Christ, why not
a rocket on the Cross? Rather than
tho recognizable Holy Family and accoutrements,
why not Miro Fish, Mary Modigliani,
and Divinity Cubes dissolving on a Guitar
Crucifix? Will we be less devout to sing
our hymns on a twelve-tone scale? But
you are not ordained to wear your cranium backward,

the vestrymen replied. The parish garden smells
me secretly: I may be a ghostly compost on
this earth. To hold one's nose is well,
unaware of the odor's source, is to be as human
as the next one, more so if his is held
more tightly. I will pray, perhaps, in a mutilated
way: that the wind blow quarterly; that the moon
give womanly orders; that the palm leaves seduce
the cobra spine. And I may be half-inclined
to listen to myself with half an ear, the net
effect more silken than we usually suppose.

THE MORNING OF A CLOWN

Tardrizzling heat, the skin sticks to the ghosts,
the moguls of an oily sky; the orchids
ogle the ripple of excreting insects.
A bleak ripe, mottled with the black slurring of
    sarcophagi.
The shadows gulp gold; a green paste in transparent
fur masticates cyanic syrup
in the lazy flarefalls of cymbals,
the meridian slopping down to dew,
my mask overpulped with mass morning
myrrh, bitter to the chaste chickle of the gum
running eye. I am too azure, too venomous
with the dactylic thrombi of rumpling slumber
to wax the alarm of laughter that floods
its own metal with gushing goitre. I
am the teased of the Clowns, and will relish roast
pompons and the marshmallow mist before I turn
informer on tragedy: she whispers odium
to the earth, while I stroke the groin of moss,
the jellyclad cougars, the gemsmeared
decibels in their scoriae of maggoted hum,
and the wounded scotmata burying the dazzles
they had hissed off the sloeeyed horizon,
The ripples in orangutan headdress are barely
resonant of the pools they come to drink
their mica from, and the flora of my recumbency
are ritual rapids in glossy senility.
My mouth slides off into plastopleistocene
flying lyres, and denuded treetrunks
in postures of exotic celibacy. The windless

resin tallows over the glassbottomed throat
of the moon, and I shall not shallow
saturation where lecherous echo glows
in mapleleaf manta under my tongue.
In such inverted dusk teething
through the morning, I cannot hear the castanets
of myelin, flamencoed on the sugarcones.

FLAMENCO: 3

spinning quartz
she salts pork, she
blowguns her heels and
cockatry wriggles shrunken heads
between pursed toes,
niggard nipples, nicked
nearsotted highhocked she
hiccups the hamstrings, quitting
quartz she mugs hard meat, salts
leaking honey, balls
on the board she
double-zeros, fit
in the finger, foaming
at the nail halfmoons, wit
in the wails girl,
slit way down to the sleet
whirl theres a bone theres a
slit way up the balls of the feet of the throat
right in the
doublequeeroed head, quartz off the top of the
heelmug, zedhock
on the board, oakgassed,
blowgun nipples knock wood,
bet
high, bet
low, eat
christ, let
go

THE DIARY OF ALEXANDER PATIENCE: 29 MAY

4:45 p.m.

What I don't understand is
it's all happening in the United
States of America where judges
and baseball umpires wear black
like the creatures of the cloth.

Somewhere there's a type who wears
his collar sideways.

Nobody is as unhappy as
the happy person out to kill
unhappiness. Known as the all-night
sucker, he's been marked by
the Psychiatric G-Men Public
Enemy Number 2, the worst offender:
Under-Ass Perspiration.

11:30 p.m.

Just about supper time the old lady
who'd been feeling lousy went out
with her family anyway to eat
in a Whelans Drugstore and in two
minutes vomited and lost the take
power in the upper limbs and
the go get in the lower
and fell in a pile of wrinkles to
the floor. Her little old man

of giddy esophagus promoted
a cot where they laid her under
a coverlet more bulky than
any ten bones she's ever had.
"God be with her" a waitress said.
The pancaked old lady's big
fat daughter looked like a stalled
trailer-truck. People ate at
the counter as if something had
happened. The old lady breathed
like she forgot air was outside;
she thought it was all inside,
and in a little while you could
see how she was creeping along
her own bottom looking for
the stuff. A great big fullback
of a doctor came, who had
the nerve to be jovial as hell
with the hooked white face of his
but got serious when he bent over
her with that metal and rubber
thing, that medical Will You Be
My Valentine. "Hamburger medium
side of french" a waitress wailed.
The old lady said something in
a softshoe rattle. The doctor nodded
and got up and jimmied his pocket
for a dime and made a call from
a phonebooth and then went away
with his great big athletic
bag to his showers. Her little old
man with the face like a scavenged
pixie lifted her fabulously
weightless arms like they really
weighed something and folded them
like she shouldn't be ashamed.
He had blue eyes. Then two great
big orderlies in white pants

and snappy brown windbreakers
and snappy encircled hospital
insignia and peaked caps for all
the world a couple of space
cadets came and suavely shifted
the old lady into an ambulance
as her little old man followed
with her handbag swinging on
her wrist. "God be with her" a
waitress said. The trailer-truck
daughter went the other way.

Tomorrow would be Decoration Day.

THE DIARY OF ALEXANDER PATIENCE: 7 JULY

1:15 a.m.

The Great Ape brought his coke
up to date at Ray's Rosy Corner
(Jack's), Fountain and Bronson, LA.
A hundred and ten in the shade.
"As a Lower Animal, the smog
doesnt bother me," he said. Jack
studied the reports on the Other Animals
at Washington Park. "Theyre my
favorites," Jack said. "The clouds
are like cream cheese," the Great
Ape said. "Thats nice,'" Jack said.
"Evolution is the subtlest form of
torture," the Great Ape pointed out;
"it requires me to wear a hair shirt."
A cab pulled over to the curb.
The harried negro driver washed
himself out of the front seat and tried
to revive the sloppy female drunk
in the rear. The Great Ape fanned himself
with a billboard and noted, with something
less than desire but more than a
rankling dream, the woman's dyed red
hair by way of her sweat-infested
thighs, and squirmed in his coke.
"Oh to be a man," thought he, "now
that summer's here." But the State had
laws about progress too quickly esteemed.
"Shes a doctor's wife," Jack said, "from

the hills," and the Great Ape shivered
down his testtube spine. A little boy,
who could not have been her daughter,
looked on his mother with frowning
hands. "These damnable moral problems,"
the Great Ape thought, "that anthropoids
are faced with, as: shall I bring
up my children to believe in
men or apes? Shall I let my
children decide for themselves? Is
my responsibility liege to
ape or man? Is God out of
apes that He must evolve man?
Should I embarrass the United
States by having children at all? in
view of certain American magazines
complaining that American art
ignores the excellencies of American
life." He sighed. "That lousy Darwin,
the Apes' first psychoanalyst,
made us self-conscious. But I
am, after all, indebted to
America: where else could an
ape get into the movies?"
"Thats right." Jack said, selecting
Nashua in the Seventh, "you
should be grateful." The hackie gave
up and went to a phonebooth to
call the cops. A trailertruck-jawed
pregnant woman came out of the
Beauty Shoppe, where her fetus had
been given a facial and its guts
a permanent wave, and picked up
the drunk's testy child to comfort
him, meanwhile evangelizing
that rummy mothers at least ought
to get potted alone, without subjecting
a child to the hideous spectacle.

"Well, I don't know," the Great Ape
reflected, "because, Oedipally speaking,
the boy has a right to see his
Womb staggering around, or dead
drunk; he had it coming to him,
the mother must have unconsciously
figured. And the kid is probably
wailing because he didnt get a
shot or two." But he didnt voice
this, for fear of spoiling his makeup;
besides, he didn't want to influence
the pregnant woman's fetus, whom he
hoped was receiving analytic therapy
in utero: he could picture the doctor
listening to the dreams through a
stethoscope. Instead, he reached a
long crewcut arm for another coke.
Jack felt suddenly samaritan:
"Maybe I can bring her to before
the cops come, so she wont be booked,"
be said, and he croupiered some icecubes
into a towel, and went unto the woman
felled by her own folly. She awoke,
fighting for sleep, her mouth as Adam
breaking in the bucking bronco of
the serpent, smeared with the bowels'
lipstick, stricken with horror at
life by icecube, screaming at
her bawling son fondled by a pregnancy
and Jack the Candystore Man's
confectionate urgency around
her skidding shoulderblades as
a Jaguar jeered by, a Cadillac
undulated, a Porsche peeped,
a Fordomatic burred in the hot
orange world of probabubbles,
leading the Great Ape in the rough
built blindly now, and spilt her

shoulder against the glass window,
betrayed by her own reflection,
stumbling, stumbling into her son
as one cop caught her, and another
the hiccupping boy before she fell.
"There will be no scandal," the Great
Ape thought, and swore in triumph
that he would invent the
Lie of the Missing Link.

M'SIEU MISHIGA: 3

ogled by bloodshot oranges,
                     I am committed.
I have a few Proclamations for the Ages —
as, we run for our hives from the uniformed coprophages,
                     I am committed.
                  What slangy eyes,
                  what slipknot hips,
                  what
brings you here inquisitors hours are over:
                              Quidditors:
if will be asked of you are you a mammal,
say youre a horizontal hunchback called a camel, and
                 see what they say, and —
                 say what they see, oh —
                 say can you see, by —
                 the fauns early light
                 that youre
committed and goggled with bloodshot oranges.
WHAT THUG OF YOUR DREAMS HOLDS YOU UP?
                 it will be asked of you,
when are the Festivals of Fickle,
how green is your pickle,
but tell them you have some Proclamations for the Ages —
as, toss a bone to Old Rover Archaeologist,
                  I am committed
and it was asked of me: was the hair that held the
                     Damocletian sword
dipped in lanolin?
confess:
YOU FOUGHT THE LAST WAR WITH YOUR PUSH-BUTTONS
    UNDONE

Oh, but it was fun,
we were all in there pushing,
you see, and when those rockets went off
and the missiles swished up
and noses touched noses from opposite arcs,
I knew the stars were mistletoe
at heaven's gate for homosexual larks
MISHIGA — MISHIGA — MISHIGA
they shouted from the launching sites:
COMMITTED - COMMITTED - COMMITTED
came back the cry.
It was I — me — they — we,
in the splitted declensions of committee
                    rolling the bloodshot oranges
down our cheeks
and the sword sticking in my throat
because it wasnt dipped in lanolin,
and the hives
from being sensitive to coprophages

love turns, sausage-souled, a sprig of vertigo,
in slidingdoor faces and bongo cravats, on
thy belly is as a heap of malt, thy
spine specifications of clavichord spittoons,
fingernail plectrums down the lizzardlyring
    lacquerlooms,
the stock-quotations antiphonal to a lads magic
    phallolamp
rubbed at the epitaphal turnstile,
love the foreign-correspondents accreditisation,
    parenthetical paradise,
the veiled cripple hobbling on thermometer crutches
to interlocking directorates of scalar mistresses,
I am a very testicle of young finance, thy
    breasts are as my twin expense-accounts, thy
    neck as of the Waldorf Towers, thy
    navel as of a rough diamond mined by a
        South African Black and withheld
        from the Market, thy
    thighs are as of near-East oil
coveted by Stereoslav and Jazzamer, thy
    rumps as of the rocket-launching
        platforms of the diplomats, love
is the preferred dividend,
the very homewrecker of the Communist State
    Comrades, I confess I loved,
Gentlemen, the Small Business of Love cannot be
    tolerated in our Industrial Reflex,
THE SEXUAL CONGRESS MUST BE ADJOURNED,
love turns, sausage-souled, a sprig of vertigo,

under the cartographers crotch, at the foot of the
    analytic
couch stood upright as at the American Wake,
Death to Love! the littleboy revolutionaries shrill
    at the barricades,
Death to Love! the conservatives pass the memomasturbators
    among themselves,
Death to Love! for there are animals in my mind
        buying and selling feel-estate
        converting fingertips to sequins
        replacing nymphs with lymphs
        haggling over bearded bombs
        charging admission to my catacombs
        full of mens low earnings
        out of pity turning the wheel for the ox
        out of pity working for God he's SUCH a
        child
        out of pity hauling up the bottoms of
        perspectives
as the mist rises from the earth it is the cold sweat
    of the men of
    low earnings crying
Life to Love turning,
sausage-souled, a sprig of vertigo,
the decalcomania of light torn from blind martyrdom,
the labor-leader calculating where shall the agony of
    my men be best applied,
the board-chairman calculating how shall the agony of my
    anus be least affected by the pinnacle,
the despot calculating how the agony of an uprooted
    population can be rooted in agony once again:
tell us how many kilowatt-hours are there in love;
        how much slag and how many coupons
initial capital investment?
communal property?
GIVE ME A BREAKDOWN ON
    republican love
    democratic love

marxist love
catholic love
mass love
upperclass love
DIDDLECLASS LOVE
in the countries with a helicopter in every heart,
an electro-oestrous engineer for every five-year cycle,
a cabinet-crisis for colonial harems,
a caste of untouchables for the very CHUNKSHEER of
        passion
these are the very cossacks riding pogroms of love
        is the
kike, the
nigger, the
        love is the
                paleolithic clown, the
                fagpicker, the
                murderer rising on his beast, the
                bacillus wearing a black bandbody
                        round its evacuole, the
air of the horse begging that its eye be pumped into
        a gunmuzzle
I LOVE YOU for the sugar cast up by the salt of the
        sea,
for the dumb spigot of the sun dealing the
                unparalleled torture of slowly-dripping
                lightdrops onto the hunchbacked black skull,
for the money printed on liberty,
for the crossed swords of the genitals as the newly-
        wed powers giggle through,
for the clothespin ICBMs nipping off the ducts,

for Jesus Christ slaking his thirst at the
        Strontium 90 waters

THE IMPECCABLE BARBED WIRE

The impeccable barbed wire blasting birds;
snarled, then, with bellowed warble,
the huddle of wings hogtied. But, trussed
to the terminals, how gorge these bleating
toggles to its own taut? Nicked to
the narrows, waspwrung, the wire wails
to rust, its own spare bloodpoisoning,
that across the arbitrary it be not charged
with next-of-kill, but the knack
of felling niche some sapped rots
away. We are clean out of powdered
red flakes, and cannot, for
the impersonal life of us, snap into song.

THE PAPERS OF PROFESSOR BOLD: 4

I must confess, according to the blobular theory
    of light,
that I could hardly have done without the long green.
I mean
cash.
I was the sort of chap who was all wool and a wad
    wide.
Condemn me not, my friends, for I could as well
    observe my reflection
in Miros
as in an integer followed by numerous zeros.
Government bonds.
Preferred stock.
In short, Americoin.
The dollar soign.
As my students might remark, I did not wish, ad hoc,
    to be in hock.
For I could not somehow be attracted to that col-
    loidal mutation
of three gold balls suspended with such pawniancy from
a frockcoated groin.
Of course I have in subtraction seen the bird
    perched atop the witty apothegm,
which forced the latter to clear its throat of the
    top white level abstractive phlegm;
a Korzybski falcon,
no doubt, doomed like Hamlet's toast to walk the
    parapets of our wrists
and haunt our overgeneralized gists.
Pray you, flay me not too harshly. Huck Finn, I

think, is ended;
the ice of Walden Pond I heard out powdered to a
    daiquiri wig
on some Sunday critic;
the New England radical become a Marxian enclitic;
Moby Dick
lynched on Faulknerian genealogy;
and the frontier —
queer.
You may wonder how my pleasure
constructed a parasol in my throat to shade my anger,
that it lean back in languor
and dab, now and again, at the ironic condensations
    on my brow.
You may wonder — at your pleasure.
It is enough to see how pockmarked is my forehead now.

THE ACTION

the action has begun
will the fart please take its seat
will the lady remove her fat
will the wing please check his bat
the cowboys holding up mt everest
what power in his gun
when villain glaciers on the run
white mustaches in the wind
no a camel making blindfold tests
nymphomania takes a bow
the gangster does a stickup with his heart
of course its jimmy valentine
my god its jesus christ with dynamite —
candles asking for a light
Ive got to get to kingdom come
I need a shave I feel like a bum
a saviour in paris is the name
shrieking hussies subtly hiss
when god and mary embrace and kiss
the immaculate daughterinlaw
ten thousand dancers revolve in crystal
shattered by an adolescents pistol
meanwhile back at the seesaw seesaw
childbride slides down the mountainside
awhoopin and ahollerin on her ass
enchanting coiffure by isinglass
the gallic priest on the american ranch
beats an atheist to death with an olive branch
the whore makes a getaway in the italian car
pursued by a saint with satanic scar

here come the marching proletariat
documented by the commissariat
what a superb high angle shot
of the world being blown apot
the scientists blaming one another
because they never meant to be down on mother
I suspect the man in the orange chemise
or maybe oedipus because hes got fleas
he loves her in the final clinch
as he gives her tickertit a pinch
her financial news is sound today
hes bet her bottom dollar for dollar
you wonder how the mans so virile
when his middle name is cyril
he beats her flays her exacerbates her
alls forgiven as he masturbates her
none of us can stand the suspense
of absolutely nothing making sense
the commander in the submarine
turning green
the father and his longlost child
meeting at last on the tower of babel
intuitively yell lets play scrabble
or one ennui to his mate
I love you Im too tired to hate
while swedish girl and gloomy boylet
stare starkly at each other
across a crowded european toilet
who will save the gorilla in distresss
forced to exercize mans noblesse
I fear my idealism must collapse
when unwed mothers take their naps
how can they possibly possibly sleep
if their vaginas are a bunch of sheep
the canadian mounty calls on the phone
somebody sabotaged my skis
but Im going ahead on my knees
jack the rippers stalking the london streets
frustrated by frozen meats

and sad monsters of every form
in shindigan headdress and dache norm
tail by adrian and hump by dior
as we look leverishly how they are hung
snap off a skyscraper to pick their teeth
but shyly deposit their dung
so american housewives keep a clean floor
american monsters are we are we
snobs toward european monstrosity
but wait the english cattle now stampede
proving theres no peace in tweed
glory glory waves the flag
the hero chokes with tears and falls down dead
the heroine bravely goes to bed
with red white blue dreams instead
up with the space ship down with sunset trail
as we dissolve an aspirin in the holy grail

I

that's not your face
it was mine for awhile
give it back
you stole it

youll regret it
because you stole an already stolen face
I took it from somebody else
and when he demanded it back I laughed in his
and told him he had stolen the face I had taken from him

somebody will steal your stolen face from you

look at it this way
somebodys got to be the first one to give the face back
no I don't know how far its going to have to go back before it reaches
                                        its rightful owner
for all I know he might not regcognize it
and even if he did he might not want it if he had learned how to get
                                        along without it
which is why it mightve been stolen in the first place
because the owner mightve wanted to learn how to get along without
                                        a face
but hes got to be given the chance of seeing if he could have it back if
                                        he wanted to
so he can really know he doesn't need it
you've got to give a faceless man the choice of regaining a face or
                                        living without it forever

because he might take his face back because he wouldn't want to
            deprive you of your chance for facelessness

you see theres really only one face to go around
when its maker saw what he had done he realized his error and never
            made a second face at all
and trying to right his error he made the rest of men a mass of thieves
since he knew by this way each man would have the passing experience
            of a face

but somewheres the man whom the face fits perfectly
and although he might take it back if it were offered to him
he might turn around and hand his face to its maker
and this possible event is something we shouldn't take the chance of
            missing
because then we should all have the chance of forgiving the maker
            his error

but our very forgiveness might be revenge
and in his fury the maker might dash the face down and break it
            into a thousand pieces
and you never know what form our vanity would take then
we might be condemned to searching for the pieces so as to be able to
            fit the face together again
and nobody would be able to tell us from the other four-footed animals

that's why the man I stole the face from finally stopped asking for it
            it back
and it wont be long before I stop asking you
I wouldnt feel right if I became an animal again
its better to be a faceless human than an animal with a face
for facelessness is your perfect reflection of another humans
            imperfect reflection

II

have you ever seen a man break a face across his knee like a slat
and then walk along his neighbors street swinging each half of the
            broken face in either hand so itll dry faster

if you watch him youll see him finally go up to a beggar and say
listen youll make a lot more money if you hold half of this face
in one hand and half in the other
that way the passerby will feel twice as sorry for you
you can also tell them youre trying to raise money enough to mend a
broken face
notice Ive hollowed out the backs of these halves so they'll each hold
plenty of coins or bills
and the empty eyesocket is convenient for stable grasping
like a lot of people I know you have no face so this ought to come
in handy
but make sure you keep it in your hands for begging
it wont do you any good if you put it on your head
id give it back to the man I stole it from but I obviously wouldn't
recognize him now

III

dont worry about your face
its not yours anyhow

what about the babys face you ask
well you say that baby looks like you or her or the grandparents or
whatever
or it looks like nobody you know at all

obviously the baby is a master thief
it goes around stealing all kinds of faces

I know I said theres really only one face
thats true
because that one face gets twisted this way and that
so what the baby really does is steal a face from somebody
and then when somebody else comes along and steals the babys face
the baby manages to steal it again after its been snatched
from several other heads

the actor as you can probably already tell is a baby
the actor more than anybosy else would like to make his stolen
face a success
something permanent
he guards his theft ceaselessly
he plays with his stolen face
he croons to it
he experiments making it black or yellow or white
he lectures it
he makes love to it
he makes hate to it
he tries to amuse it with games
all because if someone manages to steal it from him then the face
will remember where it had such a wondeful time and will
get rid of its new captor and make its way back to the actor

but the face has no memory

V

all of us one time or another think were just face for awhile
just as we are now

I know theres a head behind me
but the head itself has no face
I have only face
the head behind is faces shadow

and then suddenly theres a longing for gods sake wont somebody come
along and steal face
so that its shadowhead will come into its own again in all its
featureless splendor

to be brave as the man who broke face across his knee into two halves
but not pieces
we dare not face the wrath of faces maker

VI

even the dead mans face is stolen

VII

stealing face is the only theft not punished by law

VIII

god you know is faceless
the maker of face mustve been jealous of god and decided to make
        something you could hide behind by weeping on it and
        laughing on it and cruelling on it and pitying on it and
                        hating on it and begging on it
you could put all these things out there on face and hide behind
and everybody never would know who you really were because they
        would want to steal your face but the facemaker didn't know
        about that till after he had made the error of face
                                perfectly for one man

the facemaker knew he had made an error because he instantly felt
        that the man with face was hiding from the facemaker behind it
because in that instant facemaker knew he had been jealous of
                        himself
knew in fact he was god who had become jealous of himself because
        he could no longer bear knowing everything so that he had to
        make face on a man so that god wouldn't be able to see everything
                and that at least man could hide from god
but god knew he had made an error by having one man appear to
                need god because the man needed expressions
and god shrank in all dimensions before the expression of no need
                        for gods on the mans face
but god could not in his mercy after refusing to make another face
                        destroy the face he had
                                made
because then the rest of men seeing the face wanted the hidden feeling
the no need for god feeling
and god could not deprive them

gods mercy will cease only if we forgive him by the act of the man
whom face fits returning face to god
an event we want to see and don't want to see

so that man lives in the tension of having face and having no face
lives tense between the desire to forgive god and have face broken
into innumerable fragments so that in enormous vanity he will
become an animal altogether gods again in his search to fit all
the pieces of face together which he will never be able to do
and the desire to keep stealing face so that at intervals he can at
least show no need for god

IX

one man whom face does not fit will one day hold on to face and never
let it be stolen from him
and this will be his psalm

I am altogether hidden before the lord
I am courageous in knowing the lord cannot know me for I have by
the lords hand grown beyond the lord
I am more than the son and more than the father because I disown
featureless splendor
I am finally man because I will make face for each man like unto no
other

we will hide forever from the almighty
god will not know we have moved into him
and god shall be the face outside looking into our window
and he will wonder where we have gone

ART OF THE SONNET: 9

Bowed negress, who aghast but the light
nailed by its own decimal points?
We seem computed, and dare not shift;
we go handcuffed by shadows, despite
our fingers' skeleton-keys, and the simple lifting
of the head
above the dead.
You have said that someone touching you would be cheating;
but not many would grope about within a human dark,
fearful that its hidden snowstorm might put them all asleep.
I know you are weary as a wrestler at last in love
with the long hold,
and that children dance about you as about some inanimate object.
It is time, then, that your hands bless someone taller than yourself;
and your eyes, like moths of snowflakes, float to the white winepress.

for Lynn

Such folly of margins that may retaliate
against my separation of man and state,
to deify the one, the other to castigate,
my wife in sleep will annotate
by dreaming I leaped down one sheer unconscious
cliff at bottom to await my own fall consciously.
Let us have wives, then, before we rush
into folly, lest we become abandoned quarry
and no dichotomies ever marry.
Whatever the men of state, whatever the state of men,
I shall walk untroubled the baffled battlements
and gaze with loving astonishment upon
her impossible breathing that rises like a mist
from wherever last we slept and kissed.

ART OF THE SONNET: 43

Every time I think of the guy I feel
sorry for all us animals, because
there he is, his face full of overalls,
and hanging down like loose straps his cheeks.
He's pushing fifty. He buys drinks for his analyst
and offers marijuana confessing to his priest.
That rubs a couple giggles together to light
a laugh under the mucus of my dribbling sight.
He's lean, all right: he's catted around from Philly
to Guadalajara, and makes a girl like he would
a deadline for his paper, All-American, like his people,
who settled on the Hudson in seventeen-hundred-and-fifty.
Sure he loves his country, and hates its-guts.
"I don't get it about God," he says,
        "I've been picking up His butts."

for Lynn

Metalucent turboblue sursuddening her snowfell glisteneye
captures the hazards of imminence,
crystal bonewind of sail.
Flurring face, engineer of emerald, coming through the siddlesigh,
syzygies pump startlespurs of lyrlust glaze.
Her pangs of paean pick at me,
ricochets of rose, shaman shell,
her love refers me to blizzards of stare in the caves.
The clinging sting and satin sapphire somnolently sortie
the redolently ambushed registers,
whereby the ruffian glands disrobe umbrageously
in slurring outrage and twisted purrs,
that bits of body dissolve upon her gloom of white,
sensorial safaris swung on tusks of micromight.

ART OF THE SONNET: 67

Moved by the disappearance of my face,
I ran headlong into my barber who
thought it a great shame. I knew it had to
be somewhere, a simple obvious
place. I'd fed it, combed it, stroked it, warmed it —
why should it be angry and in hiding?
If it could get along without me, I
might never look at myself again, nor
at anybody as the final outcome.
Even if I saw it, I might not recognize
it, because by then it might be anyone's.
I simply hoped it would be taken care
of in its simple obvious place, and
wouldn't feel too much pain if it saw me walking by.

ART OF THE SONNET: 68

Nothing in particular. Perhaps mazes
of structure to transmit dust. The hose squirming
to squirt water under the water in
the bottom of the pool. Chases in faces.
Nothing out of the ordinary. Green
grapes popping through white teeth. The altitude
of tears and their longstemmed grief in the rain,
and the mazes of structure to dry them
again, and again, and again, and their
bright new colors on the wiping cloth. Nothing
I like or dislike. Cutting my fingernails
waiting for her flesh. Putting a house up for sale.
Nothing I planned for, and the mazes of
structure for that. Couldn't say, might be love.

seizure, face, crouching:
CLAM, WITH GONGS: —
(bificles, Blind Luminary
in blindsight).
rubberband insects mans each face
little goliaths revenge. SUSTAINING A GLANCING BLOW TO
TIIE WEBFOOTED BALLS OF SIGHT
man gummyweans
(diphthonged
his face)
crouching crouching crouching in the
gotnot not
in the gotnot not
... the clams beat on each others gongs with the webfooted balls ...
seizure: 9/10ths of the law: cramps.

ART OF THE SONNET: 129

All over the morning the lovers wake, even
unto the antiquities, spiking sunlight with salt
that the morning murmur meridians, and their loins
prickle at the spray of chastened chastities.
All over the morning the lovers yawn forth their sinew,
even unto the honeysuckled breasts of Aphrodite
flattened and flared by the minted hammer of Thor,
for the Race of the Beloveds is upon the world
all over the morning across the orange oceans,
each nerve now a spoke of sprint
from the arcbodies in the great gliders of their emotions
breathclad in silverfoils —
aye, even unto tomorrow's antiquities
the last of the lovers wake the morning as it dies.

ART OF THE SONNET: 130

stigmatize me baby Im on the cross for you
as the thaumaturgists traumaturgy
one looks at a clock as at a solution in a hypodermic
my roots have shining curls
my god the gods are leaving me
the devil a mass of sentimental hurt
Im waiting baby an ounce of betrayal worth a pound of threatened
        loyalty
stigmatize me baby hell Im hanging by my nails
my roots arterioscleroticed hurls
paint my wounds with iodine and I'll qualify as the communist
        christ
she's an angel who puts holes through your hands and feet and then
        fits you for gloves and shoes
for how else shall a stigmatized man his anonymity infected
        control his deadly child on the city streets
knowest thou that paradise may be administered by a physician
        in small abortive doses
stigmatize me baby please I think Im pregnant

BACK MATTER

A BRIEF BIOGRAPHY OF GIL ORLOVITZ

Poet, novelist, playwright, and screenwriter Gilbert "Gil" Orlovitz was born on June 7, 1918, in Philadelphia, Pennsylvania, to Morris and Rose Orlovitz. Morris, whose father was the chief rabbi of Lithuania, was born in 1893 and immigrated to the United States in 1892. Rose, born in 1887, immigrated in 1890. Gil was named for an older brother, 10 years his senior, who was killed as a child when, walking through a park, he was struck on the head by an errant fly ball. Another brother, Henry, was born in 1907.

According to military records, Orlovitz had two years of college education, at Temple University in Philadelphia, when he enlisted in the Army on October 31, 1941. His occupation at the time was recorded as author, editor, and reporter. He served four years in the U.S. Army Air Corps during World War II, and it was during this time that his poetry was first published; two short poems appeared in the Summer 1944 issue of *Rocky Mountain Review* (Salt Lake City). Following the war, he attended Columbia University, where he studied dramatic composition, comparative religion, and philosophy. He also studied at the Dramatic Workshop in New York under the tutelage of German expatriate stage director Erwin Piscator.

Orlovitz's first collection of poetry, *Concerning Man*, was published by The Banyon Press (New York) in 1947. Dedicated to his first wife Bettie Bennett (referred to as St. R in two of the poems), the book was well received by critics. In the July 12, 1947 edition of *The Saturday Review*, Alfred Kreymborg wrote that Orlovitz was "a poet with an amazing talent for grappling with human and superhuman problems on a wildly rhetorical basis" and with "an original gift for the elegiac mood [who] never softens his energetic drive with illusion or sentiment." Orlovitz's marriage to Bennett, later an accomplished theatrical photographer, ended in divorce shortly after the birth of their daughter.

In addition to writing prolifically during 1940s and 1950s (at least 15 copyrighted plays, 17 published short stories, and countless poems in small literary magazines), Orlovitz worked as a radio monitor, a typist for a subsidiary of Standard Oil, and in the import-export business. Three of his plays were produced off-Broadway: *A Case of a Neglected Calling Card* in 1952, *Noone* in 1953, and *Stephanie* in 1954. In 1955, he was signed to a long-term screenwriting contract with Universal Pictures and relocated to Hollywood, California, with his second wife, the actress-singer Maralyn "Lynn" Marquize, and her daughter, Audrey, from a previous marriage. The Internet Movie Database lists only one screenplay writing credit for Orlovitz, the 1956 film noir crime drama *Over-Exposed*, "a forgettable piece of 1950s sleaze" according to one recent reviewer. In 1957, he turned his talents to television, writing episodes for two ABC Western series, *The Adventures of Jim Bowie* and *The Life and Legend of Wyatt Earp*.

In 1957, *The Miscellaneous Man*, a small Berkeley-based literary magazine published by William Margolis, devoted a double issue to Orlovitz: *The Statement of Erika Keith and Other Stories, Poems, and a Play*. The issue, along with Allen Ginsberg's *Howl and Other Poems*, was purchased at City Lights Books on June 3, 1957 by two plainclothes San Francisco police officers, resulting in the arrests of store manager Shigeyoshi "Shig" Murao and publisher Lawrence Ferlinghetti on charges of disseminating obscene material. For the ensuing trial, William Hogan, literary editor of the *San Francisco Chronicle*, wrote court statements defending both publications. He described Orlovitz's *Erika Keith* as "the work of a sincere, growing, and dedicated literary talent, a talent provocative and stimulating enough to interest and excite admiration in serious critics and observers of literary craftsmanship of our time."

By publishing Orlovitz's poem "Index (3rd Series): 2," which contained the lines "a butterfly dared me to fuck it" and "your cunt split like the red sea / the jews passed through," Margolis must have anticipated some legal difficulties, as well as some subsequent publicity for his magazine. Unfortunately for both him and Orlovitz, the press at the time focused on Ginsberg's *Howl* and little mention was made of *Erika Keith*. Orlovitz went so far as to write Ferlinghetti, demanding that he address the exclusion of his work "in the press to which you are so well connected" and, further, accused him of being part of a "cheap literary cabal — with apparently no more integrity than its East Coast counterpart — which attempts to bask one author at the shadow of another." On October 3, 1957, Judge Clayton W. Horn ruled that Howl was not obscene and consequently all charges related to *The Miscellaneous Man* were dropped.

Orlovitz's poetry was again the subject of controversy later that year. The editors of Beloit College's *Beloit Poetry Journal*, on the suggestion of co-founder Chad Walsh, decided to fill out their Winter 1957–1958 issue with poems from "underground" West Coast poets, including the not-yet-famous Charles Bukowski. From several available Orlovitz pieces, the editors selected for inclusion the one they felt would be the most contentious, a poem titled simply "Not." Members of the college's board of trustees took particular offense to the poem's line "not jesus jerking off, not mohammet with his coeds" and decided to withhold future financial support for the publication.

A short autobiographical piece appeared in the Winter 1958–1959 issue of *The Literary Review* (Fairleigh Dickinson University). Orlovitz wrote that he was presently at work on four large poetry projects — *The Diary of Matthew Parson, M'sieu Mishiga, The Letters of Great Ape,* and *Art of the Sonnet* — as well as a major work of fiction, *Ice Never F,* the first installment in a series of semiautobiographical experimental novels "provisionally entitled *Now.*" However, it was its successor, *Milkbottle H,* which was published first. Shopped around for years among U.S. publishers, it was finally accepted in 1967 by Calder & Boyars in London, which had already published experimental works by such authors as Samuel Beckett, William Burroughs, and Alain Robbe-Grillet. A U.S. edition was released the following year by Dellacorte Press. The novel was very well received in the U.K.; *The Scotsman* called it "a major event in the history of the American imagination," and the *Cork Examiner* hailed it as "one of the great, if not the greatest, literary achievements of our time."

U.S. reviewers were far less enthusiastic. Thomas Lask of *The New York Times* dismissed it as a "rambling montage of words" and concluded his review with, "There have been few books in recent years that have demanded so much of the reader and yielded so little in return." Only Kevin Sullivan of the *Chicago Tribune's Book World* seemed to understand what Orlovitz was doing with his fiction. He wrote that there was "no container for the verbal energies at work here, no plot, no beginning and no end to the rush and crush of language," and that Orlovitz was creating "a new genre that no longer experiments with form but discards all form and concentrates on the presentation of immediately felt experience or, more accurately, allows that experience to present itself."

Ice Never F was published in 1970, again by Calder & Boyars. It was virtually ignored. Orlovitz gave the manuscript for a third novel in the series to his friend, the writer Anaïs Nin, who agreed to help find a publisher for it. This was likely the work titled *Will Frank Marry Mary?*, listed as forthcoming on the back cover of Orlovitz's *Art of the Sonnet,* published by Hillsboro Publications in 1961. However, Hillsboro ceased operations the following year and the novel was never released. (One Internet source states that publisher Michael Lebeck had abandoned his press and joined a mystical religious sect.) The current whereabouts of the manuscript are unknown, although letters suggest that it may have been lost in the mail between Orlovitz and James Boyer May, publisher of the literary magazine *Trace.*

Adding further to Orlovitz's frustrations, NET (National Educational Television, the precursor to PBS), had arranged to film and televise his thirty-nine-scene masterwork play, *Gray,* based on events in the life of Abraham Lincoln, but unexpectedly canceled the project after five years of negotiations. This setback, along with the lukewarm reception to his novels and his ongoing difficulty in securing a major publisher for his poetry, was likely a contributing factor to the depression and subsequent alcoholism that haunted Orlovitz during the later years of his life.

Orlovitz struggled financially during the 1960s and early 1970s and had to resort to hack writing and editing jobs at various New York paperback firms to support his family, which then included two young sons, Guy-Max and Ethan, in addition to his adopted daughter Audrey from Maralyn's first marriage. His friends Anaïs Nin and the poet Guy Daniels helped secure for him a copy-editing job at Avon Books. Thomas Payne, editor-in-chief at Avon, referred him to Universal Publishing, where he worked as an editor of soft-core lesbian pornography novels, and wrote more of the same under the pseudonym of Stacey Clubb. One of his last known jobs was a position with Marvel Comics, then a subsidiary of Magazine Management, which specialized in adventure, celebrity/film, and risqué men's magazines. Often spending twelve hours a day at what he considered degrading work, he continued to pursue his own distinctive craft, usually between the hours of 1:00 and 3:00 a.m. By 1973, his alcoholism had taken its toll; mentally exhausted and no longer able to write, he was unemployed, in very poor health, and living on welfare in a single room in Harlem, a few blocks away from his then-estranged wife and family.

On July 9, 1973, Orlovitz collapsed on the street and was taken to nearby Knickerbocker Hospital. He was in a coma with a 108-degree fever and died the next day. The cause of death was recorded as bronchial pneumonia. Police and hospital officials were initially unable to locate any relatives so he was buried in a pauper's grave at New York's City's public cemetery on Hart Island in the Bronx. His wife didn't learn of his death until July 21 when she contacted the Bureau of Missing Persons to report his disappearance; despite being separated, Maralyn and Gil had kept in weekly contact with each other. At the urging of Sidney Bernard, associate publisher of the literary magazine *The Smith*, a lengthy obituary finally appeared in *The New York Times* on September 8, nearly two months after Orlovitz's death.

Sources:

Burns, Jim, *Anarchists Beats and Dadaists*, p. 101, Preston, United Kingdom: Penniless Press Publications, 2016.

Chatfield, Hale, "Literary Exile in Residence," *The Kenyon Review*, Vol. 31, No. 4, pp. 545–553, Gambier, Ohio: Kenyon College, 1969.

Daniels, Guy, "Gil," *The Smith*, No. 19, pp. 146–160, New York, 1977.

Daniels, Guy, "Notes Toward a Bibliography of Gil Orlovitz," *The American Poetry Review*, Vol. 7, No. 6, pp. 31–32, Philadelphia: University of the Arts, 1978.

Debritto, A., *Charles Bukowski, King of the Underground: From Obscurity to Literary Icon*, p. 79, Basingstoke, United Kingdom: Palgrave Macmillan, 2015.

Internet Movie Database, www.imdb.com/name/nm0650162/

King, Andrew, "The Statement of Who?: The Narrative of the Howl Trial and its Discontents," *Berkeley Undergraduate Journal*, Vol. 26, No. 3, pp. 57–62, Berkeley: University of California at Berkeley, 2013.

Klinkowitz, Jerome, *Dictionary of Literary Biography, Vol. 2: American Novelists Since World War II*, (Richard Layman and Jeffrey Helterman, editors), pp. 388–390, Detroit: Gale Research, 1978.

Kreymborg, Alfred, "An Anthropolical Poet," *The Saturday Review*, p. 14, New York, July 12, 1947.

Lask, Thomas, "Rambling Montage of Words," *The New York Times*, p. 37, Jan. 16, 1968,

McKee, Louis, "Under the El: Some Thoughts on Gil Orlovitz," *The Painted Bride Quarterly*, pp. 68–74, Philadelphia, 1992.

Morgan, Bill and Nancy J. Peters, editors, *Howl on Trial: The Battle for Free Expression*, pp. 61–62, San Francisco: City Lights Publishers, 2006.

Newlove, Donald, "Two Line a Day," *The Village Voice*, pp. 20–22, New York, Sept. 20, 1973.

Orlovitz, Gil, "Some Autobiographical Words," *The Literary Review*, Vol. 2, No. 2, pp. 197–199, Madison, New Jersey: Fairleigh Dickinson University, 1958.

Palmquist, Peter, "Women in Photography International Galleries: Betty Bennett," Oct. 1999, www.womeninphotography.org/archive01-Oct99/print/print_index.htm

Robins, William Matthias, *Dictionary of Literary Biography, Vol. 5: American Poets Since World War II*, (Donald J. Greiner, editor), pp. 142–145, Detroit: Gale Research, 1978.

Scott, J.D., "Ulysses in Philadelphia," *The New York Times*, p. 126, Feb. 4, 1968.

Stern, Gerald, "Miss Pink At Last: An Appreciation Of Gil Orlovitz," *The American Poetry Review*, Vol. 7, No. 6, pp. 27–31, Philadelphia: University of the Arts, 1978.

"Gil Orlovitz, Poet, Died in July; Traced to City Paupers' Grave," *The New York Times*, p. 34, Sept. 8, 1973.

GIL ORLOVITZ BIBLIOGRAPHY

COLLECTIONS

Concerning Man
Banyan Press, New York, 1947

Keep to Your Belly: Fourteen Poems
Louis Brigante, New York, 1952

The Diary of Dr. Eric Zeno
Inferno Press, San Francisco, 1953

The Statement of Erika Keith and Other Stories, Poems, and a Play
The Miscellaneous Man, Berkeley CA, 1957

The Diary of Alexander Patience
Inferno Press, San Francisco, 1958

The Papers of Professor Bold
Hearse Press, Eureka CA, 1958

Selected Poems
Inferno Press, San Francisco, 1960

Art of the Sonnet
Hillsboro Publications, Nashville, 1961

5 Sonnets
Goosetree Press, Lanham MD, 1964

The Award Avant-Garde Reader (editor)
Award Books, New York, 1965

Couldn't Say, Might be Love
Barrie and Rockliff, London, 1969

More Poems
Fiddlehead Poetry Books, Fredericton NB, Canada, 1972

NOVELS

Milkbottle H
Calder & Boyers, London, 1967

Ice Never F
Calder & Boyars, London, 1970

UNPUBLISHED NOVELS

Long Flats

The Inverted Cross

Will Frank Marry Mary?

SHORT STORIES

"The Death of Sam Runnymeade"
Quarterly Review of Literature, Vol. 4 No. 1, 1947

"Lila Bohmer"
Quarterly Review of Literature, Vol. 4 No. 1, 1947

"Tears from a Glass Eye"
INTRO, Vol. 1 No. 2, 1951

"A Metaphysical Inquiry into Adam Zion Davidson
Written by Mr. R"
INTRO, Vol. 1, Nos. 3 & 4, 1951

"What Are They All Waiting For?"
Discovery #2, 1953

"Alice"
Whetstone, Vol. 1 No. 2, 1955

"The Statement of Erika Keith"
Miscellaneous Man, Nos. 11 & 12, 1957

"Ah, Kathleen"
Miscellaneous Man, Nos. 11 & 12, 1957

"— Image in Static Continuum"
Miscellaneous Man, Nos. 11 & 12, 1957

"Footnote on Willis"
Mutiny, Vol. 1, No.1, 1957

"A Fourth of July"
Whetstone, Vol. 2, No. 2, 1957

"What Will You Give Our Lord Tonight"
Colorado Review, Vol. 1, No. 2, 1957

"The Rest of the Staff Was Out"
21st Century, No. 2, 1957

"One Orange and One Blue"
Mutiny, Vol. 1, Nos. 3 & 4, 1958

"Fob at Bay"
Colorado Review, Vol. 3, 1958

"Something to Tell Mother"
American Letters Press, 1959

"A Deposition of Ben Berman"
Mutiny, Vol. 2, No. 2, 1959

"A Back Cover"
Coastlines, Nos. 14 & 15, 1960

"The Brass Plaque"
Minnesota Review, Vol.1, No. 4, 1961

"The Photographer"
Sciamachy, No. 6, 1964

"I'm Just in Sparta on a Visit"
The Award Avant-Garde Reader (ed. Gil Orlovitz), 1965

Publication unknown:

"A Louder Report"
"P.H.N."
"That Way, I Guess You're Right"
"The Simple Decision of Luther"
"When She was Alive, Did She?"
"Wild Horses in Central Park"

PLAYS

Christina, a libretto in seven scenes (1946)

Garibaldi, a play in three acts (1946)

Maneuver Incident, a play in three acts (1946)

Niggy Hyam, a play in three acts (1946)

Niggy Delaney, a play in three acts (1946)

Stevie Guy, a play in three acts (1947)
Published in *Quarterly Review of Literature*,
Vol 6., Nos. 1 & 2, 1952

Ellen Evanson, a play in four acts (1949)

Exchange, a farce in four acts (1949)

A Case of a Neglected Calling Card, a play in one act
and two scenes (1950)
Published in *Miscellaneous Man*, Nos. 11 & 12, 1957

Noone, a tragicomedy in two acts (1950)

Sharon, a tragicomedy in ten scenes (1951)

Todt and Thor, a play in five scenes (1952)

Lullaby and Goodnight, a play in three scenes for
television (1954)

But I Never Took the Money, a play in two acts (1956)

Gray, a play in thirty-nine scenes based on some of the
events in the life of Abraham Lincoln (1956)
Published in *The Literary Review*, Winter 1958–59

Do You Play Any Musical Instruments, Charles? (Unknown)

SCREENPLAY

Over-Exposed (in collaboration with James Gunn)
Columbia Pictures, 1956

TELEPLAYS

The Adventures of Jim Bowie
Season 2, Episode 2: "Flowers for McDonough" (1957)
Season 2, Episode 35: "Bowie's Baby" (1958)
Season 2, Episode 37: "Man on the Street" (1958)

The Life and Legend of Wyatt Earp
Season 6, Episode 29: "Wyatt Earp's Baby" (1961)

RECORDING

The Rooster and Other Poems of Gil Orlovitz
The Spoken Word (SW 120), New York, 1960

ACKNOWLEDGMENTS

I would like to acknowledge the following institutions and individuals who provided scans and photocopies of much of the material included in this collection: Boston Public Library, Denver Public Library, Firestone Library at Princeton University, Cecil H. Green Library at Stanford University, Lilly Library at Indiana University Bloomington, *The Literary Review* at Fairleigh Dickinson University, Robbins Library (Arlington, MA), University of Pennsylvania Libraries Kislak Center for Special Collections, Sidney Orr, and Corey J. Wetherington.

In addition, I thank the following individuals for their generous financial support which helped to defray some of this book's production costs: Reuben Andrews, Brian R. Boisvert, Jeffrey Canino, Scott Chiddister, Shane Jesse Christmass, C. Colla, Mike Corkery, Jason Crane, Nick Craske, Andrew Fearnside, John Feins, Nathan Friedman, Nathan "N.R." Gaddis, Rob Hannah, Haya K., Larry Kerschner, Hongwoo Lee, Josh Mahler, Joseph McGrath, Sidney McMahon, Doug Milam, Casey C. Miller, Steven Moore, Jonathan Morton, Geoffrey Moses, J.W. Dionysius Nicolello, Michael O'Shaughnessy, Sidney Orr, Nick Oxford, Charles Parsons, Poems-For-All, Borys Pugacz-Muraszkiewicz, Brandon Ramirez, Frank V. Saltarelli, Joelle Sasson, David Starner, Sean Stewart, Ryan Vivian, and Isaiah Whisner.

Finally, I would like express my gratitude to the Orlovitz family — Audrey C. Orlovitz Filippelli, Guy-Max Orlovitz, and Ethan B. Orlovitz — for their support of my efforts to bring their father's work back into print. At their request, a portion of the proceeds from each sale of this book will be donated to Safe Horizon, a New York-based non-profit organization providing services and shelter to victims of domestic violence.

R.S.

www.ingramcontent.com/pod-product-compliance
Lightning Source LLC
Chambersburg PA
CBHW071503110726
47908CB00003B/704